LET LOVE WIN

NICOLA MAY

Lightning Books

First published by Nicola May 2013
This edition published in 2021
by Lightning Books
Imprint of Eye Books Ltd
29A Barrow Street
Much Wenlock
Shropshire
TF13 6EN

www.eye-books.com

Cover design by Ifan Bates

British Library Cataloguing in Publication Data
A catalogue record for this book is available from the British Library

Printed by CPI Group (UK) Ltd, Croydon CR0 4YY

ISBN 9781785632969

Ever has it been that love knows not its own depth
until the hour of its separation
Khalil Gibran

PROLOGUE

Bang! Bang! Bang! Ruby sat up in bed with a start. Sluggish from her heavy slumber, she couldn't fathom where the noise was coming from. She rubbed her eyes and looked at her watch – three p.m. She was about to turn over and go back to sleep when she heard a familiar voice.

'Ruby, for feck's sake, will you open this door? If you don't come down in ten seconds, I'm gonna call the Ginger Police.' The Irish lilt cut through the silence of the warm summer air.

Ruby pulled on a stained dressing gown and hauled herself out of bed. She glanced at herself in the mirror and sighed. Her auburn hair was sticking up on end, her eye sockets were hollow, and her cheekbones looked far too pronounced.

Fi came bustling through the door, armed with a huge bunch of yellow roses and a bright green wheelie case. Her black hair was tied back roughly and she was wearing a skimpy flowery sundress. Trying hard not to be taken aback by how dreadful her best friend looked, she went straight to Ruby and hugged her as hard as she could.

'Right now, Mrs Stevens, the O'Donahue emergency cabaret has arrived. Get some vases for these flowers and then sit right down there on that couch. I'll be with you in a minute.'

Tripping over the untidy mess that depression has a habit of causing, Fi ran around, drew all the curtains apart, and opened all the windows to let the air through the beautiful Lake District cottage. She pulled rubber gloves and cleaning products out of her huge case, ran up the steep old staircase, and proceeded to scrub the bath clean.

Pouring in some fragrant bubble bath, she turned both taps on full and ran back downstairs, where Ruby was looking vacantly out of the lounge window.

'I can't do it any more, Fi, I just can't.' Her voice was flat and monotone. 'My days go into nights, my nights into days – and what for? I don't see any point in anything.'

Fi went to her side. 'I know, darling, but it will get better, it will. I wish I could take away your pain, but only time can do that, and it will. And as for running away up here, it isn't good for you. You shouldn't be on your own. Your ma, me, Sam – everyone – has been worried sick. I knew you'd come to Daffodils.'

She drew Ruby to her chest and buffeted her tiny body with silent sobs of her own.

'Now come on, let's get you bathed. I'll wash your hair and then I can make you something nice to eat. I've got all your favourites with me.'

A YEAR EARLIER…

CHAPTER ONE

'Hi, honey, I'm home.'

Ruby laughed. George's Cockney accent sounded so funny when he tried to be posh.

He sauntered into the front room of their Putney maisonette. Ruby was busy at her sewing machine. He kissed her lovingly on the forehead as she pushed her chair back.

'Don't get up now, Sarah Burton, you have designer dresses to finish.'

Ruby looked at her watch – it was only two p.m. 'What're you doing home at this time anyway?'

'I'd like to say I've come home to roger you senseless, but I forgot my wallet this morning and it's a special someone's birthday tomorrow, ain't it?'

'You're so bloody last-minute.'

'And you're so bloody old. What are you now – thirty-six tomorrow? Good job you bagged yourself a handsome toy boy, eh?'

Ruby got up and swiped him jokingly around the face. 'Thirty-five, actually, and yes, before you say it, I have seen some crows with feet this big.' They both laughed and George hugged her tightly.

'It'll be our five-year wedding anniversary soon too, blimey! I've done my time with you, bird, but do you know what? I wouldn't swap ya, not even for a younger brunette.'

He grabbed his wallet off the side and put it into his pocket.

'What do you want for your birthday anyway?'

'Well, whatever it is, it won't beat last year's gift, that's for sure. I still can't believe you did that.'

'Patrick couldn't ever leave you, I told you that. He was far too much of a character. Even I shed a tear when the old boy went, and as I said, if Janine Butcher can have one on *EastEnders*, then so can you.'

Ruby thought back to the moment when she had unwrapped her stuffed black and white moggy. He even looked like he was smiling.

'If anything ever happens to you, Rubes, I'm doing the same. I may get your hand put like this.' He rolled his hand into a wanking shape. 'Then you can still pleasure me then as well as you do now.'

'You're wrong in so many ways, George Stevens, but that's why I love you. Now piss off and go get me some Cartier earrings.'

'Cartier? I'm only going to the cash and carry.' Ruby shook her head. 'See you later. Oh, could you be a love and pick up some fish and chips on your way back? I've really got to finish these bridesmaids' dresses.'

'Sure. I may even share my saveloy with you.'

'Depends on the present, that's all I'm saying.'

'You know you want it, you dirty minx. See ya, darlin'.'

He kissed his wife on the lips and was gone.

CHAPTER TWO

The doorbell rang. Ruby checked herself in the mirror and smirked. George was always forgetting his bloody keys. She quickly threw on the green mac he liked her in and touched up the red lipstick he loved to kiss off. They could warm up the supper later.

The day they had got married had been the happiest of her life – and that happiness had continued. Since getting her fashion degree, her dressmaking business was going well, and just last week they had discussed the possibility of starting a family. Then their lives would be complete.

With a big grin on her face, and without caring if her neighbours saw, she threw open the front door.

Shouting 'Voilà!' as she did so, she let her coat drop to the floor to reveal her sexiest cream lingerie – stockings, suspenders, the lot.

'Ruby Ann Matthews?' a stern-looking policeman asked, not flinching once at her attire.

'Um, yes, that's me.' She scrabbled around on the floor and untidily threw her coat back around her.

'Can we come in?' the softer voice of the accompanying policewoman continued.

They said it had been instantaneous, that he would have felt no pain. The other driver was drunk and hit him head on as he rounded the corner to the fish and chip shop. Bloody fish and chips! If she hadn't been so lazy, and cooked, he would still be here. Her warm, loving, caring, funny husband would still be here!

Her face was contorted in grief. She couldn't do this on her own. She had to talk to someone. She dropped the orange carrier bag holding George's belongings and grappled in her bag for her phone.

'Mum…'

CHAPTER THREE

'You know what date it is, don't you?' Ruby asked, adorned in Fi's red silky dressing gown, feeling lovely and clean for the first time in ages.

'Of course I do, Rubes. I've been with you all the way through this, darlin' – even though it may not have seemed like it. But after today the first anniversary of the funeral will have passed and it will be another stepping stone.'

'Maybe.' Ruby put her head back on the armchair. 'A whole year. I can't believe it. That's a long time, isn't it?'

'It is,' Fi said gently. 'But I think you need to start making little steps into the world again. I mean, who the feck is going to make the wedding dress for Prince Harry's future bride apart from you?' She pushed a stray hair from Ruby's forehead. 'Actually, you best measure me up – it's surely only a matter of time before he realises he wants a piece of the Donahue.'

Ruby smiled. It was good to hear someone joking and not tiptoeing around her.

'But you can't run up here to Daffodils every time you feel sad,' Fi went on. 'You must talk to us.'

'Who says I can't? It's so beautiful here in the Lake District, though. It helps me see things more clearly.'

'OK, but let us know if you hotfoot it again, won't you?'

'Yes, yes, telling-off over. Now, do you know what I really fancy?'

'Johnny Depp in a thong?'

'You're bloody insatiable, girl. No, I fancy letting my hair down and having a few drinks, Fi O'Donahue – that's what I fancy.'

'You really mean that, Rubes?'

'Hell, yeah! George would be fuming thinking that I'd wasted a whole year moping about. Come on, the Maltsters pub does the most amazing homemade pies. We shall drink their finest Sauvignon and scoff pastry.'

'Shite, I nearly fell in the fecking stream!' Fi squealed as they arrived back at the cottage at midnight.

Ruby laughed. It had been a while since she'd last been drunk and she was actually enjoying herself for the first time in a year. 'You'll never guess what I've done,' she chuckled. 'I've only gone and locked the door keys inside.'

'Thank goodness it's summer – we can kip on the lawn.'

'It's fine. It's so safe up here I always keep the key in the same place dear old Lucas used to.'

Guided by the moonlight, Ruby walked around to the back garden and poked about under one of the many statues of athletic, naked Romans.

Once inside, they both sat at the big table in the beautifully fitted kitchen. Sipping on another bottle of wine that had been in Fi's 'emergency' holdall, she began to reminisce.

'I wish I'd met Lucas, Rubes.'

'Me too. He was the funniest, campest man – I actually loved him. I only nursed him for a short while, but it was enough to get to know him. I still can't believe he left me this place in his will.'

'I remember that day so well, it was unbelievable. We've had such a laugh here, haven't we?'

Ruby was thoughtful. 'Yes, it holds so many memories.'

'One of them being that I first shagged James on this here chaise longue.'

'You're such a slapper!'

'Not any more, Rubes. I'm sure he's going to make an honest woman of me soon. I can't wait to be Mrs Fiona Kane.'

Ruby bit her lip.

'Shite – I'm sorry, always putting me fecking size nines in it. I'd been doing so well, too.'

'You're fine, Fi. I've got to toughen up. Life goes on. People get married. Bring on the world, I say. Maybe I should set myself another mission.'

'Oh bejaysus. It was more than funny when you set yourself your twelve-month, twelve-job mission. In fact, I don't think I've ever laughed so hard, seeing you dressed up as Dopey on that stage. It was beyond belief, but worth it when you got your fashion degree.'

'Yes, it was so worth it. It was after my stint at Oxfam that I realised exactly what I wanted to do. Life is so weird.'

'Do you remember that wannabe starlet at Cliveden, whose birthday party you helped me arrange?'

'No,' Ruby stated. 'Nor does anyone else.' They both snorted and took a slurp of wine.

'I wouldn't be sitting here if I hadn't worked at the old people's home for ex-celebs either,' Ruby went on. 'I miss George so much. Every time the doorbell rings I think it's him coming home, and that it's all been a terrible dream. I can't sleep in our bed any more either. I had to move into the spare room the day it happened.' Fi said nothing, and instead let her friend go on. 'It's just so hard to explain. When Dad died it was bad, but this is worse. All my hopes, dreams, shot down in flames. I wanted a family with him. We'd have made lovely babies. The night it happened…we were going to try.' Ruby's face screwed up and big tears fell onto the table.

'Come on, darling. Let's get to bed, eh? We've had enough wine.'

Fi guided her friend up the stairs and into the master bedroom. She undressed her, then got into bed and cuddled up behind her, holding her tightly.

'Poor, sweet Ruby,' Fi said under her breath once she heard her best friend deeply breathing in slumber.

THREE MONTHS LATER...

CHAPTER FOUR

'Ruby, Ruby, Ruby, Ruby!' Ruby smiled as her friend Tony Choi approached her in Piaf's, her favourite Covent Garden café.

'And how is my little chickadee today then?' Tony asked. 'You are looking a lot like my old Ruby – you have some bones on the meat now.'

'Oh, Tony, you are so funny – looking resplendent in your orange corduroy ensemble.'

'Only my Chinese best to take my little freckly friend Christmas shopping. There are some lovely stalls in the market – we shall go and spend a few Lady Madivas.'

'Godivas, Tony. Lady Godivas – fivers.' His Cockney rhyming slang attempts never failed to amuse.

'What you say, Ruby?'

'Never mind, come on.'

Daphne du Mont, the Edith Piaf lookalike owner of the café, blew them both a theatrical kiss as they headed out into the cold air.

It had been a long time since Ruby had been into Central London. She had closeted herself away in her Putney flat, just wanting to feel safe with George's belongings around her. But today it felt good. The hubbub of people shopping and the general buzz that the big city offered made her feel alive again. When it was time to go home, she said goodbye to Tony and made her way to the Tube.

There was quite a scrum as she approached the escalator. Before she reached it, she suddenly felt her bag being tugged. She swung around, trying to keep hold of it, and unexpectedly, a screech arose from the depths of her red-headed feisty being.

'Get off my back, you thieving fucking little bastards!'

The two thieving fucking little bastards were so shocked that they dropped her bag. Taking flight with her purse that had fallen out in the kerfuffle, they pushed their way through the crowd. Just as she was about to run after them, she felt a strong hand on her shoulder, stopping her from going any further.

'No you don't. They could have knives or anything – you don't know these days. Here, let me help you.'

The strong-handed man bent down and picked up the remaining contents of her bag. Ruby was now crying through anger and shock.

'They have my purse!' she cried.

'It's OK, cash and cards can be replaced. You can't.'

'But you don't understand,' Ruby whimpered. 'My wedding ring is in there.'

'Calm down, it's OK.' Strong Hands had a hypnotic manner about him. 'Come with me. Let's get a sweet cup of tea in you and we can sort this out.' He led her to a coffee shop across the road.

Ruby looked up as a steaming drink was put in front of her.

The man smiled. 'I'm Michael, by the way.'

'I'm really, really sorry.' Ruby began to blub.

'That's a funny name.'

It stopped Ruby in her tracks. She wiped her eyes with her hands, sniffed loudly, and managed a weak smile.

Michael handed her a serviette.

'Ruby, my name's Ruby Stevens. Thank you, but I really must be going, Michael…?'

'Michael Bell.'

'That's got a certain ring to it,' Ruby smirked, taking in his rugby-player frame, quiffed blond hair, soft hazel eyes, and trendy horn-rimmed spectacles. She went to get up.

'Going already? You haven't even had your cup of tea.'

'You wouldn't understand.'

'Try me.'

Ruby sighed and looked him up and down. 'You're very tall.'

'You're very ginger.'

'I've had a terrible year.'

'What's made it so awful? Tell me, Ruby.'

This stopped Ruby in her tracks. This man really did seem to care.

Michael sat down and put his hand over the table to reach hers. 'It's fine, you don't have to if you don't want to, but I could probably match it.'

'My husband died.'

'Shit, that stinks.'

'It stinks, it hurts, it's not fair, and I feel like I've been drowning for the past fifteen months.'

'OK, so it makes my fiancée running off with my best friend a month before our wedding seem quite tame now.'

'Oh no, that's awful too, I'm sorry.'

'Anyway, we have to get that purse of yours back, don't we? – there's a ring to find. What's it like?'

'It's platinum, about this thick.' Ruby put her thumb and finger together to show him. 'And it's engraved inside with

"Rubes & George forever", so I'm sure no one else would want it anyway.'

Michael thought it was probably being melted down as they spoke.

'Come on, let's drink up and report it to the police. You never know. You'd better cancel your cards too, pronto.'

It was raining and dark when they stepped outside.

Six-foot four Michael towered over Ruby's five-foot six frame. He put his hand on her shoulder again. 'Come on, Ruby; I'll come with you to the cop shop.'

'No, no, honestly – I can manage on my own now, thanks,' Ruby flustered. 'I just want to go home.'

'Let me see you home, then. Where do you live?'

'Putney. But I'll be fine, honestly. I'm sorry to have troubled you.'

'Hey, slow down, I'm not an axe murderer, I promise. Take my number, at least, and send me a quick text to let me know you've got home safely.' Ruby took his card and put it in her bag. 'And what about your train ticket, did they take that too?'

'You're good, aren't you?' Ruby managed a smile. 'Luckily, for the very reason I might get mugged, I always put my ticket in a pocket.' She rifled around in her jacket. 'Here it is.'

'Good. Well, take care, and don't forget to let me know when you're safe.'

'I will – and thank you so much, Michael. You've been really kind.'

CHAPTER FIVE

Margaret opened the door to a bedraggled Ruby.

'Oh, me duck, look at the state of you. Get in here by the fire and I'll soon have you warm and dry.'

Since she had moved from her hometown, Reading, to Putney, Ruby's elderly neighbour Margaret had been a rock to her, with and without George.

Over steaming tea served from Margaret's old metal teapot, Ruby relayed the tale of shopping with Tony and the stealing of her purse. Luckily she had managed to cancel her cards before anyone had used them. However, this was all immaterial. It was the loss of her wedding ring that made her ache inside.

'There was this man as well, Margaret. He was so kind – in fact, too kind. He looked after me after those scumbags robbed me.'

'You should relish good nature, Ruby, my girl. Not everyone out there is a shark, you know. Tell me about him.'

'Nothing much to tell, really,' Ruby said nonchalantly. 'He had big, strong hands though – hands like my George.' She looked up to stop the tears from coming. 'He calmed me down, talked some sense about not chasing after the thieves, and got me tea. That was it.'

'Well, he sounds lovely to me.'

'He wanted me to text him when I got home.'

'Well, have you?'

'No. I feel weird. Like…like, I'm being unfaithful to George.'

'That can only be a good thing, Ruby.'

'Why say that?' Ruby looked bemused.

'Because Mr Strong Hands has obviously had more of an effect on you than you think.'

'Don't be ridiculous, Margaret. I don't want another man.'

'Your heart always finds room for love, duck. Gorgeous George will always be in there, but you mark my words, there *will* be space for someone else one day.'

'It's too soon,' Ruby said defiantly.

Wise old Margaret got up slowly from her chair and kissed her young neighbour on the forehead.

'That ol' devil called love doesn't have a calendar.'

Ruby walked down the steps to her flat and threw her keys on the coffee table. As she did so, the business card fell to the floor face down. She left it there, almost scared to pick it up.

She took off her coat and cast it onto an armchair. Her covered sewing machine sat there like an ornament. In fact, she hadn't touched it since the day George died. She fell back on her comfy beige sofa and rubbed her eyes. It had been quite a day. The business card was burning a hole in the floor, and she reached to pick it up.

Michael Bell – Author

How romantic.

Ruby had always loved the idea of being able to write; she most certainly had the imagination, but definitely not the patience. She then began wondering exactly what Michael wrote. Dark fantasy or thriller? Or maybe murder mysteries like Agatha Christie. In the morning she would Google him. She was too tired now.

Her father's words suddenly entered her head. *Treat others as you would have them treat you.*

'OK, Michael Bell the author,' she said aloud. 'I will text you.'

Home safe. Cards cancelled. Thank you for the tea! Ruby Stevens

Within seconds she got a reply.

Why did you hop home? It was lovely to meet you Ruby Stevens and hope I get the pleasure again

Ruby threw her phone onto the sofa as if it was a hot potato. Don't put a question! *I don't want to answer you*, she thought. At the same time, she felt a little bit excited.

She turned off her handset, went to walk to her bedroom, then stopped in her tracks. She marched over to her sewing machine, ripped the cover off of it, and threw it to the floor.

'Don't you smirk, Patrick,' she addressed her stuffed moggy, high up on the shelf in the corner. 'It's about time I started getting on with a few things.'

CHAPTER SIX

Michael unlocked the door to his flat, hung his coat on the back of the door, and put the kettle on. He shivered as he flicked the heating on. He was excited that Ruby had inspired him to get his longed-for first novel down on paper. He wouldn't tell her yet. A six-foot four, strapping man writing romance? She would laugh!

Poor Ruby. He had felt her pain, having been through the mill himself, but he just couldn't imagine how she was coping. Incomprehensible – and what a terrible shock it must have been. With sadness running through him, he began to type.

My first novel – by Michael Bell – TITLE – TBD
PROLOGUE: *Was there such a thing as love at first sight? He had never believed it before. But just being sat in front of such a sweet vulnerable girl had unlocked feelings he never thought he would feel again. He had wanted to sweep her up in his arms there and then and tell her it would all be all right. Plant a kiss on that cute nose and wipe her tears and pain away. It would be tricky for her to let anyone into that broken heart of hers, but he was going to try. And he knew exactly what he had to do first.*

CHAPTER SEVEN

Ruby stopped herself in her tracks when she realised she was singing along to the radio. She couldn't remember the last time she had sung, and almost felt guilty for doing it. This would be her second Christmas without George, the first passing in a complete blur of tears and anger. Her mum and brother just held her at different intervals during the day and let her sob.

She changed the thread on her sewing machine and concentrated on the intricate neckline of the dress she was working on. It made her happy to know that her friend Daphne, the owner of Piaf's Café, would love it – more for the fact she was moving on with her life again than anything else.

After working for another hour, she turned the heating up and started to write a list of all the ex-clients she would re-contact.

Her holiday-let money from Daffodils allowed her to pay her bills, but it would be good to have some real money coming in again. She hoped her clients would understand why she had been off the radar for so long.

Her thoughts were interrupted by her 'Jingle Bells' ringtone. She didn't recognise the number. Maybe a client had got wind she was working again.

'Ruby Stevens speaking.'

'Ruby, hi. It's Michael. Michael Bell.'

Ruby took a deep breath. She hadn't replied to his text, so she didn't think she would hear from him again. But she had to admit, she was actually pleasantly surprised.

'How are you? Recovered from the shock of the other week, I hope.'

'Erm, yes, thanks, Michael. It's just another thing to add to life's rich experiences, I guess.'

'Well, I...I was wondering if maybe we could meet for another cup of tea? Just have a chat, you know, in better circumstances than last time.'

And without even a second thought Ruby did something she never thought she would do again.

'Yes, I'd really like that. How about we go to Piaf's in Covent Garden – it's on Neal Street. I'm free tomorrow afternoon if you're around. I'm guessing you writers can pick and choose your working hours?'

'Actually, we work very hard, us creative types.'

'So that's a date then – well, not a date but...'

Michael laughed. 'I'll see you at three. And, Ruby?'

'Yes?'

'Keep hold of your bloody handbag this time.'

Ruby held her phone to her chest. She looked across to her wedding photo. George's cheeky face smiled back at her and tears began to well in her eyes. She went over and picked up the silver frame.

'It's not that I don't love you, darling. I have got to try and start to move on, and he seems nice. In fact, I think you'd like him.'

Walking to the kitchen to pour herself a glass of wine she began to doubt if she was doing the right thing. Was fifteen months too early to start seeing someone else? What would people say? She took a big gulp of her Sauvignon. It was only a cup of tea – nothing more, nothing less. No, she would go. Michael seemed like a lovely man. The bereavement counsellor had said she would probably feel like this, but she was to do what felt right and just take little steps.

The Grief Monster had been rearing his head for too long now. She would just go along and have a nice time in another man's company.

After all, it gave her an excuse to see the Christmas lights, and give Daphne her Christmas present.

CHAPTER EIGHT

Ruby tapped on Margaret's window. She peered through to see the old lady was engrossed in *Deal or No Deal*.

Opening the door hurriedly, Margaret ushered her in and bade her sit down.

'Let me just see what he's got in his box, dear, then I'm all yours.' She leaned further towards the television. 'See? He should have dealt. There's too much greed in this world, my girl, that's the problem. Now, how about a sherry, duck?' Margaret offered, slurping the remnants of her schooner.

'It's only five o' clock.'

'And? What's that got to do with the price of fish? Now come on, warm your cockles, you've got lots to tell your old neighbour, I'm sure.'

'Not really, just I've made my mind up to see Michael again. We're meeting again this week.'

'That's lovely news. It's about time you had a bit of happiness, darling.'

Margaret plonked a large glass of sherry in front of Ruby and went scurrying back to the kitchen. She shuffled back through to the lounge with a leaflet.

'I picked this up today. Think it may do you good, love. I know you're busy making bits and pieces with your dressmaking, but I think you need to do more with your time. There's still too much dark stuff going on in that noggin of yours.' She handed Ruby a leaflet.

Screwing up her face, Ruby read aloud, '"The Bow Wow Club – new year, new volunteers required." Margaret? What are you getting me into here?'

CHAPTER NINE

In Covent Garden, the carol singers' rendition of 'We Wish You A Merry Christmas' brought a tingle to Ruby's arms. She had always adored Christmas.

She arrived at Piaf's early, greeted by a massive hug from Daphne du Mont. At seventy-something (a lady never tells), Daphne still looked like she was in her fifties, with her long dyed-black hair, false eyelashes, and bright red lipstick. She was wearing her trademark lacy knee-length dress and pointy boots. Norbert, her German-actor toy boy, waved, then carried on serving customers with steaming tea and exquisite pastries. Since working here, Ruby's friendship with the couple had remained strong.

'Darling, darling, how are you? How wondrous to see you, and looking so well too,' Daphne chimed.

'I'm not so bad, actually, I'm having a good week. In fact, I'm meeting a man.'

'A *man*? Well, that's something. I hope he's gorgeous.'

'It's nothing like that. I just owe him a cup of tea, really. He was the one who helped me when I got mugged.'

'Well, even if it is "like that", that's just fine, my little darling. You deserve to have a smile on that face of yours.'

'Oh shit, here he is.'

Michael was much better-looking than Ruby remembered, and also much taller. His glasses accentuated his hazel eyes and he had crinkly laughter lines. She didn't even know how old he was. In fact, all she knew was his name and that he was an author.

'She's a marvellous woman, isn't she?' Michael commented when Daphne had seated them in Ruby's favourite window seat.

'Yes, she really is. I used to work here years ago and she's remained a really good friend.'

'So...' Ruby felt like he was looking right into the depths of her green eyes. 'It's really nice to see you not looking so distressed.'

Ruby's nervous blurt appeared. 'It was so awful that day, and I really want to thank you for helping me. If I'd had my way I'd have been hotfooting it on the Tube after them – and goodness know what would have happened.'

'It was nothing. But I have my uses.' He detected her angst and put his strong hand on her forearm and smiled. Ruby noticed how white his teeth were. 'So, I guess no luck with getting anything back from the police then?' he went on.

'No, nothing. It's losing the ring that hurt the most.' Ruby felt herself well up.

'I know. I'm so sorry about that, Ruby. I can't even imagine how you have coped with everything – at such a young age too.'

'Anyway...' Ruby immediately changed the subject. 'What have you written? I Googled you but couldn't find anything about you.'

'Did you indeed? I'm not sitting in front of some crazed stalker, am I?'

Ruby went as red as her hair. 'I was just...interested.'

'I write short stories and stuff for fun, and freelance articles for some magazines and newspapers to earn a crust.'

'So you're just showing off then, putting "author" on your business card?'

'I guess.' Michael laughed. 'Sounds better than "I will write for food", and who knows, maybe I have a pseudonym?'

Ruby laughed. 'A man of mystery. I quite like that.'

'So, what do you do then?'

'When I'm not wallowing in self-pity, I'm a clothes designer. Actually, that reminds me.' She pulled out a neatly wrapped present from her bag. 'I made Daphne a dress for Christmas.'

'That's brilliant, Rubes – two creative types together. Decision-making could be an issue.'

'I'm just having a cup of tea with you.' At that moment, the cakes arrived. 'Ooh, which one should I have?'

'See, I told you decision-making was an issue.'

Ruby laughed.

'You're almost as beautiful when you laugh as when you cry, do you know that?'

'Oh, shut up.' Ruby blushed. 'But I'm glad you noticed.' She cocked her head to one side and began fiddling with her hair. Shit, she was flirting. She was actually flirting with this near stranger and she didn't want to stop.

'How old are you anyway, Michael Bell?'

'I'm thirty-seven – what about you?'

'Thirty-six.'

'You're looking good on it.'

'Why, thank you. It must be down to the tubs of expensive wrinkle creams I plaster on at night, as I haven't really been looking after myself for the past fifteen months.'

'Do you want to talk about what happened?'

'Not really, Michael. It's just nice to be in a different place for a while. Grief is an insurmountable emotion. If you can bury it even for a second it's like a massive weight being lifted from your mind. And I haven't had many of those seconds before.'

'Here, smell this éclair – I'm not sure if it's fresh.'

Ruby bent forward and Michael pushed the creamy end right onto her nose. She squealed and Daphne beamed knowingly behind the glass counter.

'You sod! I can't believe I fell for that.'

'Here.' Michael gently wiped her face with a serviette. She looked at him as he did it and felt something she hadn't known for a long time.

By the time the cakes had been devoured and Daphne had been given her gift, two hours had flown by. Michael looked at this watch. 'I have to go soon. I'm meeting an editor in Dean Street at six.'

'OK, no problem.' She felt slightly disappointed.

'Before I go I have got something to give you, but you mustn't open it until Christmas Day.'

'A present! How exciting. I feel bad now. I haven't even got you a card.'

'It's fine. I think I've found something I knew you would like.'

Michael looked down at her as they stepped out onto the pavement and held both her hands loosely. 'So, shall we do this again?'

'Yes, we shall, definitely. Have a lovely Christmas.' She looked up at him and had a huge urge to kiss him. She knew he felt the same way too. Just as their lips were about to touch, it started to snow – big, soft flakes that floated aimlessly and gently settled on their hair. Ruby pulled away.

'I'm sorry, Michael, I just…I just can't.' She turned on her heels and started to run down the street.

'Ruby, wait!' He tried to catch her but she was lost amongst the throng of shoppers.

CHAPTER TEN

'Ruby, what on earth's the matter, my pet?'

She was sobbing against Margaret's ample bosom. A fire was roaring in the grate. Bert, the old lady's partner, was snoring in the armchair. 'Wankers!' he suddenly shouted, and twitched.

'Shut it, you silly old sod.' Margaret whacked him with a folded newspaper.

Ruby didn't even flinch. She had first met Bert when he was a tramp. He was, in fact, a very clever professor who had lost himself and taken to the streets. Margaret had kindly taken him in, initially for hot tea and the occasional bath, but over the tannin and bubbles, love had unexpectedly blossomed.

'I met that man – you know, the one who helped me when my purse was stolen. He was really nice, we got on really well. I actually think I fancy him. But then it started snowing.'

'Ruby, you're not making any sense, darling. Why has the snow upset you?'

'Because the night George realised he was in love with me and drove all the way to the Lake District to tell me – the same night he called his wedding off to Candice – it was snowing. And it reminded me of when I kissed *him* and I just couldn't do it.' She started to sob again.

'There, there, duck. It's all right. You won't ever forget George; none of us will. And you are going to have so many moments like this.'

'I know. Poor Michael. He'd done nothing wrong. He's going to think I'm completely mad.'

'No, he's not. If he cares for you, he will understand. And if you are going to take things further it will be a long, hard road for you both. But, if it's meant to be, love will conquer all, darling.'

'I will always love George.'

'I know, but you've got to start loving yourself a bit more too.'

Ruby walked across the road from Margaret's. It was a relief that the snow had subsided. She cranked the heating up and ran herself a hot bubble bath to have a good soak and think about the day's events.

She really must text Michael and explain. By the time she had dried herself, he had already texted.

You OK Ruby? Here for you if you need a chat x

Bless him, he really was so nice. She really couldn't face explaining everything to him right now; she needed to wallow.

I'm so sorry Michael, it was me, not you. I'll call you tomorrow x

She climbed into bed and turned on the television to find *Love Actually* was on. It was the bit where the adulterous one was buying the necklace for his young lover.

Ruby leaped out of bed and rushed to find her handbag. She never could wait when it came to presents. She pulled the gift bag out hurriedly, and a tiny red jewellery box fell to the floor. She snapped it open and couldn't believe her eyes. There, sitting proudly on the black velvet, was a platinum wedding band engraved inside with the words 'Rubes & George forever'.

He had missed the kiss off the end, but Ruby would never ever tell Michael that.

Feeling happy, sad, guilty and confused, all at the same time, she sat back in bed and grasped her knees.

CHAPTER ELEVEN

Slightly perturbed by Ruby's behaviour, Michael snapped open his laptop.

My first novel – by Michael Bell – TITLE – TBD

Chapter 4: *It was Christmas Day, and Michael knew that Ruby would have opened her gift by now. He had trawled the streets near where she had been mugged looking for it, but to no avail. He knew how happy it would make her if he found it so he did the next best thing; he bought one and got it engraved just as she had told him. His feelings for her had already intensified; meeting her earlier had made him realise she really was a special lady. He wasn't quite sure why she had rushed off from him, but knew he would have to try and understand her quirks if he was to be with her.*

She would text and say thank you; he just knew it. Just as he was about to check his phone again, he heard footsteps coming up the stairs. He hurriedly put his phone back into his jeans pocket.

'So, darling hubby...' The pretty blonde pulled him towards her. 'It's surely time for my Christmas present by now?'

CHAPTER TWELVE

'Happy Christmas!' Sam greeted Ruby at the door of their mother's house in Reading. 'You smell nice. Now, let me guess… Prada of some sort?'

'Damn, I didn't think you'd guess – it's new on the market.'

Ben, Sam's guide dog, nuzzled against her legs, his tail wagging furiously.

'Wow, dinner smells good. Where's Mum?' Ruby dumped her bag at the bottom of the stairs.

'I'm here, darling, slogging over a hot stove for you all as usual.'

Ruby went through to the kitchen as Sam plonked himself down in the living room to listen to the TV.

Graham, her mother's partner, was stirring the gravy. He gave Ruby a kiss on the cheek.

'How you doing, sweetheart?' asked her mum.

'Better this year than last, that's for sure,' Ruby said, giving her a big hug. 'God, I'm starving.'

'Well, that's a good sign, darling.'

'Yes. Being really skinny doesn't suit you, Rubes,' Sam piped up, sticking his head round the door. Ruby smiled. Even though her brother had been blind from birth he didn't miss a trick. His sense of touch, smell, and taste had always been heightened, and despite being nine years her junior, he had been a massive support when George had died.

'Where's Beth, anyway?'

'She's with her parents today, in Oxford – she's coming over tomorrow.'

'Isn't it time you made an honest woman out of her?'

'Shut up.' Adulthood had not altered their sibling banter or spats.

Laura Matthews piped up, 'Ooh, it would be lovely to have a wedding to look forward to. Imagine it – my number one son walking down the aisle.'

'Leave him alone,' Graham chipped in. 'He's got plenty of time to get serious.'

'Thanks, Graham, a voice of bloody reason at last. Now come on, mother, where's the turkey? There's a good film starting at three.'

'Queen's speech first, Sam, you know that.'

'Really?' Sam looked to the sky as Ben grunted and put his head on his master's feet.

Beep! Back in the sitting room, Ruby scrabbled in her bag for her phone as she heard the unmistakable sound of a text message.

Happy Christmas Rubes. Hope you liked the present

Ruby gulped. George always called her Rubes, and she wasn't sure if she wanted anyone else to do so.

She had been overwhelmed by the fact that Michael had taken it on himself to replace her wedding ring. It had only been in her purse the day that she got mugged as she was taking it to the jeweller's to get it made smaller. She had lost so much weight since George had died, and ironically she was terrified of it falling off and losing it.

She took a deep breath.

'You all right?' Sam picked up on her anguish.

'I think so.'

'What is it? Tell me.'

'Look, Sam, don't tell Mum 'cos I know she'll probably give me a lecture, but I've met someone and I actually really like him.'

'So, what exactly is the problem? George isn't coming back, as much as we all want him to, and you have to move on, you know that.'

'He – Michael, his name's Michael – bought me another wedding ring, sort of pretending he'd found the original.'

'What a decent bloke. How bloody thoughtful. I wouldn't think to do that. Go with it, Rubes, he obviously likes you. You don't have to rush anything.'

'But I still love George.'

'Why would you *not* still love him? I expect you always will. He was a fucking great bloke; we all loved him, but he'd be kicking your arse if he knew you were still moping.'

'Thanks, Sam.' She kissed her brother on the forehead and started to text.

Cannot believe you found it, thanks so much! Have a lovely Christmas

Within seconds she got a reply.

Seek & ye shall find. Call you after the festivities. Have fun xx

CHAPTER THIRTEEN

Ruby was concentrating on sewing the final button on to a New Year's Eve creation when her phone ringing made her jump. She loved her work so much that she quite often fell into a complete zone and the outside world seemed far away. It really helped, as it allowed her not to think about George every minute of the day.

'Hi, Ruby, it's Michael. How you doing?'

Just the sound of his soothing voice made her heart beat slightly faster. However, she remained cool.

'Hello,' she said. 'I'm OK, actually. Did you have a good Christmas?'

She tried hard not to think about the kiss incident as he continued, 'Oh, you know, the usual – rows over the television, my sister's kids screaming. I'm glad to be home.'

'I sort of know what you mean, but being back home makes me feel a bit lonely when I've been with company for a while.'

'Well, we shall have to put a stop to that, won't we? Look, I wanted to ask you what you were doing on New Year's Eve.'

Ruby gulped. New Year's Eve with a man who wasn't George was just too much to contemplate.

'I'm sorry, Michael, but I've got plans,' she told him.

'Oh, OK. Well, that's good. Would hate to think of you sitting on your own. What are you doing?'

'I'm seeing my friend Fi and her boyfriend James – we'll probably just go to the bar at the end of my road. I'm not a big fan of New Year's Eve, to be honest.'

'I can imagine how hard it must be. Well, if you change your mind and want someone to give you a tall hug when Big Ben strikes, let me know.'

'Michael?'

'I'm here.'

'I just wanted to say thank you so much for going back to find the ring. It meant a lot.'

'I aim to please.'

'And…' Ruby paused. 'I really would like to see you again. It's just…'

'You don't have to explain – I understand. Now take care of yourself, enjoy the night with your friends, and I'll see you next year.'

'Goodnight, Michael. It's so lovely that you're being so cool about everything.'

'Goodnight, sweet girl.'

Ruby hung up and smiled. Sweet girl, eh? He was nice. But this whole situation was bittersweet. She was excited to see him again, but also had this awful underlying feeling that she was betraying George.

She looked up at Patrick, her much-loved moggy. She was sure even though he was stuffed that he changed his expression daily.

'What do you reckon then, old boy?'

CHAPTER FOURTEEN

Michael opened his laptop on his cluttered desk/dining table and pushed some letters to the floor to make space. How he wished he could afford to get out of this one bedroom high-rise. His dream was that this novel would help him to do just that, and so much more. He sighed and began to type.

My first novel – by Michael Bell – TITLE – TBD
Chapter 6: *Michael hung up. He was keenly disappointed that Ruby didn't want to see him on New Year's Eve, but also relieved, as he wasn't sure how he could have sneaked off from the party he was going to near his Clapham home. He realised how much he had missed her quirky humour over Christmas. Odd, but this felt different: sexy, but comfortable too. Just hearing her voice made him yearn to see her, to hug her, and to make her feel safe and wanted once more.*

'Michael. What are you doing up there?'

'Just finishing off a chapter, darling.'

'Damn you and that bloody novel. We've got to be at the party for eight and you need to shower.'

Michael raised his eyes to the ceiling. Why he had got involved with this self-centred woman he'd never know.

CHAPTER FIFTEEN

'You look amazing!' James exclaimed as Ruby walked tentatively up to him and Fi in the busy Putney bar.

'You don't look too shabby yourself. I love a man in black tie.'

'Hands off, he's all mine.' Fi laughed and kissed Ruby on the cheek. 'And bejaysus you do look a picture. Did you design that dress yourself?'

'I did. Love a bit of emerald satin, you know that.'

'Well, it suits you – and you know what? It's lovely to see you looking so radiant. It's been too long. I've missed you.'

'New year, new start and all that.' Ruby smiled, but still felt like crying inside.

'Now, special ladies, what's your poison?' asked James.

'Surely it has to be fizz all the way as it's New Year's Eve,' Fi hollered above the now cranked-up music.

Two bottles of champagne later and James and Fi were already singing along to every tune they even remotely recognised. The bar was heaving and Ruby was not short of admirers. She made small talk, but wasn't in the mood for socialising. She felt drunk, but not happy drunk. In fact, she was dreading the countdown, and at thirty-six years of age, she still didn't know the words to

'Auld Lang Syne' anyway.

At ten to midnight she came out of the toilet. James and Fi were laughing and smooching at the bar. Never had she felt so lonely in a room so full of people. She looked to the door, closed her eyes briefly, and made a wish that at the first stroke of midnight George would walk right in with his East End swagger. He would flash his cheeky grin and swing her round as if nothing had happened.

Reality hit her with a thud as the first *dong!* of Big Ben resounded across the room. The big screen in the corner of the room showed Trafalgar Square. Screams went up and revellers started to shift towards the centre of the bar.

Ruby couldn't stand it any longer. She ran to the door and barged it open. She had to breathe, she needed clear air. The pouring rain ran in rivulets. *Dong!* Big Ben continued to strike his race to midnight. She carried on running, then *crash*, her four-inch heels caught on a drain cover and she went flying onto the pavement. Her hands were bleeding all over her now ripped satin dress and the contents of her bag were strewn all over the road.

The strong-handed man reached down and helped her slowly to her feet. He took off his coat and wrapped it around her shoulders. He used his scarf to wipe her bleeding hands and then held her close while she wept. When her sobbing had subsided, he pulled away, put both his hands on her wet cheeks, pulled her towards him, and planted a slow, tender kiss on her trembling lips.

'Happy New Year, Ruby.'

'Are you an angel?' Ruby blubbered.

'I've been called many things,' Michael smiled.

'What on earth are you doing here?'

'Ssh now. Too many questions. Let me pick up your stuff and

get you home and in the warm.'

Ruby nodded. 'I'd better text Fi, she'll be worried.' At that moment, Fi herself came charging up the road.

'What the feck, Ruby? You frightened the bleeding life out of me. I turned round and you weren't there, then some bloke said he'd just seen you lying in the road.'

'I'm fine, honestly.'

'And who are you?' Fi looked up at Michael.

'It's fine, he's a friend. He's going to walk me home.'

'Ruby, you're drunk, are you sure?'

'Fi, you're drunker and I'm very sure.'

'OK, darling. Make sure you ring me in the morning. Happy New Year, Rubes.' She hiccupped and steadied herself on Michael's arm. 'Happy New Year…friend – and make sure you fecking look after her right.'

'I will, and nice to meet you too.' Michael grinned at Fi's outlandishness.

Back at Ruby's flat, Michael put the kettle on as Ruby went to the bathroom to wash her sore hands and get out of her wet, ripped dress. He noticed *the* wedding photo and it made him feel sad and a bit weird at the same time. They looked so young and happy, and George was without a doubt a very handsome man.

'I'm sorry, Michael.' He was sitting on the sofa waiting for her when Ruby appeared in black jogging bottoms and a black T-shirt. 'Every time I see you it's a disaster zone. Just look at the state of me. I'm too drunk and hurting to make an effort.'

'Hey, come here. You look beautiful, and who wants mediocre anyway? Never a dull moment with you, that's for sure.'

Ruby stood in the lounge doorway looking awkward. Taking a deep breath, she went on, 'I'm sorry I ran off the other day when you went to kiss me. It wasn't that I didn't want to, it's just…'

Michael stood up and put his big arms around her. She looked up and felt lost in his hazel eyes.

'I'm glad I met you, Michael Bell.'

And then they kissed. A kiss that Ruby didn't want to end. A kiss that made her toes curl. A kiss that she never thought she'd experience again.

'Wow.' She came up for air.

'And how glad am I that I met you, Ruby Stevens.'

'I can't make you any promises,' Ruby said quietly.

'Promises are for wimps,' Michael smiled.

'Stay with me.' Ruby put her head to the side and looked at him.

Michael knew he might have to wait quite a while for the three little words he really wanted to hear, but for now these would do just fine.

CHAPTER SIXTEEN

Michael flinched at the strength of the words he was typing.

My first novel – by Michael Bell – TITLE – TBD

Chapter 8: *'What do you mean, you got fucking arrested?' Emily's eyes were glaring. 'And why is there blood all over your scarf?'*

'Oh Em, I'm so sorry. I was so drunk, I went outside to get some air and got into a fight.'

'A fight? You couldn't fight your way out of a paper bag!'

'I didn't start it – you know me. I was trying to break one up and then got involved. The police came and carted me off in the back of a van.'

'Then why didn't you call me? I've been worried sick all night.'

'They took everything off of me, just threw me in a cell and told me to sober up.'

'So what's going to happen now? It won't look too great if one of the precious papers you write for get a whiff of this.'

'Calm down, it's fine. I talked my way out of it this morning. There are no charges against me.' Then: 'It was awful, Em. I was so worried knowing you wouldn't know

where I was.'

Michael pulled his wife towards him.

'Happy New Year, darling. Come on, forgive me – it really wasn't my fault.'

Emily tried to keep her cross face on but failed miserably.

'You silly sod. Happy New Year. Now, get out of those filthy bloody clothes and I'll run you a bath.'

Michael lay back in the warm bubbles and breathed a sigh of relief. He didn't believe lying could come so easily to him. However, his guilt was completely overshadowed by another emotion. The feeling of complete and utter love for a woman he hardly knew.

The Clapham party at their friends' house had been OK, the drink was flowing, the company was old and familiar, but the urge to see sweet, beautiful Ruby had overtaken him. He just had to see her – and nothing was going to stop him.

Michael hadn't run so fast since he'd been on the rugby field five years ago. He hadn't expected in a million years that she would want him to stay with her. His intention was just to wish her Happy New Year, give her the kiss they should have had in the snow that day, and then leave – racing back to the party before anyone noticed.

And then when he had found her so crushed and upset he knew he had to be with her. Getting into bed beside her, he had wanted nothing more than to make love to her all night. But she was so drunk and so sad and he just knew her head wasn't in the right space for that, even though she said it was what she wanted.

So, he just held her close all night, kissing and cuddling her until her breathing went shallow. So overwhelmed by his feelings for her he watched her sleep. Then at 5 a.m., he had crept out of bed, leaving a note by the kettle before quietly clicking the front door shut behind him.

Michael clicked his laptop shut. 'Yes!' he said out loud. 'This is going to be a bloody bestseller!'

CHAPTER SEVENTEEN

Ruby groaned as she woke. Her head was pounding. She reached over for a glass of water and, amazingly, found one next to her. She didn't remember getting that. She then sat bold upright in bed. Oh shit. What she *did* remember was asking Michael to stay. In fact, she had actually been far more improper in her suggestion. Feeling a sharp pain in one of her knees, she was mortified to think that she must have fallen over too.

She listened for any noises – surely he hadn't just upped and gone? Then, crashing back down on the pillow, she winced at the stinging in her hands. The cuts were minimal but the skin had begun to tighten around them.

'Michael?' she called out.

She eased herself slowly out of bed and dragged on her dressing gown, noting that she was still wearing her joggers and T-shirt. She walked through to the bathroom for some painkillers then went to the kitchen to put the kettle on. She beamed when she saw a note. *I'm glad I met you, Ruby Stevens, now get some more sleep and we'll catch up later. xx*

Her phone then beeped from the other room, and she rushed to read the text.

Ruby, fecking call me as soon as you get this message

Ruby sighed. She knew she wouldn't get away with going home with a beautiful stranger for long without Fi O'Donahue wanting the full scoop. She rang her.

'Happy New Year, Fi Fi La Bouche.'

'How's it that you're so fecking chirpy when my head feels like it's been chewed by a badger?' Ruby laughed as her feisty friend groaned. 'Oh, maybe it's something to do with the six foot stranger shagging ya last night.'

'Fiona O'Donahue, don't tar me with the same brush as you.'

'Who is he, Rubes? I'm sure I would have noticed him if he'd been in the pub.'

'His name is Michael and I met him a couple of weeks ago. He was the one who helped me when I got mugged. We've got so much to catch up on. I just felt a bit weird telling you everything when I wasn't sure if there was anything to tell.'

'But you normally would tell me, Rubes. I'm hurt. In fact, I'm mortally wounded.'

'Shut up, you bloody drama queen. I've realised now how much I do like him. I could quite easily see me with him.'

'That is so brilliant, Rubes.'

'Do you think it's too soon though, Fi?'

'I'm the one who's been saying it's time to move on. You know my motto. "If you fall off one horse, get under another one as quickly as possible"!'

Ruby went quiet.

'Oh, Rubes, I'm sorry – that was heartless. This must be so hard for you.'

'It is, but it also feels right.'

'So, did you sleep with him?'

'Drunken harlot status was resumed and I actually asked him

to “fuck me”. I can’t believe I actually used those words.’

‘Good girl, Rubes. So how was it?’

‘We didn’t do it. He was lovely about it and declined the offer, saying I wasn’t in the right headspace for it and he wanted it to be perfect when we did it for the first time.’

‘Are you sure he’s not gay?’

‘Fi!’

‘Well, it was on a plate, darlin’ – and he is a man, after all.’

‘There are obviously still some decent ones out there, and he’s certainly one of them.’

‘I am so happy for you. Now, I need to get back into bed with Monsieur Kane. He just told me something has come up that needs attending to. Love you, mate. Here for you always, you know that. And Happeeee New Year!’

‘Ditto. Now go play horses, you dirty cow.’

CHAPTER EIGHTEEN

'Bet you wish your girlfriend was hot like me.' Ruby sang and danced around the kitchen to the old Pussycat Dolls' track on the radio. She had forgotten what it felt like to be happy. It was weird, like discovering a new emotion. Despite her hangover she decided to have a good clean-up of the flat. Pink rubber gloves on, she began sifting paperwork. She pinned The Bow Wow Club leaflet that Margaret had given her on to her noticeboard, telling herself she would look into whatever it was later. She lifted the cutlery tray out of the drawer to give it a scrub and suddenly stood there motionless. Lying in the bottom of the drawer was an envelope. Her name was written on it in George's handwriting.

She took a deep breath and ripped it open hungrily. It was a birthday card. One of the ones you can get personalised. Below the words, *My Own Trouble & Strife*, it had a picture of her grinning widely, wearing a bra with a dirty handprint on each breast. She smiled through the tears remembering the day George had got back from work and grabbed her as she was getting ready to go out.

Wanting to relish every single moment of being this near to George again, she slowly opened up the card.

I had to remortgage for the bloody candles this year! I love you Rubes and don't EVER forget that.
Yours forever G XXXX

Ruby fell to her knees on the kitchen floor, holding the card to her chest. He must have hidden it just before he died. The silent scream gripped her from within at the realisation that he was never coming back.

Beep! She pulled herself up slowly got up and went to her phone.

Hey Rubes, hope you're feeling better. Last night was so special. Can't wait to see you again x

She threw the phone on to the sofa with force. 'Fuck off! Just fuck off! I'm not *your* Rubes!'

CHAPTER NINETEEN

'What do you mean the tickets are booked?' Ruby said wearily to an excited Fi at the end of the phone.

'Exactly that. Me and thee are going on a little trip. I'm working on an event in Prague and you are coming with me. You actually don't have a choice.'

'I look like crap.'

'All the more reason to come. There's a spa at the hotel and it's time you stopped growing your muff down to your ankles and dragging that pretty little chin of yours on the floor.'

Ruby had to laugh.

'When are we going?'

'Tomorrow morning. Just for a couple of days.'

Ruby pulled her overnight bag down from the top of the wardrobe in the bedroom she used to share with George. The whole room was still a shrine to the man. She even wasn't able to throw any of his clothes out. There was a Porsche magazine on the bedside table. 'One day,' he always used to say as he fingered the pages before going to sleep.

The last thing she felt like doing was getting on a plane and moving out of her comfort zone, but for her own sanity she knew she had to do it.

Finding the birthday card on New Year's Day had thrown her completely back into her world of grief and longing. Days turned into nights again and she was drinking far too much. Her nearest and dearest had all tried to rally her, to no avail.

Fi, as usual, had worked her magic, knowing that Ruby wouldn't be able to resist a trip away, especially as she had booked the tickets already.

She threw clothes and cosmetics into a bag with a weary heart and then carried out her nightly ritual of smelling George's pillow. She hadn't washed the sheets since he had died, hoping that a little trace of him might remain where she could touch and smell him.

She wheeled her bag out by the front door, poured herself a glass of wine, and sat on the sofa. The lonely silence enveloped her and she was actually glad that she was getting away from these four walls.

The peace was interrupted by the beep of a text message. *If I had just one wish it would be to take your pain away right now. M x*

'Aw,' Ruby said aloud. How unfair had she been to this poor man. Five weeks he had been contacting her, not in any way pushy, just telling her how much he cared.

Fuelled by wine and loneliness, she started to tap out a message.

CHAPTER TWENTY

'Michael woke at 6 a.m. as usual. His first thought as usual was of Ruby. Well, if he couldn't see her, at least he could keep writing about her.

My first novel – by Michael Bell – TITLE – TBD
Chapter 10: *Michael nearly jumped out of his skin when a reply came through on his phone. He had got so used to texting Ruby and being ignored it felt almost weird that she had replied. In fact, he wasn't sure he wanted to know what she was going to say. He felt too much for her to let her go. He realised that staying the night with her on New Year's Eve would have evoked all sorts of emotions, especially as he was the first man she had had any physical contact with since her husband died. But George wasn't coming back, and surely when the time was right she would see that she needed to fill the George-shaped hole in her heart with someone else. A different shape maybe, but someone who felt a similar immense love for this gorgeous being.*

At least by her not responding with a negative there was a chance that he might see her again. He had made a pact with himself that if she didn't come back to him by

Valentine's Day he had one more trick up his sleeve, then that would be it.

He tentatively opened the message.

You're a good man Michael Bell, but I'm not in a good place at the moment. I'm sorry.

Right, that was it, not even a kiss. Not even anything really. She had said nothing he didn't already know. He wasn't going to sit around and wait any longer. It was about time Michael Bell got on with his life. If her husband had been alive it would be a damn sight easier, but competing with a dead man – well, how could he possibly do that?

Maybe meeting his ginger widow had done him a favour. His love for Emily had been waning for a while now but he just didn't have the balls after a mere two years of marriage to call it a day. Her parents for a start would go mad: their 'keep up with the Joneses' wedding had cost them a fortune, and the impoverished writer would have proved their fears right – that he really was not good enough for their darling only child.

But Ruby had given him the strength to do it. Whether he saw her again or not, he knew that there was a greater love than he had for Emily out there. He had to be true to himself and not waste his life with someone who just wasn't The One.

Michael sat back from his screen. Hmm. How could he leave Emily?

A lightbulb moment hit him. 'Yes – yes, that's perfect,' he said aloud and began to type furiously again.

'Michael, I'm home,' Emily called up the stairs.

'Hi, darling, won't be a minute.' Just as he was shutting down his laptop Emily came bounding into his office and threw her arms around his neck.

'Whoa, what makes me deserve this then?'

'Close your eyes and hold out your hands.'

Michael did as he was told. On opening them he could feel the bile rise to his throat. For there, staring up at him from a little white wand, was the word PREGNANT.

CHAPTER TWENTY ONE

Ruby threw herself on the massive bed she was sharing with Fi at the Hilton in Prague.

'Good work, Donahue!'

'Only an executive room for my little ginger minger.'

'I have to see the bathroom.' Ruby jumped up. 'Don't you just love hotel rooms, Fi? You can be who you want and do what you want in them.'

'After working in events so long, I know this sounds terrible but I've got a bit blasé about it, to be honest.'

Fi went to the mini-bar. 'This is what *I* always check out first.' She perused the selection of miniatures on offer. 'Time for a little livener, methinks; I haven't got to do anything until the morning. We, my friend, are going to rip the pub out of the Czech Re*pub*lic.'

With its ancient buildings and magnificent churches, the Old Town Square was picture-perfect. Wrapped up for the cold, the girls sat under a big heater at one of the pavement cafés.

'It's like being in Disneyland, Fi. I love it.'

'Yes, it's magical, isn't it? Keep your bag close though, Rubes. It's renowned for pickpockets in this touristy bit.'

'Do you know the history of this bit of the city then? You've been here a few times.'

'Well, my friend, I could quite easily bore you senseless, but we're here to drink and have fun. However, as you have asked me, this area dates back to the 12th century, and started life as the central market place for Prague. Over the centuries, buildings of Romanesque, Baroque, and Gothic styles were erected around the market, bringing with them stories of wealthy merchants and political intrigue.'

'Who needs a travel guide when you've got a Fi O'Donahue, eh?' Ruby laughed.

'Not just a mad Irishwoman, me. No, siree.'

'It could be really romantic.'

'It is really romantic, Rubes, but that isn't on *our* agenda tonight.'

'I don't think it will ever be on mine again.'

'Of course it will. Dare I ask what's happening with the lovely Michael?'

'I've been a complete bitch, actually. He texts me without fail every other week, a nice message, nothing heavy but just to let me know he's still there.'

'And?'

'And I totally ignore him because I don't really know what to do.'

'What do you think you should do?'

'I don't know, Fi. I really do like him. We click, but he's just not George.'

'He's never going to be George, mate. Like your ex-boyfriends weren't the one before and so on. You moved on from them OK.'

'Yes, but I left them not loving them like I loved George.'

'That's a lie, Rubes. You loved Dean – remember him? You left him, then you wanted him back. But you got over him.

Harsh, but true. Time will help. You never saw him again – and do you miss him?'

'No, but occasionally I may go somewhere or someone will say something that reminds me of him.'

'Yes, exactly. But that didn't stop you moving on.'

Ruby was thoughtful.

'Now, catch that waiter's eye, Rubes. He's a bit of a dish, and we need more drinks.'

'Actually, that's another thing,' Ruby told her friend. 'Michael calls me Rubes, but George called me that and it doesn't feel right.'

'I call you fecking Rubes.'

'That's different.'

'Just tell him what you just said to me. Be open, be honest, Ruby. He obviously likes you a lot – I mean, he's seen you in some bad situations. You've fallen over in the street pissed. You haven't even put out and he still wants you.'

Just as the waiter was taking their order, there was a commotion in front of them. A girl was knocked to the ground as her bag was grabbed from her hand. One of her friends chased after the thief. Ruby bit her lip and instinctively reached for her phone.

Michael, I'm in Prague. Let's meet when I'm back. Rubes x

CHAPTER TWENTY TWO

Ruby threw her keys onto the growing pile of post on the kitchen table. As she did so, the pile fell to the floor. She looked around her. The maisonette was a complete tip. Two-day-old dishes were piled in the sink, there was a nasty odour coming from the bin, and she couldn't remember the last time she had mopped the floor.

She walked through to the lounge and looked up at Patrick. The black and white cat grinned down at her in all his stuffed glory.

'Yes, Patrick – I know. I'm a dirty slut. But no more. It's about time I sorted this place out.'

Ruby went to her Bose system, found her most upbeat CD, and cranked it up full-blast. Reaching under the kitchen sink she pulled on her rubber gloves and got to work. Once every room downstairs was gleaming, she made her way up with a roll of black bags. As she entered the bedroom that she had once shared with George, she took a very deep breath.

'Right, Georgie boy, let's sort out these clothes of yours, shall we?' She pushed emotion to one side and started to create separate piles for the tip, charity shop, and to keep. She couldn't bear to look at photos just yet, so moved that box to the spare room. She threw full black bags down the stairs and then got into the bed. She pressed her face into the pillows, where her beautiful husband had once laid his head. All she could smell was the dull, musky odour of unwashed cotton. Bracing herself, she stripped the bed as fast as she could, screwed up the sheets, and ran out to put them in the dustbin. Tomorrow she would buy new ones.

Running back up to the now-clean room, she hoovered it methodically. Once she was done, she put her hands on her hips and looked to the sky.

'I will never forget you, George Stevens,' she said out loud. 'You gave me some of the best years of my life, but I have to get on now.'

CHAPTER TWENTY THREE

'You look stunning, Ruby.' Michael kissed her on the cheek as she arrived at the Soho bar.

'Thanks.' She looked him in the eye. 'It's really good to see you.'

'Well, that's a good start, I guess.' He smiled. 'Now, what are you drinking, madam?'

'Glass of Sauvignon, please.'

'Quick, go grab that free table in the corner and I'll bring it over to you.'

Ruby took off her coat and put it on the chair behind her. She glanced over to Michael at the bar and noticed other women clocking him. He really was good-looking. Tall and broad, very different to her pint-sized, dark-haired George. She liked his trendy glasses and the little quiff at the front of his hair. George had never been a clothes horse, and would have been quite happy just to wear his faded jeans and West Ham shirt every day if he could have got away with it.

'So.' Michael put her wine down in front of her and took off his coat to reveal a beautifully ironed black shirt. He smelled divine. 'How are you doing, Rubes?'

'You know me, always all right.'

'If you're not getting mugged or falling arse-over-tit in the street.'

Ruby laughed. 'I'm sorry I've been so difficult. It's just…it's so weird meeting you. I feel as if I'm being really naughty.'

'I like naughty – and for God's sake, if I didn't understand I wouldn't still be here, would I? I do have to say, though, I was just considering deleting your number, then what happens? You go to Prague and text me.'

'Really? That's awful. Please don't delete me.'

'Well, a man can only take so much of being ignored. I do have some pride, you know.'

'Look, I feel like I'm getting ready. I've been chatting to lots of my friends and they have helped me to realise that it's time I moved on. And I like you.' She paused. 'In fact, I like you a lot, Michael Bell.'

'You're not too shabby yourself, Ruby Stevens. Now, get that wine down you and we can move on to the restaurant.'

Conversation flowed freely over dinner, as did the wine.

'You're not wearing your wedding ring,' Michael noticed.

Ruby shuffled in her seat. 'No, it doesn't quite fit.'

'Oh.' Michael looked disheartened.

'Just to have it back is amazing though.' Naively, not realising that her *not* wearing it made him so much happier.

'And anyway, if I'm going to start down this road to recovery I think the time is right now not to wear it. I mean, people might think we are married.'

It was Michael's turn to shuffle in his seat. 'Perish the thought, eh?'

They walked out into the freezing February air. Michael looked to the sky.

'What are you looking at?'

'Just checking it's not going to snow.'

Ruby laughed. 'Come here, you.' She grabbed Michael round the waist. 'I've been wanting to do this since New Year's Eve.'

And on a busy Friday night on a Soho street she kissed him.

His mouth was so warm and inviting and lust ran right through her. She could feel him getting hard against her and she didn't want it to stop. It wasn't until a car full of teenagers tooted and shouted, 'Get a room,' that they broke away from each other.

'So shall we?' Michael enquired.

'Shall we what?'

'Get a room.'

'I er…'

'Don't you run away from me again, Ruby Stevens. And anyway, I've already booked a hotel.'

'Fuck me, that's presumptuous.' Ruby was wide-eyed. 'Come on then, let's get naughty.'

Michael, despite being such a big man, was soft and gentle. He reassured her that she was beautiful, despite her being aware that she had lost her womanly curves. Their lovemaking was at first fast and furious, then tender and loving. When they both lay back, completely spent, Michael propped himself up on one elbow and pushed her fringe off her face.

'Are you OK, angel?'

Ruby bit her lip. 'Not really.'

He engulfed her in a warm and comforting hug as she sobbed.

'The first time was always going to be difficult, we knew that.'

He could feel Ruby nodding beneath his strong arms.

'That's why I booked a hotel. Neutral ground.'

'It's not that it wasn't good, Michael, it was. You are bloody sex on a stick.'

'Ssh, now.' Michael rocked her gently in his arms and wondered what on earth he had taken on. This relationship wasn't going to be like climbing a mountain; it was going to be like scaling the whole of the bloody Andes.

CHAPTER TWENTY FOUR

Michael pushed open the door to his flat. He was knackered, but very happy. He wanted to have a siesta but knew if he wished to achieve his dream, he just had to keep writing, especially with such emotion flowing through him.

My first novel – By Michael Bell – TITLE – TBD
Chapter 15: *Michael pushed open the front door quietly. Emily liked to have a lie-in on a Saturday, especially now she was pregnant. She was, however, already up.*

'Morning, darling, so how was your writing course?'

'Really good, thanks. Feel I'm ready to finish that book I've always said I've had in me.'

'Thank goodness for that, we might have some decent money if you can make it a bestseller. What was the hotel like?'

'You know – nothing special. It's not really about the luxury on these courses, more about the content. A few drinks in the bar and then bed – no more exciting than that.'

'Well, I'm off shopping with Mother now. I'll be back around six – thought we could get a take-out later. I've got a craving for spicy things at the moment.'

Michael turned on his computer. How could he be so blasé about the whole situation? His wife of two years was pregnant and here was he, spending the night with another woman. Another woman who made him feel so alive. More alive, in fact, than he had ever felt in his life. The sex had been amazing. Just kissing her in that Soho street had made him want to shag the arse off her there and then.

'Hmm.' Michael grunted, then sat back and stared at the computer screen. Was that too rude? He was sure he'd read that Stephen King had said 'don't edit as you go along'. So he could worry about that later.

Loving that he had so much material now, he restarted typing.

He just wasn't in love with Emily any more. Why had he procrastinated for so long? If he had got any balls he would have ended it six months ago, but now he was going to be a father and the responsibility of it all was suffocating.

He pushed that thought to the back of his mind and concentrated on something he had to deal with sooner rather than later. Valentine's Day was coming and he had to make sure his plans were tight. Not to see Ruby just wasn't an option.

Michael swivelled in his chair. Now what would his lady readers like to see him do? Romance didn't always come easily to him, and he knew this would have to be special.

CHAPTER TWENTY FIVE

Ruby pushed open the door to the church hall in trepidation. She felt as if she was embarking on a new adventure, just like when she had set herself her twelve-jobs-in-twelve-months mission a few years ago – but that's another story.

However, this was even scarier. She was frightened as she knew she was about to face her own demons.

She had looked with interest on the internet last night.

The Bow Wow Club – from Struggle to Joy!

If you are the partner of a widow or a widower, we understand.

Come along for support and advice on how to help keep your new relationship on track.

'Love. Love, love, love, love!' A tall, well-built black man walked briskly towards her. Despite being camp as Christmas, Ruby thought his wide nose and full lips made him handsome. He reminded her of the lovely dreadlocked Justice whom she had met while working at the home for retired actors, way back when she was on her twelve-jobs-in-twelve-months mission.

Since meeting Michael, she found herself looking at taller

men a lot more. Mr Bow Wow must have been in his early thirties, and was dressed in a pair of trendy blue jeans, with a black, crew-neck cashmere jumper and brown boots. She noticed how big his feet were and how the trendy tweed flat cap suited him. He whipped it off and threw it at a coat-stand, a perfect shot.

'Thank God you're here! You must be Susie?' He had a faint Glaswegian accent. His close-cropped hair was dyed bright orange and Ruby had an urge to rub her hands through it.

'Er…no. I'm Ruby. I called you yesterday.'

'Ah, yes. That's it, that's it. Never good with names. Another kind soul to help me with all the lost ones I have to deal with. We've been up and running for six months now and I haven't managed to shift any of them. They all keep coming back week after week.'

So much for being charitable, Ruby thought, trying not to laugh.

'We meet every Tuesday at eight.' He paused. 'And don't be late. Ha ha ha, that gets them every time.'

Ruby had to laugh too.

'Beautiful face, beautiful hair. Sadness behind those eyes, though. Don't tell me you've lost one too?'

Ruby nodded. 'My husband, over a year ago.'

'Fab-u-lous. You can feel it all with them. The last volunteer was bloody useless. She was young. And spoiled, spoiled rotten. One of those silver-spooned lot, you know? I think the only thing that had ever died on her was her hair extensions. I doubt she's even swatted a wasp in her life. My name's Simon, by the way. Simon D-Y-E.' He spelled it out. 'Yes, yes, hilarious, I know but that's not why I chose to do this or my current vocation, honestly.'

Ruby wondered why, in that case, he had chosen to do this

and what exactly his current vocation was. Simon took a deep, exaggerated breath. Just listening to him was wearing her out. He carried on. 'In fact, Ruby, talking of wasps...'

'Er...were we?'

'You have to see the gravestone under the old willow tree at the bottom of the graveyard. Laugh? I needed an incontinence pad! Right, let's come to my office.' He ushered her to the desk at the front of the hall. It didn't really warrant the label of a 'hall', as it was no bigger than a larger-than-average lounge. It had windows covering two sides, covered by cheap plastic Venetian blinds. She noticed a big corkboard crammed with pictures she assumed had been drawn by the Sunday-school kids. And, on the back of the main door there were scruffy notices of Mum and Baby Groups, Zumba classes, and Stop Smoking clinics.

A picture of Jesus knocking on a door with the words 'And I say unto you, ask, and it shall be given you; seek, and you shall find; knock, and it shall be opened unto you', had been hung above the small kitchen area at the back of the room.

Ruby was quite taken aback when she spotted this, as she was sure Michael had once used the same 'seek and find' expression when talking about her wedding ring. She hadn't questioned if he was religious or not. If he was, it wasn't a problem. Everyone was entitled to have a faith. However, since George had died, it had intensified her feelings that if there was a real God then He wouldn't have ended her young husband's life so abruptly...

Simon's voice brought her back into the room.

'Here is my office.' He pointed to the messy table in front of him and sat down. 'Now, turn the heating up, Susie, honey – there's a dial in the kitchen, back of the room. Bloody January, they are usually all more depressed than usual, what with Christmas just gone. Bugger! I forgot to bring the tissues. I expect we'll get a few new ones. A new year gives people a kick up the arse.'

'Yes, it does,' Ruby said far too quietly. And, then, without saying a word, Simon reached for Ruby's hand and kissed it gently. She felt warm inside at his kindness.

'Aren't they all in relationships here, or am I missing something?' she asked. 'I thought that this was a club to help people dating other people who had lost somebody?'

'Just wait, Little Red Riding Whip, just wait. Right, heating on. Tea urn boiling. Custard creams open. Yum! Seven fifty-five, let's rock'n'roll. Oh, I nearly forgot.' He threw a scruffy piece of A4 paper at her. 'I've summarised the regular miserable lot here for you. Well, more for me not to forget their bloody names and why they're here ,really. So, I'll have that back when you're done, thanks, Susie. They hate it when I address them wrongly.'

Simon yawned and went on, 'And, as for the relationship bit, half of them are grieving. Just want the company. They read the bloody leaflet wrong. We *are* supposed to be helping people deal with relationships when they are dating someone who has lost a loved one, but we are not here to act as a lonely hearts club. However, we are almost under the Good Lord's roof in this hall – and who am I to turn anyone away who needs His and our help?'

Ruby had already fallen a little bit in love with Simon Dye. Not only for his madcap demeanour, but also for his shared love of her favourite biscuit. He was a hoot.

Goodness knows what would happen when people started arriving for their 'therapy'!

Maybe laughing at death and all the sadness that it brought *was* the answer?

CHAPTER TWENTY SIX

Ruby offered up her biggest smile as The Bow Wow Club attendees began to flock slowly in. She politely said hello as each one of the colourful assortment helped themselves to tea, coffee and custard creams. Her smile becoming even broader on catching Simon discreetly reaching into his drawer and pouring Diet Coke into whatever was already in his mug. Vodka, she suspected.

She took a seat at the back of the small room while everyone finished getting drinks and catching up on Christmas stories. When ready, they slowly scraped the old wooden chairs into a circle position. It gave Ruby a quick chance to look down at Simon's profile description entitled: *The Regulars!*

Jimmy Chislehurst: 42. Works in a roadside café trailer. Highly intelligent. Suffers from Tourette's when ill at ease. Collar-length hair. Unshaven. Bad breath. Still looking for love after losing wife ten years ago.

Eleanor Saunders (Ellie): 37. Marketing assistant. Vivacious, curly-haired blonde. Dating Danny, same age, who lost his wife last year. (Danny sounds a right bastard, to be honest!)

Nick Redwood: 29. Fireman. Hot, hot, hot! (Dating Rebecca, a glamorous woman in her late 40s who was married to an octogenarian millionaire who died in the summer.) She doesn't sound good enough for him either! But I know, I know, I just hear their side.

Cali Naylor: 51. Voluptuous. Very Zen (Always brings Fanny the wonder dog with her, whom I'm allergic to!) Dating Eric, who is the same age as her and a widower. (I think HE probably deserves better.)

Not scared of speaking her mind herself, Ruby still couldn't quite believe how rude Simon was. For fear of any of these people getting even a slight glimpse of the eccentric leader's views, she made a point of hiding the paper inside her handbag.

She looked around the room. There were seven people present and she could now pinpoint the regulars easily.

Simon was right about one of them at least. The Fireman *was* gorgeous, with his cute young face and dark, spiky hair. She wondered why he had got himself into such a tricky relationship position. But, as dear old Margaret had said, love didn't have a calendar, so why would it have a mirror, or sense, either?

Jimmy's appearance was as bad as described, but behind his heavy-rimmed glasses and unshaven appearance, she could see a lovely face. He had just let himself go, bless him. As for Cali, Simon had been spot on to use the word 'voluptuous', as she had the most magnificent pair of breasts that Ruby had seen in a while. Her size-sixteen hourglass figure suited her big personality. And her soft, round face housed smiling blue eyes. Ellie was as loud, bright, and bubbly as her long blonde curls, which appeared to dance behind her as she chatted away animatedly to the Fireman.

'Right. Now, you lovely lot. *Atchoo!*' Simon sneezed loudly.

'Cali! How many times? I really don't think I can cope with Fanny's hair for much longer.'

'She's had a shampoo this week. We thought it might make things better, didn't we, Fluffy Foo?' The woman assumed a baby voice as she lovingly stroked the little black mongrel.

Simon blew his nose loudly, then leaned against his desk. 'Anyway, enough of Cali's Fanny.' A short burst of laughter went around the room. 'Welcome, new recruits – we shall get to know you all in a minute.' The three newbies smiled nervously. 'But first to introduce our newest Bow Wow volunteer, the radiant, redheaded, sassy Susie.'

'Ruby.' Ruby's correction from the back of the room was drowned by a round of applause. 'I'm Ruby,' she repeated far too loudly as the handclapping ended abruptly.

'I'm sure he's pissed,' the Fireman whispered to Ellie, who giggled like a schoolgirl.

'Ah! Sorry – may I repeat: but first to introduce the radiant, red-headed, raunchy *Ruby*. Another round of applause for a charitable good citizen to keep you Bow Wowers on track, please. And…' Simon paused for effect '…of course, to keep you ahead of those black and white widows and widowers who are not making your life easy.'

Everybody clapped again as Ruby reddened and then cringed as Simon continued, 'Sadly, young Ruby lost her husband recently too, so she will understand from one side at least.'

A unified 'Awww,' went around the room.

'OK, so first question to the group.' Simon began pacing. 'Any sexual problems over Christmas?'

The regulars didn't flinch, the newbies shuffled, and Ruby put her hand to her face in horror. What on earth had her dear old neighbour got her into?

CHAPTER TWENTY SEVEN

Ruby was lying on her bed and flicking through a magazine when her phone rang.

She was quite content to be back in her old marital bed. In fact, she liked it a lot, as this mattress was much comfier than the cheap stained one that had originally been on George's bed before she had moved in. She really must get around to changing it. *Why did people do that?* she wondered. Whenever she had stayed at friends' houses, the spare room bed was always so damn uncomfortable. As soon as she got the money from the invoice she had just submitted, she would make sure to go out and buy a new one.

Her dress-making trade was booming at the moment. Lots of Valentines' brides had called her up, due to the domino effect of recommendations. She loved putting her creative flair to the test and adored using all sorts of glorious silks, chiffons and sequins that elevated wedding budgets allowed.

'Rubes, it's me,' came Fi's voice. 'What you doing?'

'I am lying on my bed with a pile of trashy magazines and a packet of custard creams, if that's all right with you, Ms O'Donahue.' She smiled as a vision of her unruly, dark-haired mate came to the fore of her mind.

'Jealous, I've been eating fecking dust since New Year's Day. My dry January has been wetter than expected, too. James says I've ballooned, and if I'm expecting a proposal this year I best do something about it.'

'I'd tell him to bugger off! You looked fine to me New Year's Eve. Anyway, not long until Valentine's now, is it? Is he whisking you off somewhere lovely?'

'Well, that's the point, Rubes. He hasn't said a thing and it's only a week away. What if I need to take time off work?'

'Well, he is a man and won't think logistics, and it does fall on a Saturday, so maybe you'll just stay in a fancy hotel for the night or something?'

'We'll see. I'm just gagging to get married, Rubes. I know it's hard to believe, but I'll be celebrating the big 4-0 this year.'

'No!' Ruby was flabbergasted. 'I still can't believe that – you know you don't look it.'

'I may not look it but I am it, and my womb is like a suction pad for semen. James only has to hang his shirt at the end of the bed and I'm on him like a terrier.'

'See, you'll be fine. The amount of sex you have, one of those little fellas is bound to swim to the right place. Even as ancient as you are.'

'Hmm. Well, I'm not so certain.'

'Saying that, Fi, are you really sure you want a baby? It'll stop your partying big time. Not one drink for over nine months either! All that responsibility, too.'

'Rubes, I have to grow up some day.'

'Who says?' Ruby laughed. 'Maybe getting a dog would be easier.'

'How about you, Rubes?'

'Nah, I'm a cat woman myself.'

'You know what I mean.' Ever blunt, Fi stopped Ruby in her

tracks.

'I don't know,' Ruby said quietly. 'All I ever wanted was a family with George, you know that.' She felt a lump rising in her throat.

'It's going to happen, I know it, Rubes,' Fi said gently. 'I can feel it in my water. I sounded a right bitch then, sorry. But I think what I'm trying to say is that if you let it in, you will find love again. I know you will. You're too lovely not to. And don't waste your life, angel. George would kick your butt if you did.'

'Hark at you being nice. What're you after?'

It was Fi's turn to laugh. 'Talking of love, how's Mr Strong Hands after your torrid hotel sex session?'

'I've been so busy I haven't seen him since. We've talked on the phone but…' Her mobile ringing interrupted them.

'That's him! Weird.'

'Spooky. Go, go, Rubes. Speak to him. See him tonight. He seems lovely. Ciao, darling. Lots of love.'

Damn, she had wanted to tell Fi about the Bow Wow Club. Her friend would so laugh when she heard about sex-mad Simon and his band of lonely hearts.

'Ah, Michael Bell, there you are!' She realised she was really pleased to hear from him.

'Hello, stranger.'

'I know I've been crap, sorry. Been mad busy with all these Valentine weddings I'm working on.'

'Ah, Valentine's, that's what I wanted to talk to you about. Um… I just wondered if you might be free next weekend?'

CHAPTER TWENTY EIGHT

Michael threw his arm in the air in victory, not quite believing that she had said yes so easily.

Right, a quick chapter, then he must start putting plans in place. He opened his laptop and began to type furiously.

My first novel – by Michael Bell – TITLE – TBD

Chapter 17: *Emily stomped into the study to find Michael at his computer.*

'Working again? That's all you do! Can't you find a tiny bit of time for your horny pregnant wife? Come back to bed, Pooky.'

The last thing Michael wanted to do was to have sex with Emily. He was still reeling from the feelings that making love to Ruby had created within him. He had even had to come home straight after that amazing night in the Soho Hotel and have a wank. He could do nothing but think about her lovely soft skin, pert round breasts and deft tongue.

He sat away from his screen deep in thought. Hmm. Could he use the word 'wank'? Would that offend women readers? Nah – surely that *Fifty Shades* book was much ruder? He had, however, read reviews of other romantic novels and some of the bloggers were a bit prudish. He would leave it in for now. In fact, he was already getting quite hard just thinking about Ruby as he typed. He rearranged himself and carried on, his own desire encouraging him to write a sex scene.

'I've got your favourite black lace underwear on.' Emily was relentless. He spun around on his swivel chair to face her. She lifted up her sheer nightdress and straddled him, squirming against his hardening cock as she did so.

He closed his eyes and on slipping his fingers into her, he imagined it was Ruby's wetness he was feeling and groaned in pleasure.

'See, I knew you wanted it,' Emily whispered in his ear. She roughly pulled opened his zip to reveal his hardness and climbed on top. The sex was intense and with every squeal his wife made, it made him just want to be inside Ruby more. They came together.

'Wow!' Emily jumped up. 'That was amazing. I love you, Michael. Now let's snuggle back in bed. Come on, you know you want to.' She put on the stupid baby voice which he now hated with a passion.

'Yeah, it was amazing.' Michael stood up. 'But I best have a shower.'

Right, he would tell her now whilst she was feeling like this.

'I forgot to tell you, Ems – I've got to go away next weekend. The Editor of The Sunday Review *wants me to write an article on romantic Devon country retreats, and the money's too good to miss. We need all we can get for Mr Bump now, don't we?'*

'Or Miss Bump for that matter.' Emily smiled. 'That's fine,

darling. Of course.'

'Even though it's Valentine's?' Michael feared the worst.

'We don't need a silly day to show we love each other, do we? And money is so much more important at the moment.'

Money, bloody money. Oh how he wished he could just leave her now. Material, shallow bitch!

Phew, Michael could now put his plan into action. He so feared that Emily would ask to come with him. He had prepared his response – that he just had a single room in a grotty B&B near to the posh hotels he had been asked to review.

Ruby Ann Stevens was going to have the best Valentine's night of her life.

'Oh yes!' Michael said aloud. He was excited and still a little aroused over the sex scene he had managed to write with ease.

The words were flowing out of him. Now, what could he call his developing masterpiece? He tapped his pencil on his desk. He knew how important the title was and then flash, another lightbulb moment! *A Ring for Miss Ruby!* Not perfect, or The One, but it would certainly do for now.

Oh, to be able to get out of this flat. He was sure one of his neighbours was a prostitute. She had more knocks on her door in one night than he had in a year. And the music that filtered through into the early hours was sometimes unbearable.

He still couldn't forgive his witch of an ex-fiancée Emily for luring his best mate into her wicked web. Worse than that, she had taken Barney, their black Labrador. He actually missed Barney more than he missed her. He sometimes missed his matey time with Justin, too. They had been friends since school. But how could you forgive someone when they had betrayed you so badly? Could you ever go back to how it was?

Emily was a bloody sexy girl, there was no doubt about that. Ten years younger and posh totty. They had met after a rugby match in Twickenham. Her parents had spoiled her and this had proved to make their relationship difficult. With Michael's working-class roots, he always worked hard for every penny he had earned. Losing his mum at sixteen had also made him look at life in a different way. He was of the opinion that life was for living and enjoying, and that money didn't necessarily bring happiness.

He could see why Emily had been blinded by Justin, with his City lifestyle and flash car. But he was sure she would eventually demand too much from him and he would get tired of her tantrums. Or maybe he would give her everything she wanted and cheat on her like he had done with girlfriends before.

Whatever happened, she would get her comeuppance in his novel, and that was a definite.

The night he had found out about their affair had been atrocious. He wasn't a freelance writer at the time – he had a nine-to-five job at a sports magazine. He also worked in a bar twice a week to pay off the huge credit card bill racked up by the engagement ring Madame Bitch had said she'd always wanted. On this particular Tuesday he had forgotten his bar uniform so he dashed home straight after his first job to grab it, and there they were. In the lovely two-bedroom Clapham cottage he was renting with her. His best mate with his fiancée. Her on top, the pert little bottom he used to love to squeeze bouncing away, a bottle of champagne to their side, and his favourite Athlete CD on at full volume. They didn't even notice him walk in.

Michael wasn't a violent man. Shaking with anger and emotion, instead of raising his fist, he pulled the plug from the Bose sound system he had bought for her birthday and simply walked out of the door, leaving it swinging wide open.

His biggest regret was that Barney the dog was at her parents' country retreat, as the two of them had been due to go away for the weekend the next day. He, of course, would have taken the dog there and then if he could.

He hadn't spoken to or seen the pair again. There was no need for an explanation. Maybe he knew deep down she was wrong for him, but it didn't make the hurt any less – the complete betrayal by two people he thought he knew so well and loved very much. He managed to sneak back and get his photos, CDs, and clothes, but that was it. She could have the rest. Furniture and kitchen stuff could all be replaced. His heart would heal, he knew, but at that moment the two of them had broken it in half. They of course had both independently tried to contact him but he had ignored every call.

With a betrayal of that magnitude, what could anyone say to make things better? 'Sorry' would never be enough. They were obviously so wrapped up in their own little world that Michael wasn't top of their agenda.

It still gave him a pain in his stomach when he thought about it, and he actually had to force himself to focus in order to stop the hurt from bubbling up and suffocating him.

He didn't even know if they were still seeing each other. He tried to believe he didn't care any more. He didn't want her back – they were welcome to each other. But he wished he knew why they had done it in the first place.

He blew out a massive breath, rubbed his eyes and slammed the laptop shut. His life had been dark for a long time but meeting Ruby had shone some light on it. Whatever the outcome, she had helped him to start writing the novel – something he had always wanted to do – and for this he would be eternally grateful.

CHAPTER TWENTY NINE

'Fuck, shit, bollocks. Sexual problems? You can't ask that,' Jimmy twitched. His Tourette's always got worse when he was perturbed. He looked at Simon Dye with disdain.

'It's a free country, Jimmy, so I *can* ask that, but on this occasion I am actually joking.'

The entire Bow Wow Club secretly breathed a collective sigh of relief.

'Tosser, balls, wank,' Jimmy added. The newbies smirked. They'd never met anyone with Tourette's before. The regulars carried on as normal.

'Thank goodness for that, Simon, you smut monster,' Cali said in her posh voice. 'Mind you, a turkey farm on Boxing Day would have seen more action than my bedroom over Christmas.'

'Why do you think that is?' Simon enquired kindly.

'Eric's having a bit of a wobble, I think. I mean, it's only been seven months and he was with *her* for twenty-five years. And it was our first Christmas together.'

'You've been referring to his dead wife as "her" since you've been coming here, Cali. Maybe it's time you started to let him in too?'

'Well, I can't cook roast potatoes like her, my washing powder doesn't make the clothes soft enough, and he's still wearing his bloody wedding ring! I even had all his bloody kids and their broods round for Christmas dinner.'

Ruby began to spin her ring around her wedding finger. Since getting back into the swing of working again and feeling happier, she'd begun to eat normally and had put on a much-needed few pounds. She was delighted when the ring that Michael had given to her fitted.

At first she felt weird putting it on, as it wasn't the actual ring George had lovingly placed on her finger on their perfect wedding day, but once it was there she felt whole again. And although she had said it was a good thing to not wear it, when she slipped it on it felt as if a little piece of her husband was still with her.

Cali's words made her think. She hadn't even considered that her wearing her ring would bother Michael. If it did, surely he wouldn't have gone to all the trouble to replace it for her? But that was Michael all over. So lovely. So thoughtful. She really must make more time for him, but work was mental at the moment. She thought back to their love-making in the Soho Hotel and suddenly got the urge to do it again.

'I'd shag you, Cali,' Jimmy suddenly announced in all seriousness.

Simon took a huge slurp from his vodka mug, then clapped his hands together. 'More tea, vicar, then let's get serious, shall we? The real subject of tonight is – "Can Men Only Actively Love One Woman at a Time – discuss"!'

CHAPTER THIRTY

'Blindfold me?' Ruby enquired slightly nervously as Michael pulled his old grey Peugeot into a lay-by in a quiet Devon country lane.

'Don't worry, I'm not going to rape and pillage you – unless you want me to.'

Ruby laughed.

'Let's get this roof down first, shall we?'

'Michael, it's freezing.'

'Wrap your scarf around you and put this on.' He threw a blue beanie hat at her.

'I don't get it.'

'Ooh, you will.'

'Michael! Stop it!'

'It's your mind being filthy now, not me. But you will get *that* too – with bells on it – later, I promise.'

Michael gently helped Ruby out of the car and removed the blindfold, kissing her on the tip of her nose as he did so. 'You can look now.'

Ruby blinked a few times to refocus her eyes and then bit her lip.

'Oh, Michael. This is so, so beautiful!' She jumped up and down on the spot.

They were at the top of a big hill with a view overlooking the Dart estuary, so wonderful it took your breath away. It had been one of those lovely late winter days, crisp but bright, and the setting sun made the moment perfect.

'Happy Valentine's, Ruby.'

'It's not until tomorrow, but Happy Valentine's, you luscious hunk of man.' She looked up at him and smiled. 'You're actually quite special, aren't you, Mr Bell?'

'I have my moments.' He spun her around, looked right into her green eyes, and kissed her gently.

'Now, what was that you promised me with bells on it?' she whispered.

'We've got to find the cottage first.'

'Cottage! Wow! I thought we were going to a B&B.'

'Only the best for my little ginger Sarah Burton.'

'What did you call me?' Ruby had to shut her eyes and inhale deeply.

'Sarah Burton – you know, the royal designer.'

'I know who she bloody is!' Ruby snapped. She had relived her final moments with George over and over, and this flashback washed over her like a massive tsunami wave.

'Why – do you not think she's good enough to be compared to?' Michael was perplexed by her response.

'It's nothing.'

'Well, it is obviously something.'

'George...he...on the last day I saw him...' she paused, then blurted out, 'he called me by the same name.'

'Oh, Rubes, I'm sorry. It's so hard not to upset you and I try my best. I don't know how to say this without it coming out wrong...but maybe I'm not good enough to be compared to either.'

'Michael. Don't say that. It's not about comparing. It's about coping and learning to love someone again. And when you never stopped loving the person you were in love with before, it's bloody difficult.' She bit her lip and looked to the sky. 'I don't expect you to understand, and I'm sorry. You've been brilliant with everything and I am so happy that we're here together today.'

'Really?'

'Really.' She grabbed his hand and squeezed it tight. 'Now come on, let's get to this cottage before it gets completely dark. I've just noticed there are no streetlights. Where are we anyway?'

'Questions, questions. It's a little village called Dittisham, in the South Hams of Devon. I can't wait to show you round. Dartmouth is just up the road – well, up the river, actually. In fact, the adventure starts here!'

'That is hilarious,' Ruby commented as they pushed open the low door into the quirkiest pub she had ever seen in her life. A soft toy otter whizzed up to the top of the bar on a weighted string and triggered a bell to ring as they approached the bar.

Her mobile suddenly rang and everyone stared at her. The young, strawberry-blond, and bespectacled barman pointed to the sign above the air ambulance charity box on the bar. *IF YOU RING, THE CHARITY BOX SINGS!*

Ruby dutifully put in a coin and turned off her phone. Pulling his out of his pocket, Michael noticed he didn't have signal. 'What a good idea. Phones off for the rest of the weekend. I don't want to talk to anyone but you, anyway.'

After both being convinced that trying the local Addlestone cider was a must, they managed to find a little table near the big window at the front of the pub. The black of the river was paved in light from the full moon and the blinking of the boats moored in the Dart estuary.

After a pint of her cloudy drink, Ruby started to feel a bit tipsy. She was sure the ruddy-faced boating locals were watching her reaction to their local bionic brew.

'Why have the bar staff got FBI on their sweatshirts?' she asked. 'Weird.'

Michael laughed. 'Not weird at all – the pub's called the Ferry Boat Inn.'

'Ha! How ditsy am I? I love it here. It's so cosy with the fire in the corner too.'

'It's my favourite place in the world. I had a pact with a good friend once that if ever either of us got into trouble, we would just say FBI because it's so out of the way no one would ever find us here.' Thinking of the good times he shared with Justin suddenly made him feel sad.

'That's cool.' Ruby broke his train of thought. 'Well, maybe we should have the same pact too, Michael Bell. Not that either of us will ever get into any trouble. I'm a good girl, me.'

'Hmm. When you want to be. But, yes – deal.' He high-fived her. 'Another pint?'

'I can't believe I'm drinking pints. And no! If I don't eat first, I'll fall into the river walking back.'

'Do you like the cottage though?'

'You know I do – it's perfect.'

Ruby squirmed slightly, thinking back to the amazing sex they'd had earlier. They hadn't even waited to unpack or look around. Just ran up to the bedroom of the estuary-fronted cottage and ripped each other's clothes off. The tension of earlier heightened their lovemaking.

'I'm hungry too, after all that exercise.' He kissed Ruby on the lips. 'Check out the blackboard behind you, the grub here is all homemade and usually very tasty.'

'So does a ferry run from right outside here then?'

'Yes. You can get one across to Agatha Christie's house or to Dartmouth.'

'Agatha Christie – we have to go!'

Michael was pleased at her excitement. 'It's a beautiful house – Greenway, it's called. It was her holiday home, I believe, but it's a National Trust property now. She actually based one of her novels there. Slugger, mate.' Michael addressed the young barman whom he had recognised from last time he was here. 'Is the Dartmouth ferry going this time of year?'

'You best ask old Ron. I think it depends what time he leaves here.'

Michael laughed. 'OK, thanks.'

Ruby grinned with pleasure. 'Valentine's Day with Agatha Christie and you. Maybe you can see if Daphne du Maurier's free too and I may just have to marry you!' She was slurring by now.

Michael knew he couldn't rise to it, but just to hear those words come out of his beautiful lover's mouth, even in jest, made him feel warm inside.

So warm inside that tomorrow he would tell her.

CHAPTER THIRTY ONE

'Atchoo!' Everything about Simon Dye was loud, even his sneeze.

'Bless you,' Ruby offered as she came through the church hall door. 'You can't even blame poor little Fanny for your allergy, can you now? She's not even here.'

'Susie.'

'Ruby.'

'Ruby, her dirty little hairs are obviously embedded into the wooden floor.'

'Maybe you're allergic to me?'

'More likely the moaners who come here every Tuesday.'

'Harsh. But true.' Laughing, she walked through to the small kitchen at the back of the hall.

'Diet Coke?'

'Yep, lovely.'

Ruby didn't dare say she knew that he had already poured his vodka into his mug. Mind you, maybe it wasn't such a bad idea. She was finding helping out here a lot harder than she'd anticipated. It had made her access her own loss in ways she wouldn't have thought possible.

'So are you seeing anyone again, after your husband's passing?'

'Sort of.'

'Ah, shagging someone then?'

'Simon!' Ruby turned her head to the side. 'I think it's more than that.'

'Think?' Ever the counsellor, he wouldn't drop it.

'Simon, stop it.' She took a deep breath, steadying herself. 'We've just been away for Valentine's, actually. But it's like I can't give my all to someone because I still love George.'

'So it is more than that.'

'He told me that he loved me.' Ruby welled up.

Simon ran to her side. 'Here.' Pulling two chairs to face each other, he handed her a tissue and gently held her small, pale hands in his great big ones.

'Is he a good, kind man?' His Scottish accent seemed to get stronger with emotion.

Ruby nodded.

'Do you feel he always puts you as number one?'

She carried on nodding and sniffed.

'Just take it slow, Ruby. Love is the great redeemer. If it is real, you will know. I have no doubt about that. Death; bereavement – it's a horrible business. But it will make you stronger, and you *are* strong. I can tell. It will be all right. That fella up there,' he pointed to the picture of Jesus at the door, 'He will make sure of it.' He gave her a massive bear hug.

She felt a rush of guilt as she thought back to the moment when Michael had lain his heart on his sleeve and she had brushed it down onto his cuff and right onto the floor.

He had been so excited when he had pulled her up the steps of Dartmouth Castle. It was freezing, and the sea was glistening in the winter sun hundreds of metres below. The view was magnificent and Ruby felt happier than she had in months.

He grabbed her by the hand and pulled her into a tiny

room within the gun tower. It was big enough for two, with a little ledge to sit on. The seagulls shouted their approval at his romantic gesture. The wind whistled through the viewing gaps.

'This place!' Ruby was swept away by its beauty.

'I know. All the history too. This castle was built during Henry VIII's reign, but there is proof there was a castle here in Saxon times too.'

'Imagine what's it's seen and heard.' Michael could hear the excitement in Ruby's voice. 'I'd love to go back and just be an observer. I feel like that about a lot of history, don't you?'

'Ruby?'

'Yes.'

'Be quiet a moment.' He shuffled closer to her on the ledge, gently lifted her chin, and kissed her deeply and passionately. She felt a rush of warmth flow through her and wanted to make love to him there and then.

'I love you, Ruby,' Michael whispered as he pulled away.

'No, no. Don't ruin it, not now.' Ruby suddenly shot up and began to run as fast as the tiny winding castle stairs would allow.

He found her sitting on a rock on the beach below the castle.

'I've known you less than two months, Michael.'

'And I've known from the minute I met you. I can't help the way I feel.'

'You should have waited. It's too soon.'

'Not for me it's not. I say it how it is – and how it is, is that I love you. I bloody love you.'

'You don't even know me.'

'But I know how I feel.'

'Tits, wanker, bollocks.' Jimmy pushed the door open, roughly jolting Ruby back to reality and away from her thoughts of the silent, dreadful journey back from Devon.

'Hello, Jimmy. How are you tonight?'

'Oh, you know, all right. Still waiting for Mrs Right. Sick of cooking burgers 'cause I can't find a proper job.'

'I didn't know you were looking. Milky coffee with sugar?'

'Oh, go on then, spoil me, Ruby. And yes – I've been looking for months. I've got a finance degree and worked in accountancy for years, but when Jenny died at just thirty-two, I went to pieces.'

He was silent for a moment before continuing. 'It takes quite a woman to cope with a man with this awful syndrome, you know. My self-confidence is at an all-time low.' His whole body jerked. 'When I'm happy I don't even tic. I really do think if I can get my life on track and find a decent job and a woman who will take me on, warts and all, this damn syndrome won't be half as bad.'

Ruby made a vow to herself that in ten years she would have at least made the effort to have moved on from her current state of mind. Imagine still grieving after all that time. Poor Jimmy.

Now that he had her attention, he wouldn't stop.

'I get the interviews no problem but when they see me and hear me then that's it.'

Ruby stepped back slightly as she caught the stench of the bad breath Simon had warned her about. She, for once, thought carefully before she spoke. 'Maybe you should smarten yourself up a bit before the interviews. You know – have a shave, nicely iron your shirt.'

'That's exactly what my Jenny would have said.'

'See? You can do it.'

'Can I?'

'Yes, you can.' Ruby put her hand gently on this arm.

'Will you help me, please?'

The Fireman crashed through the door with Ellie. They were

both laughing loudly.

'We share the jokes in here!' Simon shouted from his desk, then whispered to Ruby, 'Miserable fucking bastards, usually.'

Cali sauntered in with a yapping Fanny.

'*Atchoo!* That bloody dog!'

'Bless you,' the group resounded.

'Right, grab your drinks, you horrible lot.' Simon slurped from his mug. 'Tonight, my little lost lovers, the topic is…' He paused and looked at Ruby, who was clearing up in the kitchen. 'After bereavement, how soon is *too* soon to fall in love again?'

The mug that Ruby was drying slipped from her fingers and smashed to the floor.

CHAPTER THIRTY TWO

'A fecking box of chocolates and a dozen red roses. That was it, Rubes, that was *it*! No proposal of any sort. In fact, he fell asleep on me before we even got at it. I'd bought a whip and some body paint as well. Fecking bastard.'

'Blimey, Fi. I haven't heard you this angry for a while. Calm down. Let me get us another drink and we can talk about it.'

Fi took a massive slurp of her wine. The football was on so it was a busy Saturday afternoon in O'Neill's bar, but thankfully they had got in early enough to grab a seat.

'What's the matter with him, Rubes? You know James as well as I do; he's pragmatic and steady, but we've been together five years now and he knows how much I want to settle down.'

'Hmm – and he usually does like his sex as much as you do, so it was strange that he fell asleep on you.'

'Do you think he's having an affair?'

'I can categorically say no on that front. Whatever we say about James, he has always been straight up about everything. I remember when George was going to marry Candice and we knew she was fleecing him of his dad's inheritance, James didn't take sides. He just said it how it was. And besides, you can tell he's not a philanderer.'

'But what does a philanderer look like? Anyone has the capacity to cheat.'

'Not when they love you, they don't. Stop being stupid, Fi.'

'Get in there!' Three lads in West Ham shirts jumped up at the same time as their beloved team scored.

'My turn for the drinks.' Fi intuitively gave Ruby's arm a squeeze as she got up. 'He's here in spirit, I can feel him.'

She placed two large wines down on the table.

'We're gonna be pissed by six if we carry on at this rate,' Ruby said. 'What will James say? You know he doesn't like it when you get too drunk and disorderly, especially without him.'

'See – another fault we have identified, Ruby girl. But I so want children, we *have* to get married.' Then Fi pulled herself together, saying, 'Look at me going on about me as usual. How was the weekend of sex with the delicious Mr Bell?'

'It was bloody brilliant until he told me that he loved me.'

'What!'

'I know. I've known him for seven bloody weeks and those three little words bolted out of his mouth. Fi, I don't know what to do. He's the perfect gentleman. I fancy the pants off him and I feel so safe with him – but it just feels too soon to be getting so serious.'

'Oh, Rubes. Michael is so sweet. And that must have been so hard for him. Why not tell him what you just told me? You can take it slow, see what happens. At least you know he won't take five fecking years to propose!'

'That's what Simon said. Take it slow.'

'Who the feck is Simon? Don't tell me you've got another one on the go?' Fi laughed and hiccupped at the same time.

'Oh, more news I haven't told you about,' Ruby explained. 'I'm volunteering for a charity at the church hall in Eustace Street. Goes by the name of the Bow Wow Club.'

'Oh. What's that then, a dog's home or something?'

'No, it's short for Boyfriends of Widows, Wives of Widowers; it helps the partners of bereaved people learn how to cope.' Ruby took a slurp of wine. 'However, all sorts of waifs and strays turn up, even if they've just lost somebody and feel lonely.'

'Aw, bless you Rubes, that's so sweet.'

'Talking of Simon, you'd love him. He's a big black man with dyed orange hair. He's really funny. And I can tell he loves sex.'

'Ooh, how divine.'

'Only thing is, he's so camp I don't know if he's gay or not; he seems to fancy men *and* women.'

'Even better. That means he does love sex.'

'Fi! There's you saying you think your boyfriend is behaving badly – listen to you.'

'I haven't had it for a while, that's all. And on that note, come on, let's drink up. I'm feeling horny. James Kane is getting more than he bargained for when I go through that door.'

'Just make sure the football's over or you won't stand a chance.'

They put their coats on to leave and Fi hugged Ruby tightly. 'Go and see Michael. Just tell him how you feel. You like him, but want to take it slow as it's scaring you a bit.'

Ruby walked up West Hill, deep in thought. Could she imagine a life without Michael? She loved his company and the feeling that being so close to him brought. She would be hard pushed to find anyone as decent. If she was really honest with herself, she was just scared of getting close to someone and losing them as well. But she would have to face that fear head on or she would end up sad and lonely, like poor Jimmy – ten years on and still single.

OK, decision made. As soon as she got in she would arrange to meet Michael. They had to talk. So what that he said he loved her? Some women waited months for that moment. She should be happy that he cared that much.

She put the key in the door and rushed to the toilet. She really should have gone at the pub. She looked at herself in the mirror. Her face had filled out a bit now and she was pleased. Her brother was right: being bony just didn't suit her. She also liked her hair longer. Losing her trademark bob was a good thing. Changes had to happen for her to move on.

She washed her hands and rinsed off the soap that had caught underneath her wedding ring. In doing so, the ring slipped up to the top of her finger.

Leaving the bathroom, she looked up at Patrick in all his black and white feline glory and put the ring gently in a lidded pot on the side.

'Patrick, I think our Gorgeous George may be looking down and found me a proper boyfriend. What do you reckon, old fella?'

CHAPTER THIRTY THREE

Michael lit a cigarette. He hadn't smoked since the day he found Emily shagging Justin.

He had been reliving the awful drive back from Devon with Ruby all week, and when he found a stray fag in the back of his messy drawer, he had to have it.

'Once a smoker, always a smoker,' his mother used to say to him. Ironic, really, that she had died of lung cancer and had never smoked a cigarette in her life.

He hung out of the kitchen window of his poky flat so as not to stink it out.

Feeling sick after his spur-of-the-moment vice, he made a gagging noise and opened his laptop.

A Ring for Miss Ruby by Michael Bell

Chapter 20: *Why oh why hadn't he kept his mouth shut? But that wasn't him. He did wear his heart on his sleeve and at least she knew how he felt now. Bloody games! Why did people play games in relationships? And if she liked him as much as he felt that she did, why was it a problem? Maybe it was him not understanding enough about bereavement. He had felt at a loss when he split with Emily, but unlike in death* *he knew he could see her again if he really wanted to. But he did understand about bereavement. His mum dying had been the single most dreadful thing that had ever happened in his life. Thinking back to that time, he did remember the feelings of complete isolation and pain, knowing that he would never see her ever again.*

He lived for the moment because who knew when their moment was going to end – and that's why he was so impulsive. If people couldn't handle that then it wasn't his problem. If somebody loved you enough they would surely just take you how you were.

Yes, he loved Ruby but he couldn't force her to love him. That was it, decision made. She obviously didn't feel for him. He was just the rebound that is so common in any sort of split. The kindest thing for her and him would be to let her go. It was obviously too soon for her to recognise her true feelings.

If he set her free and she came back to him, then that would be it. Love would have won.

CHAPTER THIRTY FOUR

'Ruby, Ruby, Ruby, Ruby,' Tony Choi sang in his best version of the Kaiser Chiefs hit, patting the chair next to him in Piaf's. Daphne du Mont came running out, kissed a bright red ring of lipstick on Ruby's cheek, then zoomed back behind the counter as the queue lengthened.

'I have ordered hot chocolate and cold cakes. We have time for some fun together, yes?'

'We have until midday, so a good hour or so before I meet Michael.'

'Good-oh. I love a Saturday – no work, just my friends and time for play.'

'Talking of work, how *is* life in the clinic these days?'

Ruby thought back to her twelve-jobs-in-twelve-months mission and the mirth that working with Tony had caused.

'Still full of stinking kippers and warty wilberforces.'

Ruby snorted. 'You're hilarious, Tony Choi.'

'Do you remember when George came in and you thought he had the crabs, and he was just strimming the grounds?' Tony asked innocently. 'I've never seen anyone shoot under a desk so fast. Ah, dear George – we loved him, didn't we?'

'We did, Tony, but it's time I started to move on.'

Norbert, Daphne's very attractive German toy boy, brought over their drinks and cakes. He too kissed Ruby on the cheek and carried on with business.

'How is this new one, by the way?' Tony added sugar to his coffee.

'He's great, as a matter of fact, and I need to be nicer to him. I've been fighting my feelings, but just need to let them roll, I think.'

'Yes, you must. He sounds like a kind man, Ruby. Here, take this fortune cookie. Do not open it until later. I have a feeling you may need it.'

'Tony, I do love you.'

'See? You can say it to me.'

'How did you know about that?' Ruby screwed her face up.

'With age comes wisdom, my little red-headed friend.'

Ruby took a slurp of her hot chocolate and looked out to the busy Covent Garden street. She suddenly let out a gasp. Tony grabbed her arm tightly.

'Did you see what I just saw?' she said.

'Yes,' Tony replied in a whisper.

Ruby got up, sped to the door, and raced down the street. It was a Saturday morning in the busiest tourist spot in London, so she had no chance of finding him amongst the crowds.

Her face was red when she came back in, and she was shaking. Daphne came running over and held her. 'Ruby, darling, what is it?'

'I just saw George.'

Tony's face was white.

'No, darling, of course you didn't. It was just someone who looks like him. It's quite common for that to happen. It was just someone who looked like him, darling, I promise.'

Ruby took a deep breath and composed herself.

'That was awful. Tony, you saw him too, didn't you?'

By now, Tony had regained his composure. Whoever it was did look very much like George – he had been his complete doppelganger, and it had completely shaken Tony.

'Yes, he d-did look like a bit like him,' Tony spluttered. 'But Daphne's right, you just wanted it to be him.'

Ruby sat back down and fingered her mug of hot chocolate. She had identified him on that fateful day, for goodness sake. Kissed him on his cheek and said goodbye. When would this nightmare end?

Just as she started to cry, Michael walked in.

Tony stood up, saying tactfully, 'Hello, Michael. I think she burned her mouth on the hot drink.'

The eccentric Chineseman kissed Ruby and shook Michael's hand.

'You don't have to go – Tony, isn't it?'

'Yes, pleasure to meet you. I must go though. I have shopping to do.' He waved at Daphne and Norbert on his way out, slightly unsettled at what had just happened.

Michael felt nothing but love for the sweet, vulnerable girl in front of him. He crouched down next to her and hugged her tightly. But he had come here for a reason and he had to follow it through.

'Is it George?' he quietly asked.

'Yes. I'm sorry.'

'Don't be sorry.' Keeping his coat on, he sat down and held her hands across the table. He was shocked to see her wedding finger bare.

'Your ring? You took it off.' Michael bit his lip. 'Why?' He closed his eyes momentarily. Maybe he shouldn't say what he intended to say.

'Because it's time I gave you a chance, Michael, stopped being so silly. You love me. I would be foolish not to listen to my head for once.'

Michael felt sick. When did anyone ever make a decision of love with their head? He couldn't believe what he was hearing, but he had to carry on for his own sanity.

'But look at you, Ruby. Your heart is still saying George, and as much as I care about you, I don't think you're ready for this, not yet anyway. Why don't you take a bit of time for yourself?'

'I don't want to be on my own,' Ruby replied quietly. 'I've spent enough bloody time rattling around in that flat.' She sniffed.

'Oh, Rubes.' He lifted her left hand and kissed her beautiful, bare wedding-ring finger. 'Let's take time out, for both of us. My heart can't take the "will she, won't she" any more.'

'Oh, Michael. I know that it must be so hard for you, but bear with me. I've had a big think and you are such a good man. Can't we just take it slow and see what happens?'

Michael covered his face with both of his hands as if doing that would make this dreadful situation go away. He felt his bottom lip start to tremble. He took a deep breath and composed himself.

'Please don't do this to me, Rubes.' He looked to the sky to stem the tears that were pricking his eyes. It had taken him so long to come to this decision, thinking it was completely the right one. And now here she was, this beautiful creature in front of him, deciding she wanted to make a real go of it.

He squeezed both her hands tightly. 'No.' He was very definite. 'I'm going to go now, Ruby. All I want is for you to be happy, and I think this is the right decision for us both.'

He stood up and kissed her on the cheek.

'Goodbye, darling.'

Turning the corner, he was glad of the rain to disguise the tears that had begun to gently fall down his cheeks.

CHAPTER THIRTY FIVE

Ruby clicked open the gate to the Stepney Green residence that had been so familiar to her for so many years. A lively Jack Russell nipped at her heels.

'All right, gel?'

Rita Stevens had been scrubbing her step. She wiped her hands down her apron and greeted her daughter-in-law with an awkward kiss on the cheek.

'Monty!' her Cockney voice suddenly bawled. 'Get down, you little bastard. Now, on ya bed!'

Rita was how you imagined a mum should be – slightly rounded with curly brown hair and a warm, loving nature. She was a proper old East Ender and Ruby had always had a soft spot for her. She had lost Alfie, her beloved husband, only a few years before her son, and Ruby couldn't imagine how lost she must feel, being encased in this double bubble of bereavement.

In fact, Ruby had been working at a funeral directors as one of her twelve jobs when George's father had died, and she had managed to sort a proper East End send-off for him, with a carriage and black horses wearing feathers. Rita had never forgotten this.

Completely ignoring his mistress, Monty circled Ruby madly

as she entered the kitchen. He had been inherited, along with Daffodils, from the charming Lucas Steadburton. But Patrick the cat had hated him so much it just wasn't fair to keep him, and with Alfie's sad demise it seemed the right thing for Rita to have him as company. It was a partnership that had happily worked well.

'What brings you here then, love?' Rita placed a steaming cup of tea in front of her at the kitchen table.

'I was doing a fitting just up the road, so thought I'd come and see my dear old mum-in-law.'

'Less of the "old", ta, Red.' She softened. 'How you doing anyway, darling?'

'I'm feeling a lot better, thanks.' Ruby didn't think it right to mention Michael just yet. 'Work has really picked up and I seem to have a day and a night now, instead of it all blurring into one.'

'Fucking terrible, innit?' Rita wiped away a tear. 'Goodness knows how people coped in the Blitz when countless family members copped it. I mean, two is bad enough.'

'And how are you?' Ruby could see the sadness in the woman's eyes.

Rita sighed. 'I'm afraid I'm not out of the blurring stage yet. He was my son, Rubes. It's not the right way round, is it? A parent shouldn't outlive their child. He used to drive me mad with his muddy feet and his forgetfulness, but I'd live in a quagmire forever just to see his cheeky little face again.'

Ruby held back her own tears. 'I thought I saw him the other day.'

'Oh, love.'

'I was in Covent Garden with Tony, and he walked passed Piaf's. Well, whoever it was walked past Piaf's. I swear, Rita, it was the spit of George. Same height, same hair, same gait. I thought maybe I was just seeing things, as apparently that's quite common when someone dies, but even Tony said he could see the resemblance.' Ruby took a sip of tea. 'Honestly, it could have been him.'

Rita leaped up, saying, 'Well, this won't get the house bloody cleaned, us chatting like this, will it?' Ruby was quite startled at her reaction. 'I must get on, love. Pop in again, won't you?'

Ruby clicked the front gate shut, feeling slightly perturbed. *Here's your hat, here's your coat, what's your hurry?* It was so out of character for her mother-in-law, who would usually sit happily for hours and discuss 'their' George.

Maybe it was her new way of coping, and talking about him wasn't therapeutic any more. Grief was a difficult beast to handle.

Ruby headed to the bus stop, making a mental note to visit again next week. Reaching into her pocket for her Oyster card, she found the fortune cookie that Tony had given her. She pulled it out of the golden wrapper and broke the crumbly biscuit in half. The piece of paper inside fell to the ground. She didn't see the man in front of her in the bus queue lean to pick it up at the same time, and they bumped heads.

'*Love looks not with the eyes but with the mind*,' the man read aloud, looking straight into Ruby's eyes and then down the full length of her body. 'I'm not so sure.'

Still seeing stars, Ruby rubbed her head, then realising who it was, had to be steadied by the man's arm.

'I'm so sorry, I've obviously got a thicker skull than you,' the posh shire voice added.

Ruby remained mute, because standing right in front of her, with the exception of a small mole on his left cheek, was the George lookalike she had seen outside Piaf's just days before.

CHAPTER THIRTY SIX

With a heavy heart, Michael put the key into the door of his poky flat. He felt sick. He threw his coat on the sofa, put the kettle on, and opened his laptop.

***A Ring for Miss Ruby* by Michael Bell**

Chapter 22: *She had taken her ring off. A bare finger. No wedding band. A significant move for a widow – and what had he gone and done? Told her he didn't want to see her any more. Had he made the right decision? Only time would tell. He sighed deeply. Why was love so difficult? Why couldn't we be born with a homing device that drew us to just one person with whom we should spend the rest of our lives? Just put your finger on a touch screen and it would locate your match. They could be anywhere in the world. Any creed, colour, size. You would just be instantly attracted, fall in love and have babies and live happily ever after. But then again, would life be boring like that? Wasn't half the fun meeting new people, touching new bodies, experiencing different characters, places and circumstances?*

No, sod all that. At this moment Michael would be quite content with a homing device stuck on Ruby Ann Stevens's forehead with his name on it.

Her green eyes had filled with tears earlier; those tears for her dead husband had made him just want to scoop her up and protect her forever. Dead husband. You couldn't even say 'ex-husband'. This dying young business wasn't easy to get your head around, that was for sure.

Michael pushed his chair back and got up to make a cup of tea. He plonked it down on his desk and spilled some on the scraps of paper dotted all over it.

'Bugger!' To his surprise, he felt tears pricking his eyes. 'Bugger, bugger, bugger.' He sniffed loudly and went to the kitchen drawer to see if he could find another stray cigarette.

Coming back empty-handed, he took a deep breath and set his hands on the keyboard in readiness. He would wait for as long as it took. He had to submit his review on the Ferry Boat Inn to get a few quid in. Then he would get back into his book.

In fact, he would write like the wind and finish this damn novel. He had been wanting to do this for years. So now was the ideal time. He had no distraction other than the dark pull of unrequited love. So his fridge would be filled with food, he could get sexual gratification from his sex scenes, and the hours would fly by. And by the time he had finished it, his beautiful Ruby would come to her senses and be running into his arms again.

He needed sex, so began to type furiously.

Emily was waiting at the door, nipples poking through her little vest, white stockings and suspenders accentuating her toned thighs…

CHAPTER THIRTY SEVEN

The Fireman (aka Nick) was in the small kitchen at the back of the church hall when Ruby arrived with four pints of milk. Despite being taller, he was quite George-like in a way, with his London accent, black quiffed hair, big blue eyes, and boyish good looks. Today he had stubble and Ruby thought he looked even more handsome than usual.

'Here, let me.' He took the milk off her and put it in the fridge, pushing against her needlessly as he did so.

'Oi!' Ruby thought at least she should pretend to make a bit of a fuss.

'You loved it really,' the Fireman winked as he made his way out to the group, and Ruby had a sudden recollection of her pre-George harlot status. She had even slept with Bentley, the owner of the old people's home for ex-actors, who was at least twenty years older than her. And then there was the handsome, bald Adam. He had been lovely but he wasn't The One. George, who on paper wasn't her type at all, *was* The One but now he was gone and she had to find another One.

But how could you do that if the person you loved had died and you still loved them? Calling someone a 'minus one' wouldn't be fair on the new beau, would it? Maybe this would be a good discussion for The Bow Wowers. She must mention it to Simon.

Being here had, without a doubt, helped her understand more about relationships. And really, this is why she had decided to make a go of it with Michael. But that had blown back in her face, hadn't it? What could she do? The lovely, tall, and sexy Mr Bell had made his mind up. He had gone. Obviously didn't love her enough to take it slow. But part of what he said had been right. He was the first man she had slept with. Yet with age comes the wisdom that the grass isn't always greener and that people aren't perfect. And she did feel 'it' with Michael. What she called her 'love feeling' when they were making love. A draw, a magnetism. 'It' just felt right with him.

'Shit, bollocks, fuck.' Jimmy staggered through the door. Ruby intuitively poured boiling water onto half a cup of coffee granules.

'Black coffee for you today, Jimmy.' She handed it to him, his rancid breath laced with whisky, then put a mug of Diet Coke on Simon's desk.

'The bastards have sacked me.' He twitched violently, sending coffee all over the floor. Ruby ran to grab his mug.

'Oh, Jimmy! Let me just clear this mess up and I'll be with you.' She hurried to the kitchen to get a cloth, just as Cali breezed in wearing a long, pink kaftan-style dress that revealed her ample bosom.

'I saw a glimmer of March sunshine this morning, so thought I'd don a frock today.' Fanny the wonder dog barked loudly, then threw herself down onto the wooden floor, exhausted.

Ellie appeared with Simon, chattering loudly.

'Atchoo! That fucking mongrel!'

'Oh, shut up, Simon – it's not my Fanny I tell you. We all know you're allergic to us, really.'

Simon laughed. 'And can I just say, your breasts are looking resplendent as usual, dear.'

Ruby laughed to herself; nobody other than Simon Dye could get away with a comment like that.

'So what happened, Jimmy?' Ruby sat down next to the unkempt and very sad figure.

'Somebody got offended by my swearing. I was serving a burger to this woman and for some reason couldn't stop saying "tits". I must have said it about ten times. I mean, she did have a fair pair, but she took offence and the gaffer of the burger van said it was the last straw. Most people love me there though, Rubes. The truckers have all got to know me. They probably swear more than me anyway.'

Ruby squeezed his hand and noticed his filthy nails. To be honest, she wouldn't want to be served food by him and suspected that his boss had just been waiting for a chance to get rid of him.

'Oh, Jimmy. What are you planning to do for the rest of the week?'

He twitched violently again. 'I am planning to drink, Ruby, that's what I'm planning. I mean, what else is there to do?' He caught a glimpse of Cali in her dress. 'Tits, tits, tits.'

'Alcohol is not the answer, you know that.'

'It is at the moment – blanks it all out. I still miss her.'

'I do understand, Jimmy, I really do.' Ruby thought back to the nights she had drained countless bottles of wine and gone to bed in a stupor. 'But you deserve happiness. You will never forget her. And you are not betraying her by moving on. There is room in your heart for someone else, I'm sure of that.'

'I don't know if I believe you, young Ruby. But I guess I can try.'

'Look, give me a couple of weeks. I need to sort a few things and I promise to help you get back on the work and love trail.'

'You are such a darling,' Jimmy smiled.

Ruby got another whiff of his foul breath. 'Here, give me your phone. I am going to put a date in it. I need you for a whole day and you have to be sober and positive.'

'Roger that!' Jimmy clicked his heels together and saluted.

'Roger what?' Simon minced by them to the kitchen to fill his mug.

Simon cleared his throat to conclude the evening's session. 'So, that's it then. Lesson for today: if sex doesn't feel right with a new love, give it a chance, try new things. It might be your mind not letting that love in.' He drained his vodka mug. 'And, more importantly, who's coming to the pub? I don't know about you but I need another – I mean, I need a drink.'

He looked to the back of the room. 'Ruby, can we tempt you this week?' For some reason it had felt wrong mixing the traumas of the Bow Wowers with her own social life.

'I'm sorry, I can't tonight, I'm meeting a mate at O'Neill's.'

'Well, that's just where we're going, so come on – we can all walk together.'

Ruby smiled. 'OK.' They wouldn't get there until ten fifteen, so if it was awful she wouldn't have to bear them for very long. For some reason, Fi had wanted to stay the night with her, so she could catch up with her at home later as well.

Ruby signalled the universal drinking sign of a glass to lips from the bar and Fi automatically mouthed, 'Large, please.'

'Is that him? The sex-mad Simon you talk of? How hot is he?! And just look at that bulge.'

Ruby settled herself at the table closest to the bar. 'Fi O'Donahue, you are disgusting.'

'And I take it that's the Fireman, chatting to Goldilocks over there? You're right, I would do him. I almost feel like dating a widower so I can come to your Bow Wow Club.'

'You haven't seen Jimmy yet. That might change your mind.'

'Oh, I don't know...remember when Bert was still a tramp and not living with Margaret and I woke up next to him under his mac in a doorway?'

'Only because you were too pissed to see the house numbers.'

'Well, I can't say I haven't lived it. Now, I just put up with the frigidity of James Kane and his non-committed gene.'

'Fi, it can't be that bad. You two have a great relationship.'

'*Had*, Rubes. He just doesn't want sex any more, keeps harping on about me losing weight. He's got to be having an affair. I mean – look at me. Yes, I'm a size twelve but it's curves, not fat. And all the men I've slept with before have been gagging for a piece of the Donahue booty. That's why I'm staying with you tonight. He needs to miss me, needs to want me for a change.'

Simon winked over at them both.

'Bloody hell, Rubes. He is amazing. I've never slept with a black man before. Just look at the size of him! He could swing me around the chandelier with just one of those big strong arms.' She squirmed slightly on her seat.

'Fuck!' Ruby suddenly said loudly.

'What?' Fi jumped.

'I cannot believe I forgot to tell you something *so* bloody important!'

'What? Go on. Is it Michael?'

'No. Aw, bless. Don't mention Michael. He's not even returning my texts at the moment. But this isn't about him.'

'Sorry, mate. So what is it then?' Fi leaned forward.

'I went over to Rita's in Stepney Green the other day; I was dropping a dress off. Anyway, I was about to get on the bus home and I only bumped into the George lookalike. And honestly, he is his double. I felt sick. The only difference is a small mole on his left cheek and he speaks like he has a dozen plums in his mouth.'

'Well, don't people say that everyone has a double somewhere in the world? Did you get a photo?'

'Er, no. Can you imagine? "Excuse me, you look just like my dead husband. Smile, please".'

'So how did you feel?'

'It was weird. He gave me his card.'

'*What!* Why? So what's his name?'

'We both bent down to pick something up at the same time and bumped heads, and he said the least he could do was buy me a drink for hurting me. His name is Harry Bowman-Green, so there is no connection. It's just a really odd coincidence.'

'Well, no man ever gives his card out in a non-business way unless he wants to shag you. That's a fact.'

'Hmm. I want to see him again though, despite him seeming quite cocky. It is just like looking at George.'

'Are you sure that's good for you, though, Rubes?'

'No, I'm not sure. But it doesn't look like Michael's coming back, does it?'

'Well, from what you've been saying, no. I'd say go for it, but be careful of that heart of yours. Don't let it get any more cracks, not yet, eh?'

Fi got up and kissed Ruby on the forehead as Simon approached them.

'Ding dong, you must be the ravishing Fi I've heard all about.'

'And you must be sexy Simon, leader of the pack.' Their eyes locked.

'So what are you two lovely ladies doing now the pub's closing?'

'Back to mine for a coffee and bed probably,' Ruby offered.

'What – you're sharing a bed? Nice work, ladies.' His Scottish accent came more obviously into play when he was aroused.

'Simon! What are you like?'

He ignored Ruby's profession of innocence.

'So do you take your coffee black?' Simon directed at Fi.

'I might.' She ran her tongue across her lips and pouted.

Simon revealed a bottle of rum secreted beneath his jacket.

'Got any cream, Rubes? I say back to yours and we get the Jamaican coffees going.'

It had been an age since the Amerland maisonette had been subject to the sound of a full-on, mattress-squeaking sex session.

Ruby's attempts to deter them had been completely ignored. So all she could do now was put a pillow over her head and pray that the bowed Victorian ceiling wouldn't cave in, and that her naughty mate wouldn't regret her drunken antics in the morning.

CHAPTER THIRTY EIGHT

'I said it was his kid all along, didn't I, Bert?'

Bert was snoring in front of the fire, his love of *Jeremy Kyle* not quite as strong as Margaret's.

She walked slowly to answer the door to a smiling Ruby.

'Hello, love, you've timed it perfectly. Jeremy is telling them to put something on the end of it. The people on here need bloody shaking, I tell you. Oh, I'd love to be in that audience and say my piece, show 'em what's what.' Bert opened one eye and raised a hand to Ruby, grunted, and went back to sleep.

'To what do we owe this pleasure, young Ruby?'

'A strange request, but have you kept any of Bert's old trousers from when he was a bit thinner last year?'

'You know me, duck, I'd recycle toilet paper if I could. I've got everything up in the back room. What on earth do you want them for anyway?'

'There's a chap at The Bow Wow Club who needs a makeover. I haven't had time to run anything up for him – I've managed to get him a couple of bits from the charity shop, but couldn't find any suitable trousers. I know I gave some to Bert last year that were quite nice.'

'I meant to ask how you're getting on with the volunteering.

Not cursing at your old neighbour for interfering again, I hope?'

'Margaret, when have you ever interfered? You've been nothing but a magnificent support to me. I love you like a grandmother, you know that.'

Margaret dabbed her eyes with the tissue she pulled from her sleeve.

'Something strange did happen the other day though,' Ruby went on.

'Ooh, take a seat and tell me all about it.'

'I saw a man in Covent Garden who looked the spitting image of George.'

'Oh, love. I'm sorry to hear that.'

'It's fine, honestly. I then literally bumped into him again all the way over in Stepney Green. How weird is that? He even wants to meet me for a drink.'

'Well, you know me: I don't believe anything in life is a coincidence. It all happens for a reason. I told you before that it's all written, and that's why you ended up with your George. I have trouble understanding his untimely exit, but this will come to light too. I don't know when, but it will.' Margaret heaved a thoughtful sigh, then said sharply, 'Have you a got a photo of this new one?'

'That's what Fi asked too. Of course I haven't.'

'I just want to check it's not your mind playing tricks and you maybe wanting him to look like George.'

Margaret took a moment to reflect. She shut her eyes slowly, opened them, and exhaled deeply.

'Don't be fooled by this one, Ruby; don't make him into something he isn't.'

'Oh, Margaret, you are wise but that's one of the reasons why I love you. I'll be careful, I promise. Nice to have a bit of attention, anyway.'

'And what about your Michael? He sounds so lovely. Can't you try again?'

'It's him who broke it off.'

'He's just giving you space.'

'If he really wanted me he'd be banging the door down by now.'

'How many times do I have to tell you, my gel, that men are different creatures? I bet you've got no idea what he's thinking right now.'

'Well, all I know is it's not about me, and I don't like that.'

'Good.'

'Pardon?'

'I said good. If you don't like it, that means you like him more than you realise.'

'Margaret! You're a nightmare. But I do like him, you're right. Come on, let's go upstairs – you can show me those trousers.'

Ruby scrabbled in her messy bag to reach her ringing phone. It was a crisp, sunny morning and she had a spring in her step as she was looking forward to her date with Harry Bowman-Green later.

'Rubes, it's Fi.' Her friend sounded out of breath. 'Where are ya, ginge?'

'I'm about to meet Jimmy – you know, the fat one from the Bow Wow. I'm going to give him his makeover.'

'Oh feck, I need to see ya urgently.'

'Don't tell me James has found out about you and Simon?'

'No, it's worse than that.'

'Shit – tell me.'

'I'm only feckin' pregnant.'

'But that's amazing!'

'It would be if I knew who the feckin' father was.'

'Jesus!'

'The Almighty,' a whistling Simon added as he rounded the corner of the church hall – wearing a dog collar.

'Oh God, I mean gosh, you're right.' Ruby managed a strained smile at Simon and pointed to the phone. 'It is definitely worse than that. Emergency meeting in Piaf's at six. I'm meeting Harry at seven, so be prompt.'

CHAPTER THIRTY NINE

Michael carried on with chapter twenty-two.

> ***A Ring for Miss Ruby*** **by Michael Bell**
> *Emily was waiting at the door, nipples poking through her little vest, white stockings and suspenders accentuating her honed thighs.*

He felt a stirring in his jeans.

> *'Don't talk,' she demanded. She kept his gaze, pushed him hard back on the bed and ripped off his jeans. She took his now hard cock in her mouth and teased him with her tongue. 'Pooky's been a bad boy leaving his wifey for Valentine's weekend, hasn't he?' Michael nodded and gasped as his pregnant wife then gagged him. He adored it when she wore her stockings and was desperately holding back from coming even though he was on the edge.*
>
> *'Not yet, bad boy. I want to straddle you,' she whispered, lifting her sexy vest to reveal her ever-hardening nipples.*
>
> *'Want some, do you?' she asked menacingly. Michael made an affirmative noise behind the silk scarf.*

Releasing his now fully erect cock from his jeans, Michael quickly moved to the sofa.

'Ruby, Ruby,' he cried out loudly as he came with force.

Blimey, he thought. Maybe writing erotica was the way forward. Or maybe not; he had only written half a page and look what happened!

He was at the stage of missing Ruby so much he wanted to contact her, but in his head he had set a deadline of May 1st, which would give her a good few weeks to do what she had to do. If she had forgotten him by then, then love had lost.

'Please let love win,' he said in a pathetic voice.

Then, 'That's it! That's the title. Bloody brilliant! *A Ring for Miss Ruby* is not strong enough. *Let Love Win* by Michael Bell. Perfect!' The ladies would love that; he just knew it.

CHAPTER FORTY

Ruby had ten minutes before she was due to meet Jimmy. She followed Simon in to the graveyard, still reeling slightly from Fi's announcement.

'You didn't say you were a vicar.'

'You didn't ask. Is that a problem, Ruby?'

'I thought you were gay.'

'Two revelations in one day, then. I'm just a very camp reverend, darling. Every hole's a goal if it's attractive enough.'

'Simon, you're a vicar!'

'I'm also a living, breathing, hot-blooded man. A human being, just like you, Ruby. The fact that I have dedicated my life to God – oh, and the bloody Bow Wow Club of course – doesn't make me any different.'

'I never thought of it like that. Well, whatever. I'm pleased to have you as my friend.'

'Ditto. Now, enough of our mutual masturbating. How's that sexy Irish bombshell?'

'She's fine.' Ruby inwardly grimaced, not wanting to elaborate.

'Good, good. I have to say I'm not proud of the fact that she has a partner, as that does go against my moral core. However, she didn't tell me until my cock was wedged far into her mouth and it would have been rude to ask her to remove it.'

'You are so wrong, Simon Dye!'

Simon laughed. 'I know, and I won't change. And that goes for you too, Rubes. Don't ever change, girl. You're a good person. I like your heart.'

Ruby felt her eyes well up. 'What a lovely thing to say.'

'Well, believe it, my friend.'

'Right, I'd better go,' Ruby said. 'Jimmy will be waiting for me at the church hall. I'm giving him a makeover.'

'See? I know a good 'un when I see one.' He suddenly gasped and grabbed her by the hand. 'Before you go, let me show you that headstone I mentioned. Come on.' He hurried her to the bottom of the graveyard. Under a beautiful willow tree was the plainest of grey stones, and all that it said was:

Here lies Melody Pratt, she was taken by a wasp.

'No!' Ruby was in hysterics. 'I'm gonna wet myself. That's hilarious.'

'Not to her loved ones it's not,' Simon said with a straight face. Then he broke into hysterics too. 'I told you it was funny.'

'Wait until I tell Fi. She'll piss herself too.'

They could see Jimmy approaching the church hall.

'Well, give her my love and if ever she fancies another Jamaican coffee…'

Making a suggestive face, he unlocked the old wooden church door.

'I will, you insatiable beast! Now you'd better go and forgive some of your sins.'

Ruby knew she was going beyond the call of duty with Jimmy, but she remembered when she had been in a similar state and

Fi had pulled her out of the mire.

'So, have you done what I said?' she called up the stairs. Jimmy was splashing about in the bubbles like a warthog.

'Yes. Just having a little longer in here. I only have a shower at my place, so this is a treat. If you don't mind, young Ruby, that is?'

'Of course not – you enjoy.' She found it amusing that he called her 'young Ruby'. He was only six years older than she was, but grief had obviously aged him.

She put a new thread on to her sewing machine and began working on yet another bridesmaid creation.

Half an hour later, Jimmy appeared. He'd had a full shave, had trimmed his ears and nose hair, and was dressed in trousers and a smart shirt. His shoes were freshly polished and he smelled fresh and clean.

'Wow, look at you!'

'I found this aftershave in the bathroom cupboard, but I didn't…er…use it, just in case…' He held up the familiar bottle.

'In case it was George's, you mean? It was, but please do take it with you.'

Wow, another big step for her. She remembered smelling the same aftershave just weeks after George had died. The young assistant on the perfume counter wasn't sure how to react when she burst into tears.

It was funny how time changed things. As the years went by after losing her dad, she used to go to the testers just to smell the aftershave that he had worn.

Time. Bloody time. It was the main healer with grief and that was a big fact. So many people said it, because it was true. Like everything in life – broken relationships, friendships that ended, ill health – time would make you not forget, but it would lessen the intensity, allow you to move on with everything.

'So, it's just your hair now? I've booked you an appointment at Lilia's on the High Street at two. It's all paid for. Those long locks have got to go, Mr Chislehurst, do you hear me? You look amazing already, but when that hair of yours is chopped, employers and ladies alike will be falling at your feet.'

'Really?'

'Yes, really. And Jimmy?'

'Yes.'

'Have you noticed what you haven't done since you've been here?'

He bit his lip and Ruby thought he was going to cry.

'You make me feel relaxed, Ruby, relaxed and safe, that's why.'

Ruby felt a lump welling in her throat. 'Now, off with you and I'll see you next Tuesday. Short back and sides, you hear me?'

CHAPTER FORTY ONE

'I'm cross with you, Fi. You should always use a bloody condom with somebody new,' Ruby said far too loudly.

Daphne brought a big pot of tea and two long iced buns over to their table, leaving red lipstick rings on both their cheeks as she floated back to the counter.

'Well, there's a story. Just his dick alone could act as a boy band member! So the emergency one I have had in my purse for a hundred years, not surprisingly, split. And then I thought, what the feck – just be careful. I mean, I haven't used anything with James for a year. His sperm must have bloody Ferrari engines or something. What a mess, Rubes.'

'Oh, darling. It'll be all right. What are you thinking though?'

'I'm thinking the poor little bastard will be a cross between a Great Dane and a bloody Irish Setter; that's what I'm thinking.'

'But anyway, what are we saying?' Ruby screwed up her nose. 'It might be James.'

'And I might be Mother fecking Teresa. We haven't done it for weeks, Rubes. I told you he's gone all funny on me. It's definitely Mr Big's.'

'And I have something else to tell you about Mr Big – but I'm not quite sure how to.'

'Oh, no! Don't tell me he's married too, Rubes?'

'Well, in a way…but there is no Mrs Dye – just God.'

'You what? He's a fecking priest? No! No! What would my mam say? I can't believe that. Jaysus!'

'*He* is obviously not in the equation on this one. And Simon is a vicar, not a priest, so I think he's allowed to – or is that in wedlock only? Oh, I don't know.'

'Well, I disagree with you there. *Him* above has given me this baby, the baby I've always wanted.'

'Don't go all religious on me, Fi. You're going to give birth to a child who is not going to be the same colour as your partner. This is a serious problem.'

'I have to have this baby, Rubes. I'm nearly forty years old. It might be my only chance. We've had this conversation before.'

'This is hurting my head just thinking about it. OK, you could just say you are getting fat and have the baby secretly. Then I look after it and say I've always wanted to adopt.'

'There's fat and then there's a big, round, obvious pregnant belly and pendulous leaking tits, Rubes. Get serious.'

'Well, think of a better idea then.'

'I need a drink!'

'You can't have one of those for at least nine months now.'

'Shit, I didn't think of that.'

'And stop swearing. You've got a little one inside you who will have ears soon. Right, let's sleep on this. I need to think about it properly.'

'Er…and I need to throw up.' Fi charged behind the counter to use the staff toilet.

Norbert raised his eyes to the ceiling, thinking Ruby's crazy friend was just hungover again.'

CHAPTER FORTY TWO

Harry was at the bar of the trendy Soho drinking hole chatting to a couple of suits, whom Ruby assumed were his work colleagues. The heart surge she felt at his uncanny resemblance to George nearly knocked her off her feet.

She took a deep breath, straightened down her classic above-the-knee black dress, and approached him. He immediately said goodbye to the guys and went towards her, kissing her on both cheeks.

'Hey, Ruby, you look great. How're you doing?' It seemed weird he was so posh.

'Needing a drink, that's how I'm doing.'

'Here.' He put his hand on the small of her back and guided her over to the bar.

He didn't smell like George; she wasn't even sure if she liked how this impersonator smelled. She had loved the smell of her pint-sized gardener. Even when he was sweaty, he didn't smell bad. In fact, that was when she liked him best. Straight in from work, a bit muddy, a bit sweaty. She suddenly felt the emptiness in her stomach again. But no, she must be positive, Ruby told herself. Margaret had said that gap could be filled with another love, so she had to give love a chance. Let love win.

‘Cheers.’ Harry chinked their glasses and Ruby became aware that he was dressed in a very expensive, well-cut suit.

‘Great tailor, by the way,’ she complimented him. She could tell he was pleased she had noticed that his suit was bespoke.

‘Yeah, thanks. If you can afford it, why not, hey? The City bonuses do have their advantages.’ His brashness left a bad taste in the unmaterialistic Ruby’s mouth. She wished she could wave a magic wand and put him in George’s beloved West Ham shirt.

‘Back in the room, Ruby.’ Harry waved his hand in front of her face. ‘You were miles away. Are you OK?’

‘Fine, fine. You just look uncannily like someone I once knew, that’s all.’

‘Was he debonair and handsome too?’

‘He was, actually. He was my…’ She paused. What on earth should she say? She couldn’t say “ex-husband”. Because he wasn’t. ‘He was my husband.’

‘A crazed divorcee, not sure if I’m ready for that.’ He threw his head back and laughed, revealing two unsightly fillings. George didn’t have any fillings.

‘He died.’

‘Oh no… Ruby, I’m so sorry.’

‘It’s fine. It’s just weird how much you look like him, that’s all.’ She showed him a photo on her phone.

‘Whoa!’ Harry took a massive slurp of his beer. ‘Whoa,’ he repeated. ‘That’s mad. That’s me!’

‘I know – it’s freaking me out.’

‘I can see why.’

‘But even weirder, I saw you walk by a café in Covent Garden and then bumped into you in Stepney Green, miles away. It must be fate or something.’

‘Maybe it is, Ruby.’ He lurched towards her and kissed the

back of her neck. She wasn't sure if she liked it and pulled away quickly, on the pretence of needing the toilet.

On her way back, she got them another drink.

Harry had started drinking an hour before her and he seemed quite drunk already. He had managed to wangle a table and called her over to it loudly, not even attempting to get up and help her, despite her juggling drinks and a handbag.

'So, this husband of yours…' he began.

'George. His name was George,' Ruby butted in, uncomfortable that they were talking about him despite her bringing it up.

'Good old English name, a bit like Harry. We could be brothers.'

'You could have passed as siblings, that's for sure.' Ruby felt as if she was going to cry. She had to get out of here – and fast.

Thankfully, one of his workmates was beckoning him back to the bar.

'Well, Harry, it's been lovely to meet you,' she said, standing up. 'I've got a really early start tomorrow, so I'll be off. Bye.'

He kissed her clumsily on the mouth. 'Goodnight, kitten chops. We really must get to know each other better.'

Ruby felt immediate relief as she double-locked her front door and kicked off her shoes. Bloody kitten chops! Who the hell did he think he was? She put the kettle on, flopped down on the sofa, and scrolled through the messages on her phone.

She noticed the last text from Michael, sent when they had returned from the dreadful drive home from Devon.

If my only crime is loving you, then I'm sorry

She suddenly craved his big, strong arms around her, telling her how beautiful she was and that everything would be all right. She then looked at the two-seater sofa opposite and remembered George lying there, one leg draped over the end in his cocksure fashion, and felt confused.

'Bloody hell!' she shouted up to Patrick. 'Why does life have to be so difficult?'

CHAPTER FORTY THREE

'Fuck, shit, bollocks.' Ruby smiled from the kitchen of the church hall as Jimmy made his entrance. Then, 'Tits.'

'You dirty bastard.' Cali swiped the air as he took in her ample cleavage.

'*Atchoo!*' The intensity of Simon's sneeze behind made her nearly drop the cup she was holding.

'Simon! Put your hand up.' He raised his left arm in the air and she whacked his bum with a tea towel.

'Put your Fanny down, more like.'

Cali was mute in disbelief.

'Jim, what have you done to your hair?' the Fireman piped up, grabbing three custard creams from the biscuit tin.

Peering out of the kitchen hatch, Ruby noticed that Nick looked slightly red-eyed. She then looked to the back of the room and remained open-mouthed for a good thirty seconds. For there, bold as brass, was Jimmy Chislehurst, stroking Fanny the wonder dog and sporting a bright red Mohican. Not even a Mohican a few millimetres long. No – it was a huge plume of unruly hair.

'Jimmy! I said short-back-and-sides!' No one even noticed his smart clothes or clean-shaven appearance. Even his breath would probably now be fresh. No, all of the good work she had done was overshadowed by his clown-like hairstyle.

Ruby marched over to him. 'How on earth are you going to be taken seriously in the workplace with *that* on your head?'

'What do you mean? I thought I'd go the same colour as you. You do all right.' He jerked violently in a full-boy tic and she managed to catch the spilling coffee with the tea towel she was still holding. 'And it's not far off from the Rev's either, is it?'

'Right, come on, you lovely lot,' Simon boomed, filling his vodka mug with Diet Coke. 'Let's sit down and Bow Wow now, shall we? We've wasted half an hour on Jimmy's barnet already.' He pulled his chair round to face his disciples and put his serious face on. 'So, tonight I wondered if any of you wanted to tell us your story. I know it might be difficult, but sometimes hearing how other people cope in a challenging situation will resonate with your own struggles.'

Nick tentatively put his hand up. Ruby thought that tonight, the usually cheeky and chirpy twenty-nine-year-old looked like a lost little boy.

'I'm afraid I've got a confession to make.'

'Well, you're in the right place, pal,' the vicar input gently.

'There *is* no Rebecca – the glamorous older woman I talk of. Nobody has lost an octogenarian husband. She was purely in my imagination.'

'Go on,' Simon urged.

'I didn't think I could come here if I was honest with you, but I saw the leaflet and I…I…just didn't know where to turn.' His eyes filled with tears.

Ruby, who was sitting next to him, reached for his hand. It seemed out of character for someone usually so lively to be so sad. But that was life. She guessed that many people put a brave face on, that they felt they had to. Sod bravado. A man should feel he could cry too. Too many people didn't, and drowned in sadness.

Nick cleared his throat. 'But now I know that there are people here who are widows and widowers too, I feel ready to share my story.'

Ellie sniffed loudly. Ruby took a deep breath. Simon drained his vodka mug. Fanny farted loudly.

'Cali, will you take that bloody dog of yours outside!' Simon shouted. 'She stinks.'

'How many times do I have to tell you it's not my Fanny that stinks!'

Jimmy laughed out loud.

Simon turned to Nick. 'I'm sorry, pal, please share with the group.'

The Fireman nodded. 'I've been a fireman for eight years now. It had always been my dream, the same as my dad and granddad. All on the same watch, in fact. I met Milly four years ago. She worked at base camp, as we called it, taking emergency calls. She was so proud of what she did. I loved her so much…' He paused to swallow and Ruby squeezed his hand again.

'The wedding was amazing. The boys did a guard of honour and everything. Then Annabel came along ten months later and life was just complete, really. Until last October.' His voice cracked.

'I was on nights.' Nick blew out his cheeks and looked up. 'The panic in Milly's voice shocked me when she phoned to say that Annabel was poorly. The emergency doctor on call had said it sounded like meningitis. We agreed she would drive straight to A&E and I would meet her there. I didn't think anything of it when the fire engine shot past me on the motorway. In fact, the boys gave me a special whoop with the siren when they saw it was me they were passing. And that's when I saw it. Milly's car.

Rammed against the central reservation. I was sick as I ran to the wreckage.'

The Bow Wow Club gasped in unison.

'An ambulance was already on the scene. My mate Andy tried to stop me but I had to go to my beautiful girls. I'll never forget their faces. Annabel didn't have a mark on her, she looked like an angel. Milly was literally covered in blood. The lorry driver was in total shock. Said that the car had shot on to the junction at such a speed, he had no chance to avoid it. He said it was as if the woman driving hadn't even looked.'

Everyone had tears rolling down their faces.

'Bollocks, wanker, cock!' Jimmy howled.

'So there you have it. I'm here because I'm so, so sad and so, so lonely and don't know how I'm ever going to get over this.' Nick began to weep and ran out of the church hall.

'I'll go.' Ruby raced after him, calling his name.

The Fireman stopped in his tracks.

'Hey, slow down, come here.' Ruby went to him and held him close while he sobbed. 'Do you want to come back in?'

Nick shook his head. 'No. I'll come back next week, but I can't right now.'

'You live down by Putney Bridge, don't you?'

When he nodded, Ruby said, 'Come on, I'll walk with you.'

They walked silently arm-in-arm to his flat, and she hugged him again when they reached the entrance.

'Would you come in for a coffee?'

'Sure.'

Ruby took in her surroundings as Nick went to the kitchen. *The* wedding photo had pride of place above the fireplace amongst photos of baby Annabel. Ruby was in her second year of grieving, and still couldn't take her own photographs down. Poor, poor Nick. He was in the awful, all-consuming first months of grief, and it made her realise how far she had come.

Nick put a coffee down on the side table next to the sofa. 'You don't take sugar, do you?'

'No – sweet enough, me.'

'You are certainly that.' Nick came and sat next to her, then in an instant his lips were pressing hard on hers and his right hand crept between her thighs.

Ruby pulled away, shocked. 'Nick! What do you think you're doing?'

'Ruby, I am so sorry. I thought you fancied me?'

'You're a good-looking man, but…but you are so not ready for this, even if you think you are.'

'It's been so long since I had any female company – or sex, for that matter.'

'Oh, Nick. I understand completely where you're coming from. I didn't feel the sexual urge thing, to be honest, but I guess for men, that's probably different. I did feel so alone. But you're not. Your family sound great, and it was a brave step coming to the Bow Wow. And now you've told us the truth, the people there will be a great support too. Simon comes across as useless at times, I know, but you couldn't ask for a better person when you need help.'

'And you, Ruby. What can you be?' He sighed deeply. 'You're such a great girl, and if I was ever to have a relationship again I'd like it to be with someone like you.'

'Exactly, someone *like* me, but *not* me. It's not the right time, Nick. Get yourself back on track and then you'll be ready to let someone in. It's nearly two years for me now and I'm almost there.'

'So, do you have a boyfriend, then?'

'Well, not really. There is this guy who did adore me but I fucked up. And now he's gone, saying I need to sort my head out.'

'And is it sorted out?'

'Well, I am thinking about him more and more, which I guess is a good start.'

'So, could you go back to him?'

'I don't know. He's probably got bored of waiting by now – and maybe I do need to have a fling or two first before I commit to another proper relationship.'

'Really? You're thirty-six now, aren't you? I think if you've found a good 'un you should hang on to him. Why waste any more of your life searching for something that probably isn't even out there anyway?'

'Look at you, Mr Wise Man.' Ruby smiled and vowed to contact Michael that evening. 'Come here.' She pulled Nick towards her in a massive bear hug. 'Sometimes a hug is enough, especially at this stage, and I am always on hand for those, you hear me? And chats and tears and rants. Just throw it in with an odd cup of tea and a custard cream and you've got a friend for life here.'

Nick pulled away, held her at arm's length, and looked right at her.

'You are so strong, Ruby – it's a deal. I'd be honoured to call you my friend.' She reached for her coat and Nick helped her put it on. He walked her to the door and he pecked her on the cheek.

'So, just to check, are you sure a shag's out of the question?'

Ruby pretended to swipe him with her hand. 'Yes! Well, not now, for sure.'

The Fireman clicked the door shut and tears began to roll down his face. But this time, they were tears of relief. Relief that he had jumped yet another of the huge hurdles that the grizzly grief monster had thrown at him.

CHAPTER FORTY FOUR

Michael sat at his writing desk staring at his computer screen. He found the words difficult to type without Ruby to give him inspiration. It hadn't even been three weeks yet since he'd last seen her, but it felt like an age. He missed her. She was always such fun to be with. Plus, he was horny.

She had sent a couple of texts just saying *Hope you're OK.* Neither of which had a question mark so he didn't think she was that bothered for an answer.

Thinking of texts, he realised his phone had been very quiet this evening.

'Damn,' he said. It had run out of battery and he suddenly remembered he had left his charger at the *Rural Writers' Magazine* offices earlier today. He would have to retrieve it tomorrow as they would have all gone home by now.

Ruby rounded the corner to Amerland Road, feeling entirely drained. Her moment with Nick had taken it out of her. But on a bright note, she was glad that she had moved on so much. It hadn't been that long ago that she had fallen over in the street on New Year's Eve. The night when Michael had appeared as her knight in shining armour and picked up the pieces.

She saw Margaret's curtain twitch as she walked past her neighbour's house.

'Ruby!' the old lady shouted from her front door. 'Took a parcel in for you today, duck.'

Ruby doubled back. 'Oh, thanks, Margaret. It's probably the special sequins I ordered for the cocktail dress I'm working on.'

'Not quite!' Margaret appeared with a huge bouquet of flowers.

Ruby gasped. 'They are beautiful.'

Bless Michael, he had been thinking of her after all. She couldn't believe that he would just dump her like that. It seemed so out of character that he hadn't even replied to her texts.

'See. I told you he was a good 'un, Rubes. I must get back in, *Coronation Street* double bill tonight. Catch up soon.'

'Yes, we shall – and thanks so much for taking the flowers in.'

Ruby walked to her place with a spring in her step. She placed the bouquet on the kitchen table and ripped open the mini-envelope that accompanied it, excited about reading the message that she knew Michael would have really thought about. Instead of being delighted, however, she was slightly perturbed.

Sorry if I was a bit of a dick the other night, too much of the funny juice. Dinner Friday at 8 to make it up to you? I'll send a car. Enjoy the flowers. Harry X

How lovely to get flowers – but she would much rather they had been from Michael. He had said he loved her, and love was strong. Surely he must still want her? But why had he not texted her back? She would text him now and put a question mark so he would have to answer. If he didn't answer, then she would know.

Ruby bit her lip, and after drafting and re-drafting the text countless times she decided that simplicity was the way to go.

I miss you. Let's meet soon? X

CHAPTER FORTY FIVE

'I don't like being pregnant, Rubes. I can't drink, I'm nauseous from dawn till dusk, and I keep getting sharp pains where everything's moving into place.'

'Oh, Fi. I did say getting a dog would be easier.'

'Thanks – that's really helpful now when I've got the Rev's rugrat cooking in here.' She pointed to her stomach where a perfect little bump had formed. 'Make me a ginger tea, can you?' From her lying-down position on Ruby's sofa, Fi rustled about in her handbag and threw two tea bags at her friend. 'Have one yourself, mate – or would that be like cannibalism with your colouring?'

'Ha bloody ha. Not too sick to take the piss, are you, Ms O'Donahue? But on a serious note, have you thought any more about what you're going to do?'

Fi put her hand to her forehead. 'It's such a mess – I don't know. I have to have this baby, Ruby, you know that. So that is one major decision made. If I tell Simon, it would be scandalous for him and he might lose his job...but then again it was him who dipped his huge dick in without so much as a by your leave.'

'And if you tell James it will destroy him. How's he been lately?'

'Just his same horrible self. Still no sex. Pushing me away completely. It's making me seriously think about leaving him and going it alone.'

'I know you love him though, Fi. You're just putting on a brave face because he's being so awful at the moment. Try talking to him. Maybe he's got problems at work or something. I'd hate you two to split up.'

'Well, if I tell him this and he understands, then he is a keeper for sure. But who in their right mind would want to take on another man's baby? Especially the result of a one-night stand.'

'Well, it would certainly be something to sell to one of those sensationalist magazines: "40-year-old Irish vixen sleeps with black vicar and keeps it from her white boyfriend".'

'I'm still fecking thirty-nine!' Fi had to laugh. 'But do you know what? Just talking this through has made me realise what I have to do. I am going to tell James tomorrow.'

'The truth?!'

'No, of course not the truth.'

'But I thought you said you hadn't had sex with him for weeks?'

'I thought we hadn't either, but during a recent argument when I said we never did it any more, he reminded me of the great session we had had the Saturday after my shenanigans with Simon. Rubes, I was so fecking drunk I'd forgotten! So I have my alibi.'

'Until baby Simon pops out in all his ethnic glory.'

'I'll deal with that then. I feel too rough for the explosion that telling the truth will cause.'

'I don't think that's the right thing to do.'

'It's the only thing I feel I can do at the moment, Rubes.'

'Then of course I will stand by you. But what a mess.'

'Lovely flowers, by the way,' sighed Fi. 'I told you Michael would come running. Men are like bloody elastic bands. Let them go for a while and they come twanging back with a vengeance.'

'They're from Harry. He wants to take me out for dinner on Friday – said he'd send a car.'

'Bloody hell, send a car? He must be loaded.'

'He's a typical City boy. Not scared of flashing the cash whenever he can.'

'You don't sound as if you like him much?'

'He annoyed me the other night, but I guess he was drunk. Maybe I should give him another chance, seeing as Michael has definitely disappeared.'

'Michael hasn't disappeared – he said he wanted you to take some time out.'

'Yeah, but I sent him a text last night – *with* a question mark – and nothing! Maybe I should move on. I keep thinking about him, Fi.'

'Well, tell him them! I hate to bring up Gorgeous George but we had exactly the same conversation about him. I remember it vividly, because I believe it was the night that Basset hound you were looking after shat under the table in the pub. Fecking hilarious.'

Ruby laughed out loud. 'Yeah. We kept feeding him pork scratchings to shut his howling up.'

'But going back to Michael: men aren't mind readers, Rubes. You have to spell it out to them. They think in terms of sport, beer and sex. If you can speak in any of these languages then you'll be just fine. Just phone him!'

'Fi, you're bloody mad.'

'I'm bloody right, you mean. Hmm, what should you do first? Ring Michael or reply to Harry's dinner invite?'

'It's OK, dear friend. I know exactly what I am going to do.'

CHAPTER FORTY SIX

Ruby looked out of the window and smiled. A black Mercedes. Young Harry was certainly pulling out all the stops. She hadn't even asked how old he was, but he looked younger than her, that was for sure.

She reapplied her lipstick, put on her coat, and headed out into the chilly evening. Once settled in the back of the comfortable car she checked her phone. Still no text from Michael. Well, that was it. If he was playing it this cool then he must have either met someone else or just didn't care any more. Thank goodness she had someone in the wings. She smiled, thinking of Fi, who always said that it was essential to have a man on stage, plus one in the wings and one in rehearsal.

The Mercedes pulled up by a smart Soho restaurant. Harry was outside, stubbing out a cigarette. He hurried to open the car door.

'Madame!' He took her hand. 'I hope your carriage was to your satisfaction?'

Ruby smiled. He seemed softer tonight. Maybe because he was sober. He guided her to a table in the back of the restaurant. 'I didn't think you'd mind if we started with this?' He winked over to the waiter, who immediately poured them a glass of pink champagne.

'Cheers.' They clinked glasses in unison.

'Look, Ruby, about the other night...'

'Hey, it's fine, Harry, you were drunk, I was in a bad frame of mind. It's good to see you again.'

She actually meant it too. Just looking at Harry made her heart lurch because it was so like staring at her George. His teeth were slightly crooked and his hair was longer, and of course he had the little mole on his cheek, but that was it. If she half-shut her eyes, it was him.

'How old are you by the way?' she asked.

Harry squirmed slightly. 'Coming up to the big 3-0 this year. September, in fact.'

'Please don't say the seventeenth.'

'Yeah – how did you guess?'

Ruby felt sick. 'This is just too weird, Harry. That's the same day as George...' and then she said it, the word that she hadn't been able to say since her beloved husband had died. 'George, my *late* husband. His birthday was the same day.'

'That is quite a coincidence.' Harry's voice sounded genuine. 'I really am sorry about your loss, Ruby. But I take it George left you all right, did he? Money-wise, I mean.'

'Yes, he did. His dad had passed away not long before and left him a tidy sum. We bought his place in Putney together and the life insurance covered that, so yes, fortunately I'm fine.'

'Plus, of course, being a successful businesswoman in your own right, you must be raking it in? I looked on your website, actually. Great designs. You should be proud of yourself.'

'Thanks,' Ruby blushed. As she got to know this imposter, he didn't seem half as bad.

'Another glass of champagne?' Harry enquired.

'Lovely.' Ruby was beginning to feel quite heady. She excused herself and went to the ladies, where she checked her make-up and phone. Three days and nothing from Michael. Well, sod him – he'd had his chance.

Harry and Ruby shared lobster and the most beautiful cherry cheesecake that Ruby had ever tasted. She flinched as she caught sight of the bill that Harry insisted on paying.

'Nightcap back at mine?' he asked casually, lighting up a cigarette as they stepped out into the thronging Soho street.

'I'd love that,' Ruby hiccupped, knowing already that she wouldn't be heading back to Amerland Road anytime soon.

CHAPTER FORTY SEVEN

Ruby felt slightly sick as she got out of the taxi the following morning. The Amaretto had flowed when they got back to Harry's place – a very smart apartment overlooking Tower Bridge. She had tried to shut herself off from thoughts of George, but when Harry started to undress her hungrily, she couldn't help it. The sex had been hard and intense. And that's all it had been – pure sex. A need for both parties to satisfy themselves. When she had sat astride Harry and looked down, all she could see was George, but it didn't put her off, just made her more aroused.

And then, when the drunken tussle was all over, she lay back and thought of Michael. Gentle, kind Michael, who pleasured her in such a way it made her feel warm and wanted. He wouldn't have turned over and gone straight to sleep. He would have held her in his arms like he always did. Said she wasn't allowed to be alone with her thoughts after they had made love. He wanted to be with her so she felt safe.

She needed to sort her head out. George was dead, Michael might as well be, and Harry, although the spitting image of George, was just that. A lookalike of her late husband. She thought back to their first meeting and Tony Choi's fortune cookie message. *Love looks not with the eyes but with the mind.* Deep down she knew that Harry was not a potential suitor. He didn't make her heart flutter and her mind blurry like George had. But the sex was good enough and she was beginning to warm to him slightly, so surely a bit of fun was allowed?

She waved to Margaret, who was polishing her knocker, and was startled by someone calling her name as she put her key in the door.

'James? What are you doing here?' she said. 'Is the mad one with you?'

'No, she's at home. I need to talk to you, Rubes.'

Ruby went cold. Fi must have told him that she was pregnant. Maybe he had worked out it wasn't his. No, Fi assured her they had had sex the same week as Vicargate, so there could be no dispute. Well, not until a miniature Simon Dye popped out the other end, anyway.

Ruby put the kettle on and sat next to James on the sofa. It was weird thinking that he used to live in this very flat with George when she had first met her husband-to-be. James hadn't changed much; just a few more lines around his eyes. He was doing really well as a solicitor now in his own partnership. They'd shared a lot of laughs together and, more recently, some tears. She and James used to be as thick as thieves, in fact. They had shared an awful lot as friends and in a way Ruby missed it, as things naturally changed when he got together with Fi.

Ruby noticed how tired James looked. He looked different in a way she couldn't quite put her finger on. And then she realised what it was: he was sad. He had no light behind his eyes.

'What's up, mate?' Ruby enquired as breezily as she could, placing two cups of tea down on the coffee table. 'Seems weird having you here without Fi – a bit like the old days, eh?'

'Yes, we had some laughs here, didn't we? I miss George too, you know. He was such a good mate.'

Ruby started to well up. 'Don't get me going, but is this why you wanted to talk to me? You know it's always good to get it out.'

'No, it's something current.'

Oh shit, Ruby braced herself. As much as she cared for James and she truly did, her loyalties had to lie with Fi. James cleared his throat. She gripped on to the cushion on her lap. It was as if they were about to set off on the highest, most terrifying rollercoaster in the world.

'I'm sterile, Rubes. Firing blanks. I'll never be able to father a child.'

'Fuck!' was all Ruby could muster.

'I can still do that.' James managed to smile. 'I've been just so horrible to Fi and this is why. I thought if I kept on, she would just leave me for being a bastard. But she's hung in there. I believe she must really love me, or maybe she's just plain stupid, because whatever I throw at her she takes it and tries to see the good in me. Tries to help me through whatever is bothering me.'

Ruby took a noisy slurp of tea. At least Fi hadn't told him yet. Hopefully she'd had second thoughts.

'I didn't want to tell her what was wrong because I knew that she would feel she had to stand by me – and I know how much she wants children. I gave her a get-out clause so she could leave me without feeling guilty, and typically, our lovely Fi hasn't taken it. Although saying that, maybe she has. She called "a meeting" today in Piaf's. Said we have to talk. Goodness knows why we couldn't just talk at home.'

Ruby made a funny whining noise with her throat.

'Are you all right?' James looked concerned.

'Fine, fine. Shit, is that the time? I need to phone my brother. I'm off to watch Reading play Chelsea at Stamford Bridge with him.' She jumped up. She had to act quickly.

'I'm sorry, James, I'm not being much help, I know.' She was gabbling her words. She always did that when under stress. 'All I know is that she loves you deeply. Maybe you could consider adoption, or even better a sperm donor. That's it! Sperm from a different man, so you would still have a baby together. Fi could still go through the pregnancy. I mean, if you agreed on that then you would have to sort it out quickly as Fi isn't getting any younger. In fact, what a brilliant point of discussion today. Talk to her, James. She loves you. And if it's all meant to be, then love will win.'

James got up and hugged her. 'I knew you'd say the right things, Rubes, you are such a good friend. And I'd really appreciate it if you'd let me tell her first. I just wanted to see what you thought. But now you've made it all seem – well, not so daunting somehow.'

'Of course you must tell her first, and I'm sorry to be so short but I really need to get a move on.'

She virtually bundled him out of the door and ran to her phone. 'For goodness sake pick up – pick up!' Why did her friend never answer her bloody phone? She started to redial over and over. Surely then her mad Irish friend would realise she did need to speak to her, and urgently.

CHAPTER FORTY EIGHT

Michael's phone started to come to life as he plugged the charger into the wall. It had actually been quite a treat not having to be beholden to it. Text messages began to beep in. He felt popular for once.

Alrite Bro, long time no speak. Let me know if you fancy babysitting soon.

No 1 son, I need a lift with putting something in the loft next time you're up.

Michael, it's Jean Tiverton, Rural Writers' Magazine here, could do with some of your editing time if you're free this week?

And there it was, the message he had been praying for weeks that he would receive. His heart began to beat faster as he read over and over the most beautiful words he had seen for a long, long time – *I miss you. Let's meet soon? X*

He even felt a slight stirring in his loins. It was quite unbelievable what an effect Ruby Stevens had on him. He couldn't waste another second. Picking up the phone, he rang her number, but it was engaged. He kept trying and got a busy signal each time. After trying an hour later and still getting the engaged tone, he assumed that her phone must have a fault. He couldn't take the risk of her not receiving a text message. No, he would surprise her. She would love that. He would get her some yellow roses from the wonderful flower stall at East Putney Tube and turn up on her doorstep. If she was out, her nosy old neighbour Margaret would no doubt know where she was – and he could just leave the flowers with her, or wait.

CHAPTER FORTY NINE

After an hour, Fi still wasn't answering her phone. Ruby looked up to her stuffed black and white moggy on high.

'Oh, Patrick, I'm going to have to go and intercept that scatty friend of mine, aren't I?'

It was a three p.m. kick-off and she wasn't meeting Sam until two at the pub in Fulham for a pre-match drink, so she had plenty of time. She hadn't been to see Reading play for ages and was actually quite excited. Now they were back in the Premier League, it usually made for a great game. She was also looking forward to seeing her brother, as they hadn't met up since Christmas.

She worked out the logistics in her head. She would just have to get to Piaf's early and somehow apprehend Fi before James saw either of them. Easy!

She had a quick shower, got dressed, and threw her blue and white scarf around her neck. Just as she was pulling her boots on there was a knock at the door. She screwed her face up, wondering who on earth was visiting – and was completely surprised when she opened the door.

'Harry? I've only just left you. I thought you'd be sleeping in for ages?'

'Sleeping in? Not when you invited me to the Chelsea game, no chance.'

Ruby suddenly remembered why she had made a pact with herself to not drink so much wine. The recollection of inviting him as they had arrived back at his flat came to the fore.

'We are *obviously* in the away end.' She had wanted the chance to catch up with her brother and hoped this might deter Harry.

'I will just have to bite my tongue then, when we so *obviously* thrash you.'

Ruby smiled. For one second Harry *was* George. Sharing the same banter when he talked of his beloved West Ham. Thank goodness there was a spare ticket on offer, as Sam's girlfriend had decided against coming.

If Michael had bothered to reply to her text, then she would have invited him. Sam was a good judge of character and she already knew that he and Michael would have got on like a house on fire.

Saying that he loved her in Devon must have simply been a whim. After all, it had been Valentine's Day and they were in such a romantic setting. They hadn't been together long enough for him to think she was The One, surely? If he had truly loved her, he wouldn't have ignored her. She had actually said that she missed him and wanted to see him soon. How could he ignore that, if he 'loved' her?

'Look. Being really honest with you, Harry,' she said bravely, 'I was so drunk I had forgotten I had invited you.'

'Oh.'

'No. It's cool. Luckily, I *have* got a spare ticket. But I'd arranged to meet a friend for coffee first in Covent Garden and then was heading to Fulham for two-ish.'

'No worries. I can meet you at the hotel at Stamford Bridge if you like. Mates of mine are going anyway. I'll have a beer with them beforehand. Just text me when you get there.'

He opened the front door and then, turning around to face Ruby, he pulled her towards him and gave her a big kiss on the lips.

'These lips give great head, by the way.' He winked and did a funny little side kick as she watched him walk down the road.

Ruby slammed the door shut behind her, mortified. She hadn't remembered that either!

Michael put the roses in front of his face as the smartly dressed, dark-haired man walked past him. He crossed the road at speed and started to walk in the other direction. Margaret's curtains twitched. Seeing Michael and then George's doppelganger, she had to sit straight back down in shock.

I miss you! Let's meet soon! That's what she had said. So what on earth was going on? Michael felt sick. He was confused. Surely she couldn't have lied to him, made up the fact that her husband had died? No, not his dear, sweet Ruby. She didn't have it in her to be so heartless.

CHAPTER FIFTY

'Where's the fire?' Ruby virtually bowled Norbert over as he set a table in Piaf's.

'What is it, darling? Quick, come round the back.' The red-lipsticked, glamorous figure of Daphne Du Mont opened up the counter door.

Ruby was out of breath. 'I need to talk to Fi before James talks to Fi. It really is urgent.'

'OK, OK, beautiful girl,' Daphne du Mont soothed. 'Are they both coming here?'

Ruby nodded, then gasped and ran to the back room as James' bespectacled figure pushed open the glass door. As fast as a cat, Daphne was at the front.

'Hello, James darling. Large cappuccino as usual?'

'Oh, hello, Daphne, how are you? And yes, please.'

'All good here, thanks. Norbert, sort it for me, will you, lover? I need to show the lovely Fi something out the back.' She steered the approaching Fi straight behind the counter and into the room behind.

'What the feck?' Fi was shocked to see Ruby sitting there adorned in her Mighty Royals scarf.

'You can't tell him, Fi,' Ruby burst out. 'He's just been around to see me. You have to hear it from him, let him speak first. But just think along the lines of a surrogate child. Putting someone else's sperm in you to make a baby. It won't take much thought.'

'Fecking hell.'

The worldly Daphne didn't even bat an eye. 'Lemon Danish, darling?'

Fi nodded, following the older woman as she scurried back out to the front of the café.

CHAPTER FIFTY ONE

Michael had to put his intense feelings down on to a page for fear of saying something that he might regret forever.

***Let Love Win* by Michael Bell**
Chapter 21: *Michael smiled as he watched the beautiful yellow roses being wrapped. He had a spring in his step as he headed towards Ruby's place. The fact that she was missing him and wanted to see him was like a dream come true. His plan had worked. Leave her be and let love win. She had come back to him. He was the man for her, after all. He loved her so much. He had done nothing but think about her, ever since the day he had set her free in Piaf's a few weeks ago. He had been prepared to wait for months, not weeks, and was just so relieved and happy.*

Turning into Amerland Road, he smiled to himself as he noticed Margaret's curtains twitch. From what Ruby had said about the old girl, he was sure she would be pleased that Ruby had made a decision to have a relationship with him. He may not be George, but he too was steady and dependable and would do anything for his ginger lover.

And then BANG! He stopped in his tracks and did a

double-take. Because there, bold as brass, was Ruby with George! He had only seen the wedding photo once, but there was just no mistaking it. There she was on her doorstep kissing her husband. The duplicitous bitch! How could she have got away with it? The tears, the drama. Telling him that George was dead. Even her sex-mad Irish friend must have been in on the story. But no, surely not. He began to doubt himself. Tony Choi, Daphne and Norbert from the café... That meant everyone would have been in on it and Ruby's emotion had been so real when she lost the ring. Maybe he was going mad. Love had made him paranoid and, granted, he had only seen the photo once.

Michael took a large drag from a cigarette that he had had to buy through stress on his way back to his flat. Paranoia aside, Ruby Stevens was still kissing another man on her doorstep. It may not have been long and lingering but it was a kiss nevertheless.

She was playing him whatever the situation and he loved her too much to just let it go. Maybe it was a grief thing that you went for men who looked like your dead partner. He wished he understood more about bereavement. His mother dying was different. He of course had felt the complete distress and loneliness that losing someone you loved brought, but he couldn't even imagine what it was like to lose someone you woke up next to every single day.

Michael stretched his arms in the air and drew hard on his cigarette. He opened the window and, not caring if the whole place filled with smoke, puffed away furiously. He loved her too much to hurt her in real life, but he could write about it at least. Release his emotion in more ways than one.

Emily walked in behind him quietly at his desk.

'Shit, Em, you made me jump! How are you feeling?'

'Oh, you know, still a bit sick and a bit fat but also quite randy.' She pulled open her shirt to reveal that she had no bra on.

'You're insatiable, wifey, but I'm not complaining.'

'You're not? I feel you've been a bit off with me lately – is everything all right?'

Michael knew if he was to get what he wanted he had to lie.

'Of course it is, babe. You know, it's stressful being freelance, and with a baby coming along too, I just want the best for us all. Now come here and let me touch those beautiful breasts of yours.'

'They are massive now!' Emily laughed, feeling for once at peace with her husband.

'So is this.' He pulled her hand to his erect cock and she undid his zip hungrily.

'Let me suck you.' She teased him with her lips until he was moaning in pleasure.

'Bedroom, now!' he demanded.

Their lovemaking was passionate and frenziedt.

'I'm gonna come!' Michael gasped.

'Goal!' Sam shouted as his beloved football team scored. Ben the guide dog sat quietly by his feet.

'Lucky,' Harry whispered, as Ruby squeezed his hand warning him not to upset the away supporters. She'd had a bad enough experience years ago when James had called out against Newcastle, and Sam had to give him his glasses and white stick and pretend it was him who was blind.

'So how did you meet my sister?' Sam enquired at half-time. Ruby was annoyed that she hadn't been able to tell Sam anything about Harry before the match. She'd had to wait for Fi and James to leave the café before she could depart, as Norbert had misplaced the key for the back entrance.

'We literally bumped into each other, didn't we, Ruby?'

'Yeah. I was just leaving Rita's, I dropped something, and we bumped heads and that was that.'

When Harry went off to the toilet, Sam said, 'Rubes, you haven't mentioned this one before. What's happened to that guy Michael you were seeing? He sounded really nice.'

'He is really nice, and even told me that he loved me, but then he turned around and said he should give me some space. I mean, I was mucking the poor guy around. You know how confused I was, and still am, about George. He said I was to go to him when I felt I was ready.'

'So why haven't you?'

'I have. I texted him and said I missed him and wanted to meet him soon. And – nothing.'

'Have you spoken to him?'

'Well, no, I haven't.'

'He could have just not got the text or anything. The new smartphones aren't infallible, you know.'

'I didn't think of that – but anyway, he knows where I live.'

'Ruby, people just don't turn up on other people's doorsteps unannounced these days.'

'If they loved you they would, and he said he did.'

'Blimey, sis. You've read too many Mills and Boons. This is the twenty-first century and Mr Darcy isn't going to suddenly appear from the water and rush to you, dripping all over with a bouquet of flowers.'

'He might.'

'Talk to him – it's probably just a silly misunderstanding.'

'But I slept with Mr Smooth last night.'

'Oh God, what are you like? Sometimes you are like a bloke. You've only just met him.'

'When did you become the Pope? I have needs as well, you know.'

'You also have a man who sounds like he adores you. He could fulfil those needs – if you just stopped being so bloody childish and talked to him, that is.'

Sam stroked Ben and gave him a doggy treat. Ruby went quiet. 'And stop sulking!'

Ruby smiled and kissed her brother on the cheek. 'I love that you can see more about me than I can.'

'I'm just not sure about Harry, Ruby. I can't put my finger on it at the moment, but I know that he smells wrong.'

Ruby felt a massive surge of love for her younger brother. 'You and your smells.'

'Have you not seen *A Midsummer Night's Dream*, Rubes?' In theatrical voice, Sam quoted, '*Love looks not with the eyes, but with the mind; And, therefore, is winged Cupid painted blind.*'

'That is *so* spooky.' Ruby thought back to the fortune cookie message.

'What's so spooky?' Harry returned to his seat.

'Nothing, really,' Ruby flustered. 'Just that being blind has a lot of advantages, that's all.'

CHAPTER FIFTY TWO

Bubbly blonde Ellie came bounding through the doors of the church hall and kissed Simon right on the mouth.

'Wow, that's quite a greeting,' he beamed. 'Maybe we should have a two-week Easter break more often.'

'I can't tell you why I am so excited but I have an announcement to make when everyone gets here.'

'Ooh, sounds exciting. Is Nick not with you?'

'No, he's working nights this week.'

'Fuck, tits, bollocks.' Jimmy's red Mohican preceded him.

Simon was pleased to notice that he was still clean-shaven and was wearing a lovely new suit. He even appeared to have lost a fair bit of weight.

Cali shimmied in, wearing one of her brightly coloured kaftans. Her voluptuous breasts were on full show.

'Tits!'

Cali put her hand in the air for effect. 'Jimmy Chislehurst, that is enough. Just one "tits" today is plenty, thank you very much.'

'But you have two and might I say they are looking very fine this evening.'

Cali had to laugh. She wasn't sure who was ruder, Simon or

Jimmy.

'Where's Fanny the wonder dog today then?' Simon asked, making his way to the back kitchen to retrieve his vodka mug.

'She's at the doggy parlour. I am collecting her later.'

'Good. It may stop me bloody sneezing if she's clean.'

'I don't know why I bother coming here,' Cali said, offended, and put her hand in the biscuit tin to dig out two custard creams. 'Biscuit, Jimmy?' She offered him the tin.

'No thanks, I am on a diet.'

Cali looked him up and down. 'Actually, you look great. You must have lost at least a stone. What's the secret?'

'You're the secret.' He winked and Cali felt annoyed that he had actually made her blush. She blamed it on the fact that since Christmas her Weeping Widower was still not happy to have sex with her. She had always been rampant in that department and since starting the menopause was gagging for it even more than usual.

'Where's young Ruby?' Jimmy enquired, rubbing his eyes. It was taking him a while to get used to his new contact lenses. 'I have something to show her.'

'It's quite a night for revelations, isn't it?' Simon looked to Ellie and smirked. 'She's just getting us some late Easter treats. Won't be long.'

As he spoke, Ruby arrived and Jimmy rushed to relieve her of her goody-laden bags.

'Wine, beer, cakes, chocolate. Party time, everybody!' Ruby announced to the group.

'So are we not having a serious discussion this evening then?' Cali asked, secretly pleased.

'No,' Ellie piped up. 'Get those drinks poured. We have something to celebrate. Danny has only gone and proposed!'

A plethora of congratulations flew around the room. Ellie

was beaming.

'I would like to raise a toast to Simon, because without him and the rest of The Bow Wow Club, I never would have got this far. It's been bloody hard dating a widower, but I've managed to keep the faith, keep the patience, and now I know that I am moving forward with a long-lasting love. I am *so* happy.'

'That is brilliant, and I am so pleased for you.' Ruby kissed her on the cheek.

'Actually, Ruby, I wanted to ask you a massive favour.'

'Go on.'

'I will pay your train fare, of course, but I was wondering if you might pop along to a wedding I'm going to next week? It's a good mate of mine. She's shown me a fabric sample of the bridesmaids' dresses and a simple design and I adore them. I wouldn't mind you taking a look as it's the sort of style I'd love for mine. And I guess it's always better to see these things in the flesh, rather than in a photograph?'

'Are you sure she won't mind you copying her?' Ruby checked.

'I won't be getting married for at least eighteen months so it's fine, and it's just the initial ideas, really. And, of course I would love you to make them for me once I settle on a design.'

'Thanks Ellie, that's really sweet of you. Whereabouts is the wedding?'

'The Guild Hall in Windsor. Do you know it?'

'Ooh, nice. And don't be silly about the train fare, it's only half an hour from Putney and I've always wanted to see the Queen Mary's Dolls' House at the castle anyway. There are also two remarkable French dolls there. The clothes and accessories were designed and made by the leading Parisian fashion houses, including Cartier, Hermès, and Vuitton. So it will be a lovely adventure for me.'

'Atchoo!' Cali whacked Simon's bottom as he let out a

magnificent sneeze.

'See? I told you it wasn't my smelly little Fanny.'

'Little, you say?' the vicar quipped.

In less than an hour the party was in full swing. Cali was dancing as if she had been tasered, while Ellie was getting down to some sexy shimmying with Simon. With Britney Spears booming from the stereo, Jimmy suddenly ran up to the front of the hall and leaped onto Simon's desk.

Everyone stared in disbelief as he pulled hard at his head to remove a plastic Mohican wig!

Hysterics ensued. Cali was speechless; under all that fake hair and swearing was, in fact, a very handsome man. His hair *had* been cut into a smart short haircut, which suited his new slimline look perfectly.

She limboed towards him, wobbling her big boobs, singing as she went, 'Hit me baby one more time!'

'You only had to ask.' Jimmy jumped down and grabbed Cali's substantial rear end.

'How's Fi?' Simon asked Ruby, when the last regular and newbie had left the party.

'She's all right, thanks.'

'Good, good. I really like her, you know. And, that doesn't often happen to me.'

'I know. But I'm sorry to tell you that she's staying with James by the look of it.' Ruby wanted to get off the subject as all she could see in front of her was the cause of Fi's sweet little bump.

'Well, as long as she's happy.' Simon drained his glass of wine. 'And how about you, young lady? Are you happy? You've seemed a bit low recently.'

'I'm OK. Just having trouble understanding men, that's all. Michael was all over me two months ago and now nothing. I've tried to call but he doesn't pick up and he never replies to my texts. I don't understand what I've done.'

'That's not good.'

'I've been sleeping with this other guy who looks just like my late husband, but he's so far from him in personality that I know that I'm fooling myself.'

'So, what are you going to do?'

'Just leave it for a bit, I think. It's good to have company and sex on tap sometimes.'

'But that can be so shallow and worthless too. You have a big heart, Ruby. Fill it back up with some proper love. You deserve every little flutter to be real. Why don't you go to Michael's house? Ask him what's wrong face-to-face. At least then you'll know how you feel, and his eyes will be able to tell you so much more.'

'Maybe I will. I do miss him – and thanks, Simon. I'm glad I met you.'

'Likewise, you old tart. Now let's get out of here.'

They walked out into the graveyard and heard a terrible squealing noise. Ruby grabbed Simon's arm.

'Foxes rutting, probably.' Simon shone his torch around and then, trying not to laugh too loudly, clicked it off.

There, bold as brass, kneeling next to where poor old Melody Pratt had been taken by a wasp, was the buxom Cali being taken from behind by the freshly refurbished Jimmy Chislehurst.

CHAPTER FIFTY THREE

It was a bright, sunny Saturday when the train pulled into the old, ornate station in Windsor. Ruby had at least an hour to kill before the wedding party was due to emerge, so took it upon herself to look around the local shops. Ellie said she would text her when the wedding party were due to appear from the Guild Hall, as she thought that would give Ruby the best effect of seeing all the outfits together.

Ruby headed towards the river and wandered along the path, not quite believing how many swans there were. She had read somewhere that swans mated for life and wished that it could be that easy for humans too.

Taking a seat on one of the many benches lining the river, she pulled her scarf up to her chin and did something she hadn't done in a long time – she gloried in her solitude. She no longer felt lonely without George. She still missed him, but time was beginning to heal and a new life had begun emerging for her.

When he first died, every waking thought was of him for months and months. Now, this was no longer the case. She couldn't even think when that had happened, or why. It was the same as when you broke up with someone. First you thought you would never ever get over it, would check your texts, your phone messages relentlessly. Cry at sad songs, relive every moment of the love affair. And then suddenly that was over too. You picked yourself up, dusted yourself down, and went in hunt of another love.

George's death had made Ruby understand that life is transient and happiness infrequent. That when a good spell happens, you need to grab it by the balls and relish every single golden moment.

Now, when she heard people planning their lives and talking of retirement, it made her smile. Yes, of course, most people did plan, but not one person could be certain of their future. It was quite ironic that George had always said to her that life was a rollercoaster and if you were on it until the end, then you should count yourself lucky. They had made a vow to live every second of their life as if it was their last. This had led to a wonderful and exciting marriage.

The beep of a text message awakened Ruby from her thoughts: Ellie's ten-minute warning to her. She walked up the hill, passing the castle on her left, and headed towards the Guild Hall. A small spattering of Japanese tourists, alerted by the awaiting wedding cars, were craning their necks to try and get the first sight of the bride and groom.

Ruby had brought her camera along and poised it ready as the door opened to cheers and confetti-throwing. She smiled at the thought of her and George's wedding, which had taken place in her hometown of Reading, following by the most perfect honeymoon at Daffodils, her cottage in the Lake District.

Flash! She snapped as the happy couple appeared.

Then *crash, bang, wallop* – the sound of her heart sinking as she identified the handsome groom, resplendent in light grey tails and top hat, as none other than Harry Bowman-Green!

CHAPTER FIFTY FOUR

Simon was just locking up the church hall when he noticed Fi walking up the path.

'Hello, stranger.' He greeted her with a kiss on the cheek. 'Don't tell me you've come for me to forgive your sins. We have a service in six hours so you'd better get a move on.'

He knew something was wrong when the usually effusive Fi didn't comment.

'Have you got a second to talk, Simon?' was all she said.

'I have as many seconds as it takes. Come with me.' He led her to the vicarage opposite the church. Once sitting comfortably in his kitchen, with a ginger tea she had brought along, Fi began to talk.

'I won't beat around the bush, Simon. I'm pregnant.'

The vicar could tell congratulations weren't in order. 'And is that the problem?'

Fi had to stop and think about this simple question.

'Actually, no.' She looked to the ceiling. 'No, it's not.'

'Well, that's a good start. It's one less decision you have to make at least.'

Fi was in awe of this man's direct compassion and understanding.

'Do you know who the father is?'

She nodded slowly.

'You don't have to tell me, Fi.'

'It's you. You're the father.'

'Whoa, OK.' He put his hand to his head. 'Shit, Fi.'

'I'm in it to be sure, Rev.'

'Oh, God!' Simon got up and started pacing around.

'You can't say that, you're a vicar.'

'A vicar with a scandal afoot in the parish. Right, so it's happened. There's no point screaming and shouting, we just need to deal with it now. Oh, and poor you. How are you feeling?'

'Not good, to be honest. Sick as a dog every day.'

'Bless you.' He kissed her on the top of her head.

'But this is such a longed-for baby, Simon. And if it wasn't for deceiving James, I would be elated.'

Simon sat back down. 'OK. Let's talk this through. It can be as easy or as difficult as we want to make it. There is a solution to everything except death. Him upstairs will guide us and love will win whatever happens, Fi.'

'Unless James kills me first.'

'By the sound of it, he adores you. I can feel a lot of love in this room. Me for you, and you for that baby. It's going to be fine.'

If relief were red smoke Fi would resemble a Red Arrow in performance flight at this moment.

'Have you told James you're pregnant?'

'No, because he's just announced that he is, in fact, infertile and wants us to have a surrogate child via IVF.'

'Jesus. It's like *Jeremy* bloody *Kyle*.'

'I know; tell me about it. But I guess why I'm here, Simon, is to get your blessing.' Fi took a noisy slurp of tea. 'I love James,' she went on. 'I always have. And I want to spend the rest of my life with him. Initially, I was thinking I was just standing by him because I so desperately wanted a child, but now it's come to the crunch and he's given me the option to walk away from him, I don't want to. He is a good man, Simon.'

'There will be a lot of lying involved, Fi. You'll have to say you're going to the fertility clinic alone.'

'I know – and I realise that dishonesty must go against your grain.'

Simon laughed. 'The vicar of the parish has just got you pregnant by sleeping with you out of wedlock when you are co-habiting with another man. Who am I to ever judge?'

'And that is why you are such an amazing man, Simon. People flock to you because you're real. You say it how it bloody is. Sugar-coating is for wimps, I say.'

'Just one tiny problem though, Fi. This baby is not going to be fair-skinned like its beautiful mum.'

'So, I didn't have my contacts in when I looked at prospective fathers' details at the clinic. And your mum is white – right?' Simon nodded. 'And with my translucent Irish skin, you never know. We can deal with that when it happens. James will be happy if I'm happy, and to know that I am bringing a human being who is half of you into this world delights me.'

Tears pricked Simon's eyes. He cleared his throat.

'If you need any money, please let me know.'

It was Fi's turn to get emotional. 'You're fine. James is a solicitor, so money will never be the issue. I just want to make sure you understand why I am doing this. You can see me and the baby whenever you want to, but nobody will ever know, just me, you, and Ruby – and I trust that girl with my life. You won't get a say in this baby's upbringing and I know that is a tough ask and I'm sorry for this.'

'Look, Fi. This child will have the love of two strong parents, I know that. And that is half the battle won. I have no doubt you will be an amazing mum.' He squeezed her hand. 'In truth, I need to get married and be respectable and have a family of my own, but I haven't been totally honest with you. I do like men and women, but fundamentally I know I *am* gay. I have only ever slept with one woman before you, and that was when I was at school, but there is just something crazy about you. You're a great girl, Fi.'

'That makes me feel better somehow.'

'What, that I am gay?'

'Yeah, it sort of makes my decision even clearer, since I know that a "proper"' –Fi made speech marks in the air with her fingers – 'relationship would never be on the cards with me and you.'

'Good. I will come out when I am ready, but at the moment it's just not the right time for me. I have only been in this parish a year and it's not easy when the Good Book doesn't think we should be allowed to love another man. There are too many bigots in this world, but I chose to follow God. I know that I am here for a purpose and none of us are perfect, eh?'

'Well, apart from me, of course,' Fi laughed. 'I want you in my life, that's for sure. There's nothing wrong with you being an amazing godfather, now, is there?'

Simon stood up, his huge frame making Fi look like a fragile bird, and hugged her tightly. 'Love has many aspects, Fi, and it doesn't have to be the all-consuming, passionate kind. That is probably last on the list to make things work, to be honest. I've only met you once before, but I know I love you. You're a special girl, Fiona O'Donahue.'

'And do you know what, Simon Dye? You big, religious, gay, blaspheming bastard, I love you too.'

CHAPTER FIFTY FIVE

'I can explain,' Harry mouthed to Ruby as he got into the wedding car. He was as white as the lilies in his new wife's bouquet.

She had managed to keep it together long enough to say goodbye to Ellie and wish her a good day, but she was fuming so much when she got to the station that she literally felt like she was going to explode.

'Bloody married!' she said. Fearing she was a complete weirdo, the woman opposite put her book in her bag and moved quickly to another seat. Ignoring completely the fact that she was in a quiet zone carriage, Ruby rang Fi.

'You will never guess what's just happened,' she burst out.

'You slept with a vicar? Oh no, that was me.' Her friend didn't even giggle, so Fi knew it was serious. 'Just tell me, Rubes, are you all right?'

'No, I'm fucking not. You know I was going to that wedding in Windsor to look at the dresses?'

'Yep.'

'Well, none other than Harry Bastard Bowman-Wanker hyphen Green was the groom.'

'No!'

'Yes! Bold as brass. He saw me, went white as a sheet, and just mouthed, "I will explain". Fi, this time last week I had just got off his knob!'

'Oh, Rubes. I am so sorry.'

'I'm not, actually. Sam said he smelled wrong – and you know Sam is always right when it comes to people. But why? That poor woman. I mean, if it had been a one-night stand, you can almost understand it. Some men are born cheaters and I know they would do that. But it was the beginnings of *something*. We had sex a few times; had dinner together; went to the football. It may not have been a perfect union, but it was a relationship of sorts.'

'Well, you just need to draw a line under it now, Rubes. It is a lesson. He may have looked like George but he was so far removed from him, it was untrue. You need to follow your heart now.'

'I want some answers from Harry, though. It just seems weird for someone to do that.'

'He'll be on honeymoon from tomorrow I expect, so just let it be.'

'I feel so used!'

The woman who had moved from opposite looked up in annoyance. Seeing Ruby's angry face made her far too scared to say anything.

'I've had quite a day too. I told Simon the baby is his.'

'What!' Ruby shouted. The book-reading woman got up quickly to change carriages.

'It's all cool, Rubes. Just another secret to take to our graves, I'm afraid. And we know we can the trust the vicar. Even though he just came out to me as gay.'

'Bless Simon, how hard must that be for him?' Ruby relaxed and gave a chuckle. 'He must think you look like a bloke.'

'Yeah, thanks for that, mate. Anyway, the plan is in place. You are coming to the pretend clinic with me on Monday to get me spermed, so to speak, and we go from there. I will, of course, be going into labour six weeks prematurely, but James *is* a man and I've kissed the Blarney Stone so we can blag it as and when necessary.'

'Oh, Fi. How lovely that you are expecting a baby. I cannot wait to cuddle them!'

Ruby jumped up and did a little dance around the carriage. Which had now thankfully emptied or she would surely have been committed by now.

'Can I be godmother? I mean, the little one already has a godfather. Ha!'

'You can be whatever you like, madam, as long as you move out of the quiet zone immediately,' a frosty-looking ticket inspector butted in.

'Gotta go, mate. Being told off. Catch up later. Lots of love.'

CHAPTER FIFTY SIX

Michael's initial anger had subsided over the 'front door incident', as he liked to call it. Maybe he had jumped to conclusions. He hoped he was a good enough judge of character to know that Ruby wasn't capable of being unfaithful in a marriage. Yes, that man had looked like George, but he had only seen one photo of the poor bloke. Maybe his mind had taken over rational thinking because his heart was so drawn to this amazing woman. Maybe he too hadn't taken the chance to understand enough about grief, in particular losing a partner. He had Googled 'dating a widow' the night before and couldn't believe the amount of stuff that had come up. There were even special forums relating to the topic. And he found it heartening to see that he wasn't the only one struggling with it.

So that was it, he would see Ruby again. He would be gentle and ask her how she was coping. He had to be with her, there was no question, but first he would arm himself with knowledge. Learn from people who had been through the same as him.

He had one mission – to be the best boyfriend of a widow that he could possibly be.

CHAPTER FIFTY SEVEN

Monty barked loudly as Ruby clicked open the gate to her mother-in-law's East End house.

'Hello, Red, what a lovely surprise,' Rita said, her welcome genuine. 'Fancy a cuppa? The kettle's on. How you been?'

'I've been all right, although the man I mentioned who looked like our George and who I dated once or twice didn't work quite how I expected. Tea would be lovely, thanks.'

'Ooh. Last time you had just spotted him in the street. Tell me more.'

Ruby reddened. It felt weird telling her about it.

Rita could sense her angst, and said, 'Just 'cos I've chosen to be a dry old spinster from now on don't mean you 'ave to be, Rubes. You're young, got your whole life ahead of you. I couldn't be 'appier to hear of you finding love again. Don't get me wrong, if it had been minutes after our boy had gone I might 'ave 'ad a word. But not now.'

'I've got a photo of him. It is just so spooky.'

Rita viewed the photo on Ruby's phone and began to shake. Ruby steadied her and led her to a kitchen chair.

'I know! I felt the same. It's like looking at George.'

'Except for that little mole on 'is cheek, ain't it?' Tears rolled down Rita's face.

Ruby wasn't sure how to react. Rita Stevens's wasn't a crier and she was sure she wouldn't want to be consoled.

'It's 'im – I know it's 'im,' the woman sobbed.

'No, no,' Ruby soothed, tears in her own eyes. 'It's not our George, it's someone who just looks like him.'

'That's what I mean, darling. I've done summink terrible.'

Ruby screwed her face up. 'Terrible? What do you mean?'

Rita sniffed loudly. 'I was pregnant with twins, see. Me and Alfie were poor as church mice – that was before we set up our business and made a go of it. We made a pact that we would just keep one of 'em. Keep the one who looked like he needed more looking after.' She could barely speak for crying.

'Little George was just so tiny. Just three pounds, had to go into an incubator.'

'The other little boy – I couldn't even bear to name him – was a much healthier five pounds. I knew he'd make it through, you see, so I let him go for adoption. It was the most terrible decision I've ever made in my whole life, and I regret it every minute of every day.'

Ruby welled up. She gripped Rita's hand. 'I am so sorry.'

'I said to the adoption lady that I didn't ever want him to find me because I was so ashamed. I asked that they send him to an affluent family so he would want for nothing, get a good education – you know. Make summink of himself.' She shuddered with grief. 'For twenty-nine years I've tortured myself, and when our boy was taken, that was my penance. The Good Lord took my Alfie and then George because I was so wicked.' Her voice was high-pitched with emotion, and she wept.

'No, Rita, no,' Ruby implored. 'You are such a kind woman. You did what you thought was right.'

'But it wasn't right, was it? We would have managed. People

do. And, now I can't ever change it. I know that is 'im. I just know it.'

'I think it must be him,' Ruby whispered. 'He's going to be thirty on September the seventeenth.'

'Oh, no!'

'Do you want to meet him? I'm sure I could arrange it.'

'No, I don't.' Rita was adamant. 'It wouldn't be right.'

Ruby breathed a sigh of relief.

'Promise me you will never tell a soul,' her mother-in-law said.

'I promise,' Ruby vowed.

'So, what's he like, love?' Rita went on, sounding stronger now. 'You said earlier that he didn't turn out how you expected.'

'He didn't turn out how I wanted him to be because he was marrying someone else. How dare he, eh?' Ruby attempted a smile. 'He is lovely, Rita,' she lied. 'Not our George, of course, but he's a credit to you as his natural mother and to his adoptive parents too.'

Rita laughed through her tears. 'What does he do?'

'He works in the City, a big finance job. He's doing really well.'

'So he's having a good life?'

'Oh, yes. He is a great person and wants for nothing.' Ruby took another deep breath, fearing that if she told any more lies she might be struck down.

'That is enough for me, Rubes, coming from your mouth too. I can die 'appy now – and what a coincidence for you to meet 'im of all people!'

'I know, it's millions to one. Our George must be looking down on you. He wanted to put you at peace.'

Ruby put a comforting arm on Rita's shoulder. And, at that precise moment she realised that her meeting with the City slicker was no doubt a far cry from a perfect coincidence.

CHAPTER FIFTY EIGHT

Michael pushed open the door to the church hall in trepidation. This had seemed the perfect solution. A self-help group to see you through the trials and tribulations of dating a widow or widower.

The website had stated "*The Bow Wow Club – From Struggle to Joy!*" Well, he was definitely due some joy, that was for sure.

Greeted by a tall, friendly black guy who made him feel completely at ease, it looked like he was the first to arrive.

'So, Michael, if it's OK with you, I'm lacking in content today, so do you mind if we start with your story? Are you a widower?'

'Erm, no. I'd been dating someone who has lost a husband. That is what this group is all about, isn't it?'

'Bloody marvellous, pal.' Simon shook his hand. 'Yes, yes, this is why I set this menagerie up. But it seems that the world and God's dog turn up thinking it's a bereavement centre. Which is fine.' He touched his dog collar. 'We listen to everyone here, but there are people more specialised than me to deal with grief itself and I don't think I always send them away with the right message.'

Michael took in Simon's cropped hair and Glaswegian accent, and thought he would make a great character in his novel. An eccentric vicar – every parish should have one!

People started drifting in and making their way to the kitchenette. He noticed a clean-shaven man in a smart suit who seemed to tic slightly as he sat down. A voluptuous fifty-something tried to bring her scruffy black dog to heel, and a good-looking lad who he thought smelled vaguely of woodsmoke mouthed 'Hi' as he walked past.

He wondered what their backstories were. Life was a funny beast. You had to deal with all sorts of obstacles as they cropped up, usually without warning. It would have been so much simpler for him to fall in love with someone who hadn't been bereaved – but then that would be too easy. There was only one Ruby Stevens, and it was she whom he had chosen to love.

'Right, chop chop!' the leader shouted. 'Our delicious red-headed volunteer is en route from the East End and is going to be a bit late, so you have to help yourselves to tea et cetera. She'd break my balls if we didn't start on time.'

Everyone grabbed a drink and custard creams and settled into the semi-circle.

'So, today everyone, I want you to welcome Michael. Say hello to Michael.'

'Fuck, shit, bollocks,' Jimmy burst out with, and Cali glared at him. When they were together in the bedroom, there was never so much as a 'tit'.

This was to be the couple's last session. But they had wanted to give Simon and Ruby a gift before they left, as they felt they owed it to them both, for transforming Jimmy into a fanciable creature and bringing them together in such a bizarre circumstance.

Luckily, Eric, the widower whom Cali had been dating for a matter of months, had actually seemed quite relieved to be rid of such an insatiable beast.

The Fireman smiled warmly at Michael and gestured for him to go on.

'So, er. Yes. I'm Michael. I'm thirty-seven years old and I live in Clapham. I've been dating a widow since December.'

It felt like he was at some sort of addiction meeting. Well, he was, in a way – addicted to somebody he loved.

Ruby quietly let herself into the back door so as not to disturb the meeting. On seeing the new Bow Wow member, she froze on the spot like a rabbit in headlights. No, she had to be mistaken. It couldn't be, surely?

She dived into the kitchen and peered over the hatch, then began ducking up and down like a meerkat. She couldn't let him see her, he would be mortified. It must have taken him such courage to come here. She tried to catch Simon's eye and mouth that it was him. She was worried that everyone present was able to hear her heart beating through her chest.

Michael went on. 'Her husband had been dead just over a year when I met her and I felt like I was in a tug of war, but with somebody who didn't exist any more.' Michael cleared his throat. 'One minute we were sailing along nicely and the next, we'd got shipwrecked with no chance of ever carrying on with the voyage. It was then I decided to set her free. You know – let her go and see if love would win. It was a long, agonising wait but I knew it had to be done if I was going to stay with this beautiful creature.'

Simon made a sympathetic face.

'I thought we were making progress recently because she texted me saying that she missed me and wanted to meet. I couldn't get through to her on the phone, so I decided to go to her house with her favourite flowers.'

'Yellow roses?' Simon was completely absorbed in Michael's story and missed Ruby's cut-throat signal to him behind the hatch.

'Yes, how did you know that?'

'Don't all women like yellow roses? They are a sign of... um...a transitioning relationship, I think,' Simon blustered, wishing that Ruby had never told him that they were her favourite bloom.

'Ah, right, you vicars must hear all the stories and know these things.'

'Please go on,' Simon urged. The group was transfixed.

'Well, I rounded the corner to her place and she was on the doorstep kissing a man.'

A united groan.

'And it wasn't just any man,' Simon managed. 'It was – I think...her dead husband.'

Ruby was so shocked she fell backwards and knocked into a mug tree, causing three of them to smash to the floor with a ginormous clatter. She lay on the lino hoping nobody would investigate, but it was too big a commotion to go unnoticed.

Nick looked over the hatch. She smiled up at him.

'Ruby! What on earth are you doing?'

She knew her cover was blown. She stumbled up and appeared in the hatch, looking dazed.

'Ruby? What the...?'

Glowing with embarrassment, Michael stood up, grabbed his open briefcase, and ran to the door. In his haste to leave, papers flew out all over the graveyard.

Ruby leaped over the hatch and began to run after him.

'Michael, I can explain!'

He turned around with tears in his eyes. 'Explain!' he shouted from ten feet away. 'This is something else I didn't know about you, Ruby. You're obviously the "delicious red-headed volunteer". So are you shagging someone here too?'

'Michael, stop it!' She ran to him.

'So who *was* that man? I get a text from you saying you missed me and wanted to see me, and then I see you kissing *him*? Please tell me the whole dead husband thing is not a charade.'

'How bloody dare you, Michael Bell? You know how much grief I've been through. You have felt it through my skin. Don't you ever say that again.'

'So who is he, then?'

An owl hooted and the leaves rustled on the trees surrounding the graveyard.

'He's…' Ruby remembered her solemn promise to Rita. 'He's just someone I know, that's all. Look, this is too much.'

'Have you slept with him?'

Her anger, combined with guilt, rose as bile in her throat. 'I don't feel that you deserve an explanation. How could you think I would be so cruel as to lie to you about George being dead?' Ruby turned and stropped back towards the church hall.

'But you were kissing him!' Michael screamed at her.

'Yes, yes, I was, because you weren't exactly knocking my door down, were you? I texted you, you ignored me.'

'My phone wasn't charged, yours was constantly engaged. I was on my way to see you.'

Ruby pushed her way through the Bow Wowers, who were now dining out on their argument. Michael walked back towards the hall.

'I don't want to talk to you.' Ruby shouted from the doorway.

'Don't flatter yourself, love. I've just come to pick up my papers.' He stormed towards the church gate. 'And to think we had something special. I must have been mad.'

'OK, show's over.' Simon handed Ruby his vodka mug, which she promptly drained.

'I'm sorry to have mucked up your evening, everyone,' she

said, shamefaced. 'I'm going to head home.'

'Tits!' Jimmy shouted, and rushed up to Ruby to give her a hug. 'If it's any consolation, I can tell that he loves you. He cared too much about you sleeping with the other guy not to. Who is the other one anyway?'

'Men!' Ruby shouted on her way out, noticing a stray piece of Michael's paper that had blown into a tree outside. She unceremoniously stuffed it into her handbag.

Stomping up West Hill to home, she clocked a fire engine coming the other way and thought of Nick.

Bless the Fireman. Whatever happened, he would always understand her.

CHAPTER FIFTY NINE

Margaret was putting a charity bag of clothes outside her front door when Ruby stomped past.

'Oi, little lady, what's wrong?'

'Margaret, it's far too late for one of your in-depth chats.'

'It's never too late for you, missy. Come on in for a sherry. It looks like you need one.'

Ruby curled her legs up in the familiar chair in front of the fire and took a sip of sherry from the schooner Margaret had taken from her old-fashioned china cabinet.

'Where's Bert?' she asked.

'Already gone up with his crossword – you know what he's like.'

'I'm glad I sort of got you two together.'

'He's an annoying bugger half the time, but I do love him. I still can't believe he was homeless.'

'Well, they do say that some people are just one pay cheque away from homelessness. If you don't have a good support network, that is.'

'Thankfully, young Ruby, that is what you've got, and with what you've been through, you've bloody needed one. So, tell me, why are you looking so troubled, duck?' The ever-wise

Margaret waited for Ruby to tell her about the other morning, rather than jump in.

'I'm confused.'

'Men?'

'What else? And my head is exploding. I have a massive secret I know I can trust you with, Margaret.'

'Of course you can. Now come on, just tell me, get it off your chest, duck.'

'George had a twin brother.'

'Do you know what? I saw somebody walk past here the other Saturday and had to sit down because it was such a shocker. He's a dead ringer, ain't he?'

'Yes, he is. It's such a sad story.'

'You don't have to tell me if it's too difficult.'

'I need to tell you. I just feel for Rita so much. She didn't think that she and Alfie could financially cope with bringing up two babies. Harry, that's his name. They had him adopted.'

'That poor woman! So, this all makes sense now. He was the one you saw walk past Piaf's and bumped into at the bus stop in the East End. Doesn't sound like a coincidence to me.'

'I don't think it is either. And to top it all off, I went to a wedding in Windsor – bearing in mind this is after I slept with him.'

'Oh, Ruby, you never learn. How many times do I say keep your bloody legs shut? You hardly know him.'

'I know, I know. Well anyway, it was him getting married at this wedding.'

'No! The little toe-rag. What a complete wrong 'un. So do you think he tracked you down on purpose?'

'Yeah, I do, actually. The fact he was near Piaf's and then so near Rita's in Stepney Green…as you say, it would be too much of a coincidence.'

'But why, duck?' Margaret drained her glass.

'The root of all evil, of course.'

'Money? I don't get it.'

'And nor will he, Margaret, nor will he.'

CHAPTER SIXTY

Michael awoke and groaned at the awful memory of the night before. The last time he had cried himself to sleep was the night his mum had died. Not even Emily's philandering had hurt him as much as the Ruby 'graveyard incident'. He pulled himself out of bed, reached for his glasses, and lit a cigarette. At least he would get a novel out of this painful experience. He had so much bloody material now.

***Let Love Win* by Michael Bell**
Chapter 24: *Michael opened his briefcase and began straightening out the pages of his novel that had been strewn all over the church hall and graveyard. Thank goodness he had managed to get them all. Well, he hoped he had anyway. Then 'Damn it!' Page 85 was missing. It had been windy so he guessed he was lucky only to have lost one. He would just print it off again when he was at* Rural Writers' *next week. He just found it so much easier to edit in hard copy rather than on the screen.*

This aimless task, however, didn't distract him from his inner turmoil. This had to be it now. She would hate him. The hurt and anger in Ruby's eyes had been so great. I mean, how could he have been so stupid to accuse her of lying about George being dead? Yes, he had only seen the wedding photo once, but that other guy had looked identical to George, he was sure of it.

Oh, why had he been so stupid? He lay back on his bed and thought through the whole sorry scenario of earlier. Ruby had been right. He had felt her grief through her skin. Had held her beautiful soft body whilst sobs of pure emotion had engulfed her. And the embarrassment of The Bow Wow Club. Why hadn't she mentioned that she was volunteering there? Such a lovely thing to do. He then remembered accusing her of sleeping with the vicar too. I mean, as if a man of God would sleep with a woman out of wedlock!

'Michael, Michael – I'm home.' Emily's whiny voice rose up the stairs. 'What are you doing, pretending to write a book again?'

'Yes, I'm writing.' His voice was monotone. He closed his eyes momentarily and thought of the very first night he had spent with Ruby in the Soho Hotel. When he had made love to her it just felt so right. Like they fitted together. And her smell. How he loved her smell. He loved cuddling up to her from behind when she was just dropping off to sleep. They fitted together perfectly, like Lego bricks. And when he woke at half-light and looked over to the contours of her sleeping face he just felt warm inside. In his eyes, she was the most beautiful woman in the world. She felt right. It felt right – and despite the fact he had seen another man so obviously kissing her, now he had made everything irredeemably wrong.

Emily bounded into the bedroom and threw several coloured shopping bags on to the bed.

'Darling, I've found the most amazing maternity-wear

shop. Everything is just so trendy. Even the underwear is to die for.'

'Show me,' Michael said quite roughly, annoyed that she was frittering away money they really didn't have again.

She began to pull clothes out of the bags.

'No – show me the underwear on you now.'

Emily looked at him and could see his sexual hunger.

'Michael? It's not like you to be so naughty on a Friday morning. I like it.'

'Just do as you are told.'

Emily was already aroused at his demands and quickly got herself into matching a cream and pale pink lace bra and panties, her perfect pregnancy bump evident now.

It was over in minutes. There was no Lego brick spooning afterwards. Emily just jumped straight off the panting Michael and ran to the bathroom to shower.

Michael lay back on the bed feeling thoroughly depressed. Without Ruby his life was a darker place. He had no escape route now. His love for her would have made him make the step to leave his selfish wife. But now, perfunctory fucking with no real love and a baby he didn't even want was his future and he would just have to man up and get on with it.

Michael had an appointment with the editor of a magazine so didn't have time to address his arousal. He couldn't believe that every time he wrote a sex scene, he got a hard-on. While wondering if writers of erotic fiction spent half their days masturbating, his mobile rang, making him jump.

He didn't recognise the number, but on sudden recognition of the voice, he felt his heart shift like a tectonic plate.

'Michael? Is that you? It's Emily. I really need to see you.'

CHAPTER SIXTY ONE

Harry sheepishly pushed open the gate to the East End graveyard. The bunch of flowers he was carrying was nearly as big as him. He turned left and walked down to the bottom fence, where a row of tall fir trees protected the many souls within. He saw Ruby; a lone figure crouched down chatting away to a white marble headstone. As soon as she saw Harry, she leaped up and brushed herself down.

'I don't think there are enough vases.' She blushed at being caught in such a private moment.

'No, these are for you. Let me lay them down here.' He put them gently down onto the grave and noticed the wording on the headstone.

George Stevens. Dearly beloved husband and son. Sleep softly in our hearts.

He sniffed loudly. 'That's beautiful. Did you choose those words?'

Ruby nodded and exhaled deeply, thinking how sad it was that she couldn't have added the words 'brother' or 'father'.

She felt at peace here, and if she was visiting Rita, she would pop along to the Stepney Green churchyard and leave a single yellow rose on George's final resting place. When he had first died she would make a weekly pilgrimage, despite it taking nearly three hours out of her day. As time had gone on it was monthly, but this year she had made the decision that she would visit on birthdays, at Christmas, and their significant anniversaries, plus of course whenever she visited Rita.

George's mum religiously kept the plot immaculate, which put Ruby at peace and alleviated her guilt at not visiting as much any more.

Ruby ushered Harry to a nearby bench. He noticed the plaque along the back of it. *In memory of Ralph Weeks, still taking wickets in Heaven.*

'Why are people so mean to each other in life when this is where we all end up?'

'You tell me that, Harry.'

'I set myself up for that one, didn't I? I am so sorry, Ruby – I hope I can explain.'

'Explain away. All I can say is that I am glad what we had was just a casual fling or I might not be quite so calm now.'

Ruby noticed his shiny new wedding ring as he started his sorry tale.

'I found out I was adopted when I was very young. Mum and Dad are great, and have always been completely open. When I got to eighteen my inquisitive nature got the better of me and I *had* to know who my real parents were. The fact I was informed that my real mother did not want to be contacted made me even more determined.'

'I took it on myself to find out everything I could about my heritage without anyone else knowing, so I wouldn't cause any hurt. I even saw George when he was alive.' Ruby gasped. 'It was before you two got together, when he was at college. I knew that we could never meet face-to-face because he would obviously suss we were twins, and Rita would get hurt. I sat in the back of a student bar, astounded at how alike we were – in looks, anyway.'

Ruby couldn't believe how surreal this was. Here she was, sitting on a bench with somebody who could quite easily pass as George. She had made sure that Rita was doing her shift in the local charity shop before arranging to meet Harry. It would have just been too distressing for the woman to be faced with her other son.

'I love Rita, Ruby. She's a good woman. I am proud to call her my real mum. I've seen her from afar in so many situations it breaks my heart. I was even behind the trees here at my real dad's funeral.' He pointed to the fir trees. 'But I also respect her wishes. I know she would be ashamed if it came out in the community about me, but she has no need to. It's sad, but I do understand. She is a proud woman, too. It would be too much to bear if people started judging her for her decision. I know that.'

'So why have a relationship with me? You must have seen how hurt I was if you were still stalking us throughout our marriage.' Ruby put her hands through her fringe. 'I can't believe you did that, Harry. It's too weird.'

'I don't expect you to understand. Look, I'm going to be honest with you because I like you, Ruby. I didn't think I would. I mean, I've never been out with a ginger in my life before.'

'OK, OK, stop the shallow, unfunny crap and be honest with me then.'

'In a word, money.'

'I bloody knew it, you scheming little shit. All those "innocent" questions when we were out for dinner, about me being looked after by George financially. You just wanted a piece of the pie.'

'I thought that I would surely get some of the inheritance, what with being a one-hundred-per-cent blood brother. I had lost track of where George was living as he was renting for a while, but I followed you from Rita's one day and saw that you seemed to visit that Piaf's café a lot. That's when I hatched my plan. I knew that if I could get close to you, you would be so overwhelmed by my similarity to your George that you would spill everything about your finances and I could take what I could.'

'You complete and utter bastard.'

'Yes, I'm a wanker. But things didn't go quite to plan, as not only do I like you, but I fell for you too. Mad, I know. I've been with Lucy for seven years and don't regret marrying her for a second. But, then there was you. Spirited, funny, feisty Ruby Stevens. My brother was a lucky boy. And if you hadn't busted me at the wedding, I would have tried to sleep with you again, married or not.'

'Your poor wife.'

'She doesn't deserve me, I know. I am completely ashamed now at my behaviour. You, George, Rita, and my real dad are all bloody good people. So all I can do is say how truly sorry I am. You'll never see me again, I promise that. I won't check on Rita any more either. If she had ever caught sight of me, I know that it might have killed her. We – me and Lucy – are flying to Geneva tomorrow. I've got a new job. The plan is to build a new life, and for me to earn as much money as I can so that we can start a family.'

Ruby was beyond anger. She stood up silently and walked towards George's grave. Harry followed.

'Say goodbye to your brother,' she whispered venomously. 'Because what you just said means you can never come here again.'

'I know that.' Harry's voice was cracked with emotion. He touched the marble headstone. 'It's never goodbye, mate. Just see you later.'

Ruby started to cry. It was like having to say farewell to George all over again. Harry rushed to comfort her and she halted him with her hand. 'No. Please don't. I don't need anything from you. Ever. Goodbye, Harry.'

'Be happy, Ruby,' he replied. Then he discreetly dropped something into the bouquet of flowers that were still lying on the ground. Leaving Ruby deep in her thoughts, he walked back to the car park.

He hoped she would be pleased when she found it. It was an act of kindness of sorts, he thought – giving something back when he had been so wicked.

The day he had set up the stealing of her handbag in London, he had expected to find her address and bank details.

But what he didn't expect to find was the treasured wedding ring his twin brother had so lovingly given to her.

CHAPTER SIXTY TWO

Ruby opened her front door and threw her keys on to the kitchen table. She looked at herself in the mirror above the fireplace and grimaced as her red-eyed, blotchy face looked back at her.

Harry would be packing up his life in the UK. It was such a relief for her that he was moving overseas. Then she could put the whole sorry affair behind her. Guilt flowers as well? What was he thinking? She couldn't bear the thought of having them in the house – it would remind her too much of his ways. So she had just left them on George's grave. She didn't like bouquets on graves as a rule, but as there were no spare vases she thought it wouldn't matter this once, and Rita could clear the old paper and dried stems away when she next visited.

She picked up *the* wedding photo from the fireplace and held it to her chest.

'Oh Georgie boy, what a mess. How you would have loved to have had a twin brother, and how different he might have been if you'd been brought up together.'

She was hungry, and scrabbled in her handbag looking for a cereal bar she had put in there that morning. Along with a couple of used tissues and an old train ticket, she brought out a screwed-up piece of A4 paper. The terrible memory of her recent fight with Michael in the graveyard crossed her mind. She flicked on the kettle and unfurled the crumpled document.

On noticing the page header she gulped, then began to read hungrily.

***A Ring for Miss Ruby* by Michael Bell**

Chapter 22: *She had taken her ring off. A bare finger. No wedding band. A significant move for a widow – and what had he gone and done? Told her he didn't want to see her any more. Had he made the right decision? Only time would tell. He sighed deeply. Why was love so difficult? Why couldn't we be born with a homing device that drew us to just one person with whom we should spend the rest of our lives? Just put your finger on a touch screen and it would locate your match. They could be anywhere in the world. Any creed, colour, size. You would just be instantly attracted, fall in love and have babies and live happily ever after. But then again, would life be boring then? Wasn't half the fun meeting new people, touching new bodies, experiencing different characters, places and circumstances?*

No, sod all that. At this moment Michael would be quite content with a homing device stuck on Ruby Ann Stevens's forehead with his name on it.

Her green eyes had filled with tears earlier, tears for her dead husband that had made him just want to scoop her up and protect her forever. Dead husband. You couldn't even say ex-husband. This dying young business wasn't easy to get your head around; that was for sure.

Ruby wanted to read more. What a dark horse that Michael Bell was. Mind you, she hadn't told him she was going to the Bow Wow Club. It was quite a nice quality in a new relationship that you didn't feel you had to share everything in your life straight away. Kept it fresh. Her mum always said to her to keep a bit back at first, to let them wonder.

She made herself a cup of tea, reached for the custard creams, and reread the page again. Bless him, wanting to put a homing device on her. And bless him, wanting to scoop her up and protect her forever. He obviously *did* love her. And as for the wedding ring, she had no idea how much of a barrier that had been. He had been so patient with her, it must have been painful for him too. And there she was, so wrapped up in her own grief and misery she didn't even notice. Why on earth had she not given this kind, lovely man a chance? But no, in true pre-wedding Ruby Matthews style she had cast aside a deep love for a shallow dalliance with someone who took her eye. Granted, he was the spitting image of the love of her life, but it had still been wrong. Why hadn't she taken heed of Tony Choi's so obviously fixed fortune cookie? '*Love looks not with the eyes, but with the mind.*' If she started using her head and not that butterfly heart of hers, she would find true love again. In fact, it had been staring her in the face all along, and because of her bloody-mindedness and her grief, she had mucked up again.

Michael had every right to be angry. Harry could quite easily have passed as George and he *had* kissed her at the door. Now she truly realised how much he loved her, of course he would be upset and jump to conclusions. But even after that he had taken it on himself to go to the Bow Wow Club to try to learn how to make things right. What a man!

A man writing a romance novel as well. She loved that idea. From the little piece she had read, he was good. Rather than being annoyed that he was using their love affair as the main plot, she was rather flattered. Who wouldn't want a book written about them? She just hoped he wasn't too graphic about their sex scenes. Her mother might read it!

She had to give Michael another chance. He gave her 'the love feeling' when they were in bed. He was sexy, good, and kind – and most importantly, he loved her. Yes, that was it. She would finish the wedding dress she had been working on and have a good night's sleep to try and make herself look a little more human. Then, in the morning, she would go to him.

She always harped on about men coming to her. But this was different. She had wronged Michael when all he wanted to do was make her happy. Now, to find his address...

She ran to her messy drawer and began to hunt for the business card he had given her all those months ago on that cold December day.

'Watch out, Mr Strong Hands,' she said aloud. 'Ruby Stevens is coming to get you.'

CHAPTER SIXTY THREE

'You sound weird, Rubes.' Fi always called at inappropriate moments.

'I've just put on a face pack. It's drying and I can't open my mouth properly.'

'I *so* need a bit of pampering. I've got three huge spots on my chin, must be my bloody hormones. The way I feel, they must be having some kind of pregnancy party inside me every night.'

'Still not good then? Poor you.'

'I threw up in the street yesterday; mortified. Luckily I have a slight bump now, so anyone who saw me would hopefully have realised it was because I am with child. Or should I say with elephant. I've been looking on the internet and my bump is far bigger than it should be at this stage.'

'Well, Simon isn't a small fellow so your Great Dane, Irish Setter analogy probably isn't far off the mark.'

'Ha! And James is being so lovely. I feel so guilty.'

'Well, James will never know of your illicit sex session, and you are both getting the child you wanted. I mean, the only difference is that a penis was inserted rather than a turkey baster.'

'Ruby!'

'What? I know it's morally wrong to have an affair but what you did could almost be justified. James pushed you away on purpose and was cruel, so you went elsewhere. Purely physical. It doesn't count.'

'I do love Simon, in a way.'

'I love you in a way, but the thought of getting jiggy with you isn't exactly a turn-on.'

'All this love,' Fi laughed. 'But to make it a hat-trick, as it happens I love you too, Ruby Stevens. Anyway, enough about me – how are you?'

'I'm going to give it a go with Michael.'

'Wow. Where did that come from? I thought you were never going to speak to him again after accusing you of lying about George.'

'I know, but things have moved on. He's writing a novel, Fi, about him and me. I found a page of it and realised how much he loves me. I would be a fool not to at least try again with him.'

'I am so pleased! I like him, Ruby. And you're the one who shagged another man. He hasn't done anything other than love you, has he? And that's hardly a crime.'

'I know. It's funny. I feel like a smoke screen has suddenly cleared. I've said goodbye to George properly and it's time now to start my new life.'

'So what's the plan then? With Michael, I mean.'

'I'm going to pitch up at his place, show him how much he means to me. I always harp on about men not caring enough unless they are knocking my door down. Well, it's time I put my money where my mouth is and showed him just how much I do care.'

'Blimey, Rubes – when is all this happening?'

'Tomorrow morning. I thought I'd go nice and early just in case he's going into the office in town.'

'Ooh yes, catch him all warm and snuggly in bed. You can then get in with him and show him just how much he is forgiven.'

'Fi O'Donahue, you are a slut but I like the way you think.'

'Good luck, mate. To see you smile properly again will mean a lot to me.'

Ruby washed off her facemask and plastered herself in her favourite Clarins moisturiser. She put on her dressing-gown and looked up at Patrick in all his feline stuffedness.

'It's time, old boy, to let somebody in now.'

CHAPTER SIXTY FOUR

Michael hadn't been up at seven a.m. for quite some time. The joys of freelancing meant never having to set an alarm. He stretched and yawned his way to the bathroom in order to shave. It would be painful to see Emily, but he wanted to look his best when he did. Make her realise what a mistake she had made. She had been very cagey when they had spoken – just said that she needed to see him urgently and would really appreciate it if he would agree to meet. After all she had put him through he should have just told her to fuck off, but that wasn't Michael's style.

She had sounded slightly distressed on the phone, and despite what had happened he wished no harm on her. Time had healed his intense anger and, in a way, he was quite intrigued to see her. He couldn't even imagine what she wanted to see him for. If it was money she was after, she could whistle as he barely had enough to keep himself going. He still had a bit of freelance work but the internet had affected journalism greatly. Thankfully, because the magazines he wrote for were quite niche, he would be OK. At least until he could get his novel out there.

She said she would come to him, that it was only fair as it was she who wanted to meet up in the first place. But in true Emily fashion, the timing was on her terms: to meet at seven-thirty as she had to be at work for nine.

They had arranged to meet at a café near Michael's flat in Clapham. He didn't want her to know he was living in a highrise block. No, he wanted her to regret her decision. Get his own back slightly.

Barney almost knocked him over as he turned the corner and saw Emily waiting outside the café for him. Despite their time apart, the loving Labrador hadn't forgotten him and Michael found himself holding back the tears.

'Good dog, Barney boy.' He fussed him as Emily looked on.

'You always did love him more than me,' she eventually managed.

Michael took in her petite frame and pretty face. She'd had her blonde hair cut into a short elfin style and it suited her small features. Her deep sapphire eyes were accentuated by a sparkly blue scarf. She had obviously made a special effort, but there was no way Michael was going to acknowledge it.

'You look great, by the way,' she added. 'You've lost weight – and those are nice jeans. They look expensive.' Michael realised now why he would never take her back. Ruby wouldn't have cared if he wore tracksuit bottoms and a smile all day. She would love him regardless.

The café didn't allow dogs so they grabbed a take-out coffee in silence and started to walk, Barney still overexcited at seeing his master of old.

'What do you want, Emily? There has to be something. I mean, this isn't a social call, is it?'

'I wanted to say sorry. It was inexcusable, what happened.'

Michael said nothing. He was desperate to find out if she was still with his ex-best mate. He didn't have to wait long.

'Justin struggled with it. In the end, it broke down our relationship. He was so guilt-ridden he couldn't stop talking about you. I couldn't stand it any longer.'

'I'd like to say that was a shame, but what goes around comes around, Emily. You didn't have it so bad with me.'

'I realise that now. Time makes you think, doesn't it? The grass isn't always greener.'

'No, it's not. You did me a favour, actually. I've met someone. She's an amazing woman. Accepts my writing. Loves me for who I am. Isn't materialistic.'

'Ooh, twist that knife a bit harder, will you?'

'As if you really care.'

'She's a lucky woman.'

'Why are you really here? I know you too well. You wouldn't go out of your way to come to this side of town, especially at this hour.'

'It's Barney.'

'Oh, no – what's wrong with him?' Michael stopped and stroked him lovingly.

'Nothing at all. I'm moving out of the flat I shared with Justin and my new place doesn't allow pets.'

'So you take on the long-term commitment of a dog and then because it doesn't fit in with your plans, you want to dump him?'

'Not dump him, just give him back to you.'

'Just like that. Hand the lead over. Off I go. Good old Michael, takes the dog back despite his ex shagging his best mate.'

'I thought you'd be delighted. I mean, I guess you're still freelance so you can fit walks and feeds around your work?'

'What about dear Mummy and Daddy – they've surely got room?'

'No, Mummy's getting brand new sofas imported from France, says she can't bear the hair.'

Michael kept playing her. He knew that Barney could go to no one but him, and he was secretly delighted.

'Well, I guess it's Battersea Dog's Home then. I've not got much on today, I can take him up there.'

'You can't do that, Michael.'

'Well, OK then – why don't you find a flat that takes pets?'

'But who would walk him?'

'Who walked him before?'

'Justin did.'

'So it's a recent thing, you splitting up then?'

'Yeah, a few weeks ago. And this flat – you should see it. It's got marble bathrooms and carpets you sink into. I couldn't possibly not have it.'

'Emily.' Michael didn't even raise his voice. Just kept it at his same calm level. 'You are a spoiled bitch. You think of no-one but number one. I am so pleased that you did what you did, because I would have been a poorer man if I had stayed with you.'

'Don't say that, Pooky.'

'I was never your fucking Pooky. Just give me Barney. You know I'll do right by him. I don't suppose you brought his bowls?'

'I couldn't fit them in here.' She pointed to her designer handbag.

'And I guess you wouldn't dare ruin your look with a carrier bag. You'll never bloody change, will you, Emily?'

'Can't we just kiss and say goodbye nicely?' Before he could reply she leaned in to kiss him on the cheek. He turned his head away quickly, so she ended up giving him a full-on smacker on the lips.

She laughed. 'See? That wasn't that bad, was it?'

'Say goodbye to Barney and go, Emily. All I can say is that

before you commit to having kids, think long and hard as it won't be as easy to give *them* back.'

Emily petted Barney, then within minutes waltzed up the road with a spring in her step, shouting, 'Byeee!' as she went.

'Good riddance to bad rubbish,' Michael said under his breath. Then, 'Come on, boy. I can barely swing a cat in my place, let alone fit you in, but we'll manage, won't we?'

Barney barked his approval as they set off for home.

CHAPTER SIXTY FIVE

Ruby got off the bus at Clapham Junction and checked Google Maps. It must be that highrise over there. No wonder he never invited her to his. Bless him. He probably felt a bit embarrassed, as it wasn't in the best area. He obviously didn't know her well enough, as she would not have cared a jot. "The ornaments in a house are the friends that frequent it" was something that dear old Lucas Steadburton had written in a letter to her – and how true that was. You could have a bigger bath, a comfier bed, but at the end of the day, did any of that really matter? Health and happiness were far more important. And of course, love – never forgetting love.

She had wanted to get him a present, but it was too early for any suitable shops to be open. She thought a pen that wrote nicely would be the ideal gift for a novelist. She would say he should save it for his first book signing but there would be plenty of time for presents. That was, if he would take her back. That thought had crossed Ruby's mind. What if he thought he had given her too many chances to redeem herself? She would have to use all of her womanly charms and convince him that this time it would be right and she would not go off the rails. She had even put on the favourite white lacy underwear that he loved and the perfume he always used to comment on. In fact, she couldn't wait to make love to him, tell him just much she really did care.

She rounded the corner and walked towards the base of the flats. It was then, from a distance, she saw him and her and the black Labrador he had made a fuss about missing. It had to be Emily; petite, ten years younger, blonde, and bloody beautiful. Ruby watched in shock as Madame Bitch kissed Michael on the lips and jauntily walked up the road, smiling as she went. Damn, she had missed her chance. He had got back with Emily, within minutes of having a go at her for kissing Harry on her doorstep. Ruby felt sick. She began to run in the opposite direction. In her haste she caught her heel in a loose paving stone and went flying on the pavement. She picked herself up and could see blood through her tights. Last time she had done this, big, reliable Michael had picked her up, dusted her down, and soothed her back to calmness. This time, a homeless chap just laughed at her and shouted 'While you're down there, love…'

She couldn't face the bus – she needed air. It was only three miles to home so she began to walk in a sorry state, the ladder in her tights getting bigger and the blood oozing through with every step. She cried as she stomped. Then, as she got to Putney fire station she heard her name being called. She looked to her left. It was Nick.

'Ruby, what on earth has happened?' He took in her bleeding leg and streaming eyes. 'Here, wait a second. I'm off shift now, let me give you a lift. You're just up West Hill, aren't you?'

'Honestly, it's fine. I don't want to trouble you.'

'It may be fine for you, but I'm not leaving you like this.'

Once back at her flat, Nick insisted she got out of her bloodied tights. She washed her face and reappeared wearing her dressing gown. He had brought a first-aid kit in from his car and gently bathed her sore knee and put a neat dressing on it.

'Look at me, wearing this. What must you think?'

'I'm a fireman, Ruby. The sights I have seen, nothing phases me. Now, does that feel better?'

'So much better. Thanks, Nick. I really appreciate it.'

'Dare I ask what's up? Is it Michael?'

She nodded.

'You didn't sort it out after the row the other night then?'

'No. And, I was so ready to give it a go with him.'

'So what happened today then to put you in this state?'

'I feel such a fool. I thought I'd go to his house – you know, make an effort. Show him I really did care. Anyway, I turn up and there he is, kissing his ex! Playing happy families with the dog. I thought I was going to be sick. I ran away and fell over. I always bloody fall over.'

'Oh.' Nick couldn't think of anything positive to say.

'And the fact it was so early can only mean that she must have stayed at his. She went off to wherever she works, I guess, and kissed him goodbye before leaving *their* precious pooch with him.'

'It might not be the case, Ruby. You don't know the facts.'

'I saw enough. She's younger than me, too. Skinnier, blonder, prettier.'

'That's enough of that, Ruby. Don't you dare put yourself down. You are beautiful. You are far from fat and all I know is that I think you are amazing company.'

She smiled as she remembered back to the incident at his flat. She then took all of her sexy companion in. The fact he was a fireman was a turn-on in itself. His dark hair, good looks, and pecs to die for, just sealed the deal.

There was no going back to Michael on any account, so what

the hell. Fuck him and that blonde slut. He was welcome to her. How dare it take only seconds to get over her?

Dear old Lucas had told her to only regret the things she didn't do, so she got up, walked to the kitchen, and let her dressing gown gape open long enough for Nick to get a glimpse of her sexy white underwear.

He walked up behind her and began kissing her neck. She didn't resist.

'Are you sure?' he asked softly.

She led him to the front room, lay back on the sofa, and placed her hand on her white panties.

'Fireman Redwood, I think there is a fire down here that needs seeing to.'

Nick laughed. 'Oh, really, Mrs Stevens? I best get my hose out ready then.'

He began to kiss her gently, then more hungrily. But on feeling a wetness on his nose, he stopped immediately.

'Oh, Ruby.' He held her tightly as she began to sob. 'It's OK. I did ask if you were sure.'

'I know,' she blubbed. 'I'm just so cross with Michael. How dare he?'

'Maybe it's just the wrong time for you now, that's all. You're doing so well, but emotions are so unpredictable; love is so powerful and grief is so overwhelming.'

'It's got nothing to do with grief.'

'Really?'

'I don't know. It's just so unfair, Nick. If your Milly and my George were here still, we wouldn't have to feel like this.'

'But they're not, are they? So we've got to get on with it as best we can.'

'I'm sorry.' Ruby sniffed.

'For what?'

'Just then.'

'I got to see you in your underwear, so no apology required. And just look at you.' He glanced down at her. 'You're beautiful, Ruby. Inside and out. Don't forget that. Never sell yourself short.'

She snuggled into the crook of his muscly arm.

'You're not so bad yourself, Mr Fireman. Thank you for understanding.'

'I'd be some sort of dick if I didn't, you silly mare.' He kissed her tenderly on the forehead. 'Now, why don't you run yourself a nice hot bath? I'll leave a clean dressing on the side in case that one gets too wet.'

Ruby lay back in a deep bubble bath and sighed. What a good man Nick was. He had lost not only his wife but his baby daughter too. His strength amazed her. She would be strong now too. If Michael wanted a cheating blonde bimbette with no morals, he could have her. No more stress. She would throw her heart into helping others at The Bow Wow Club. Bloody men could wait for now.

CHAPTER SIXTY SIX

'You got nigh on naked with The Fireman? You lucky cow.'

'Shh, we don't want the whole of Piaf's to know.' Daphne blew them a big kiss from behind a plume of steam from the coffee machine. 'What am I like though, Fi? I'm returning to my pre-George serial-shagger status. I've slept with two men and got naked with a third.'

'You're a single girl in her mid-thirties,' Fi said stoutly. 'And Harry doesn't count because he was a bastard.'

Ruby laughed. 'How are you, anyway?'

'So much better. I'm over the three-month mark and the sickness is definitely waning. Look, here's the scan.'

'Aw, bless. I want one!'

'Let's get you in a stable relationship first, shall we? And look, if that's not a boy, then I am Mother Fecking Teresa. That's got to be his willy.' Fi pointed to the grainy scan picture.

Ruby laughed out loud. 'Hilarious, he's Simon's boy for sure. You're not supposed to see it until twenty weeks either, are you?'

'No, and he's three centimetres bigger than the average baby already. He's going to be a monster. It'll be like shitting a football.'

Ruby screwed her face up. 'You are so vile.'

'Any word from Michael?'

'No, why would there be?'

'I still don't think he'd go back to her after what you said.'

'I do. Men are strange. They don't like being on their own and I think some of them compromise because of this fact. There is no doubt she's a very pretty girl and she's got youth on her side.'

'She's not that young and I bet she's shit in bed. Probably doesn't like to mess her hair up or her vajazzle.'

'Vajazzle? What is that?'

'Norbert, you really don't want to know.'

'Girl talk. I see. Would you like some more drinks and cakes on the house from my angel?' Norbert glided back to the counter and Daphne got their order ready.

'I would, you know,' whispered Fi.

'What – Norbert?'

'Yeah, too right.'

'Fi, I think you need to marry James and get this baby out of you before you even have one unchaste thought about another man.'

'Darling Rubes, the day I stop having unchaste thoughts about men is the day I die. Anyway, spill. What about you and Nick? Are you seeing him again?'

'We're just friends.'

'What's his cock like?'

Ruby shook her head in mock disbelief. 'He kept his jeans on.' Then, smugly, 'But I could tell that he's hung like a horse – or should I say fireman's hose.'

CHAPTER SIXTY SEVEN

Rita Stevens whistled as she walked down the churchyard path. She stopped at her husband's grave and tidied the flowers she had arranged in the vase just yesterday. It was her little boy's turn today. As spring had well and truly sprung it was time for one thing – to decorate his grave with the daffodils that she had lovingly grown herself. The idea was to plant them, so there would be an abundance of the bright yellow flowers every year.

Oh, how excited George used to get when he told her about the amazing times he had at Daffodils. His love for Ruby had been so great that when he found out at his own wedding that his wife-to-be, Candice, had been after him for his money, he literally flew up to the Lakes, wedding suit still on, to tell her how he really felt. It had been a real love story that Rita would proudly tell to anyone who would listen.

She got to the grave and screwed up her face. Who had put a bouquet there? She hated when the flowers died and just the old wrapper was left. It looked so forlorn and untidy. She knew it couldn't have been Ruby as the girl hated that too.

Rita shook the water off the plastic and took it with the dead flowers to the rubbish bin to the side of the graves. Filling a watering can, she wandered back to commence the planting.

Just as she was about to start digging a hole, she saw something glint against the sun and leaned forward to get a better look. When she realised what it was, a tear slowly rolled down her cheek. 'Bless her heart.'

She remembered the day George had come running into her kitchen asking her if she knew any good engravers. He wanted to get the job turned around in a day, so that while Ruby was out he could slip the ring back in his box and it would be a surprise for her on their wedding day: to see the engraved words, *Rubes & George forever X.*

She was surprised that Ruby had wanted it away from her, but guessed it brought her closer to her husband if it was on the grave. Rita wondered why on earth she hadn't put it in the actual coffin, but she knew only too well that you didn't think rationally during the first stages of grief.

It was such a private thing that she wouldn't mention it; she would just make sure the ring wouldn't be disturbed again. So when the daffodils were proudly singing their bright song on top of George, the grieving mother carefully placed the ring just under the top layer of earth so it wouldn't be found. The two of them could be together again in their own private Daffodils.

Rita finished up and packed her garden tools back in the carrier bag she had brought them in. Sitting for a quick rest on the bench near to George, she suddenly felt a peace she had not experienced for quite some time.

After wondering and questioning for twenty-nine and a half years, she could finally let it all go. At last she knew that her other son was happy.

A white feather floated down, gently rested on her cheek, and then, with a slight puff of breeze, drifted back up into the sky.

Both her beautiful boys had gone forever, but her memories of them, however fleeting, would never fade.

CHAPTER SIXTY EIGHT

'Rubes, is that you?' Laura called from the kitchen as she heard the front door open.

'Yeah, hi, Mum. How's it going?'

'All the better for seeing my favourite daughter.' The woman wiped her hands on a tea-towel and kissed Ruby on the cheek. 'It's great to see you, darling.'

'Well, the offer of Sunday lunch with you and Sam couldn't be resisted. Where's Graham anyway?'

'He's training today.'

Ruby thought back to all those years ago when Graham had met their mother and fallen in love with her. Sam had, in essence, brought them together. He always knew what was right, that boy.

She heard Ben let off a little bark of approval as he recognised the smell of the Matthews' house – or more likely the scent of roast beef in the air.

Sam appeared in the kitchen and smiled at them both broadly. 'Don't tell me, Rubes, it's that Prada perfume. D'Iris, isn't it?'

'How do you know it's not Mum wearing it?'

'Because I've told you before; all fragrances are distinctively different when they're mixed with a woman's own smell.'

'You're such a show off.' Ruby pushed the back of her hand against his cheek. It had always been the way she greeted him, somehow seeming more meaningful than a kiss on the cheek.

'I hate to admit it, but I've missed you. Ages since I saw you.'

'Gosh, you're both getting all grown up, aren't you?' Laura mocked. 'Being nice to each other and everything.'

They sat down at the familiar dining table and tucked into the scrumptious roast in front of them, Ruby secretly feeding Ben bits of beef under the table and getting scolded by Sam. She sometimes wondered if he really was blind!

'So, did you get it together with Mr Smooth?' Ruby knew it would only be a matter of time before she got a grilling from her sibling.

'Er, no. I don't want to talk about him.'

'What's the matter, Rubes? You can tell us, we're family.'

'There's nothing to tell.' She took a sip of wine and let out a deep breath. She felt like she was going to cry and Sam felt put his hand on hers.

'It's all right.'

'No, it's not really, Sam.'

She burst into tears, and Laura ran around to hug her from behind, saying, 'Oh, darling, don't cry.'

'I promised Rita I wouldn't tell anyone.'

'Ruby, telling this family is like a confession to the Pope, you know that. We stick together. Just these walls, Sam, and Ben will be the only ones to know.'

'Well, and Margaret.'

'But she's in effect family so that's all right. What is it, love?'

Ruby held her mum's hand loosely as she sat back down next to her.

'George had a twin brother.'

'Fucking hell!'

'Language, Sam!' Laura shouted.

'Yes, I know – it's unbelievable. To cut a long story short, Rita and Alfie didn't think they'd cope with twins so had Harry – that's the brother's name – adopted. He tracked me down after George died in the hope he could get some money out of me.'

'Shit, that's terrible.' Laura took a large gulp of water.

'It gets worse,' Ruby carried on. 'I fell for him.'

'Ruby!'

'It's OK, Mum. He's gone forever now. He didn't realise he'd have feelings for me too and he's married. Luckily he's got a job overseas now.'

'And what does poor Rita think about that?' Sam butted in.

'She never met him, said she didn't want to. I told her what a lovely man he was and how successful he was. It seemed to give her a sense of peace, which I'm so pleased about or she wouldn't have forgiven herself otherwise.'

'That poor woman,' Laura had tears in her eyes. 'Losing two of her boys – well, three, with Alfie going too.'

'She's a tough old bird.' Ruby felt better for getting it off her chest. 'So, that's it, really. He looked so like George, it made my heart literally hurt.'

'But he so obviously wasn't George.' Sam squeezed her arm. 'I met him, I knew he wasn't a good person. I'm glad he's gone. I think by the sound of him it's Michael who is so right for you.'

'And here lies another story. I did listen to you, Sam. He treated me so beautifully, understood about my loss. So I went to him, as you said I should. And I saw him with his ex and their dog outside the flat, kissing.'

'Oh no! You have been through it, love.' Laura topped up her daughter's wine glass.

'Maybe you need a bit of time out – can you take some time off work? You haven't been to Daffodils for a while. That might do you good. Clear your head of these awful men.'

Her brother never let up. 'Have you spoken to Michael about what you saw?'

'Of course I haven't. I know what I saw and he accused me of George being alive because he saw me with Harry. I mean, how much of an insult is that?'

'Gosh.' Laura went to the kitchen to check on the dessert. Ruby thought if she was to tell her about Nick, she would be more than 'gosh'-ing.

'I think you should talk to him, tell him how you feel.'

'Sam, shut up now, please. Too much has happened; if we were meant to be together, it would have happened by now. I always think if it feels right with no difficulties then it is right. There have just been too many obstacles.'

'The course of true love never did run smooth, Ruby. Don't tell me to shut up, because you know I'm right and the only obstacle I can see is you!'

'Children, children.' Laura brought in a steaming apple crumble. 'Come on, I don't see you both much. Honestly, think about some time out, Ruby, love. You've been through the mill and back by the sound of it.'

'Yeah, sorry, sis. It's great to see you getting on with it again, whatever the outcome. I only shout because I love you.'

'Me too, you little shit.' She gently pressed the back of her hand onto her brother's cheek and tucked into her pudding.

CHAPTER SIXTY NINE

Barney let out a grunt at the side of the bed, stirring Michael from his restless slumber. A one-bed flat was *not* ideal for a pet, but it was good to have the comforting company of an animal. And the exercise of walking a dog could only be a positive.

Michael rubbed his eyes and yawned. He glanced at his alarm clock: eight a.m.

'All right, old boy. I guess we'd best get you outside.'

He rolled out of bed and pulled on his tracksuit bottoms. He was relieved it was Saturday. He had submitted all his freelance copy to *Rural Writers*', so he could go for a run along the river without worry and then come back to write more of his novel.

He had found it hard to get back into it after his row with Ruby. Seeing Emily had completely thrown him.

Love was such a funny business. You could be so into a person, would know them mind, body, and soul. Then, where and how does it all go wrong? How do the roses and sunbeams turn into dandelions and storms? The quirky little twitch of her nose, once so sweet, becomes an annoying habit; the pet name she calls you becomes repulsive; and sex is a chore rather than a treat.

Barney barked his approval as his new, more attentive owner

grabbed his lead from the kitchen. They took the lift down to the ground floor and Michael was relieved to find a sunny June day in front of him.

He was getting really into his running. It allowed him to think deeply, and without interruption. He had come to some of his best plot ideas this way, plus it completely relaxed him.

In a way, seeing Emily had been a good thing. Yes, she was sexy, there had never been a doubt about that. But although the shell was perfect, inside she was a bad egg. It had taken him to his thirties to realise that kindness counted for so much in a relationship. The little things mattered. The odd cup of tea in bed, finding your socks on the radiator on a cold morning. Opening the fridge to your favourite tipple after a hard week at work. Emily would never have thought of any of those.

He reached Putney and started to follow the river. Every time he got here he hoped that he might find Ruby power-walking around her favourite park, but to date he had never seen her. It was eight-thirty now. Would she be up, he wondered. Should he just go and knock on her door and put things right over a cup of tea? No, it would take more than that. He had lost her for sure. She had been so angry when he had accused whoever that man was of being George. And she had every right to be angry. But, then again he had seen her kissing him. And, if she had really wanted him, then she surely wouldn't have seen anyone else…

Just then, a pretty red-head jogged past him and smiled.

He missed Ruby. Her quirkiness, her sense of fun. The way she could talk with those bright green eyes of hers. He had seen love in those eyes, he was sure. He had also seen incredible sadness. Yes, she was independent, but also vulnerable. Like everyone was, in a way.

He stopped as Barney decided to do a poo in the most open part of the path and then cursed himself that he had forgotten his bags. He couldn't leave it. He saw a woman walking towards him with a black dog.

'This is very embarrassing, but could I trouble you for a poo bag?'

'I've been asked for a few things in my time.' She laughed, then stared at Michael's face. 'Don't I know you from somewhere?'

'Um, I don't think so.' Michael clocked her voluptuous chest and smiley eyes and then cringed as he recalled that she had been at The Bow Wow Club on that awful day when he had rowed openly with Ruby.

'I remember! You're Michael – Ruby's Michael.'

He reddened.

'I miss young Ruby. I must look her up soon. Have you made up with her yet?'

'Um. I…er…'

'She used to talk so highly of you. We all make mistakes, you know.' She put her hand on his arm. 'It's hard to date someone who's been through a bereavement. But me and Jimmy? Well, all I can say is, he was just waiting for the love of a good woman.' She laughed. 'You have to try and gently fill the holes in their hearts that were blown open by grief.'

Cali handed Michael a green plastic bag. 'Shit happens. Clean things up with her if you haven't already. I truly believe you have something there.' Fanny the wonder dog barked loudly. 'Right, I'd better get her ladyship home.'

'Thanks,' Michael said warmly. 'For everything.'

Once he had dealt with Barney's offering he started to run, the dog beside him with his tail wagging madly. Maybe there *was* a chance. He thought back to his novel. How should he finish it? He knew what the perfect happy ending should be – it was just a case of getting there.

CHAPTER SEVENTY

'Ruby!' Simon opened his long arms and embraced her warmly. 'I've missed you. *We've* missed you.'

'It's only been two bloody weeks. I know it's not very charitable, but I just couldn't face it.'

'Wanna talk about it?' Simon asked casually.

'Michael again.'

'Oh.'

'Yes, oh. And, no, I don't really want to talk about it. It's not meant to be and that's it. He's obviously jumped back into bed with the ex. Saw them together.'

'Dear, dear. That's not good. Have you spoken to him since?'

'God, no. Oops, sorry. Gosh, no.' Simon laughed. 'It's fine honestly, Simon. I'm going to help out here, concentrate on my work and just have a bit of fun for now. Maybe it's too soon still after George. He's a hard act to follow.'

'Follow your heart Rubes.'

'You're a fine one to say that.'

'Hmm, I know. However, between you, me, and Him upstairs, I've met someone.'

'That's brilliant, Si, what's his name?'

'Derek – he's a carpenter.'

'Good with his hands then?' Ruby smirked.

'Darling, he's good with everything.'

'I'm really pleased for you. You deserve happiness, you're a good man.'

'Really? Saying that, how's Fi getting on?'

'She's good actually. You've made a big baby. You can imagine already what she's saying about the birth.'

'Ha, yeah. The poor midwives should be warned. The delivery room air will be blue, that's for sure. But honestly, is she OK with everything?'

'Please don't worry. James is oblivious, just completely excited about the whole thing. Their decision was the right one. They do love each other. You have done a wonderful thing for both of them.'

'I do hope so. I will always be here for her, make sure she knows that.'

'She knows. She loves you.'

'Do you think they will get married?'

'I think so, but Fi will want to wait until after the baby comes, of course. It'll be a massive Irish knees-up, I expect.'

'I can't tell you what a relief that is, Rubes. I don't think I could have stood up and married them. Imagine it – I would be struck down there and then.' And as the church hall door was pushed open, he went on, 'Here comes the happy crew.'

'Jimmy, what are you doing here?' Ruby questioned. 'I thought it was your last session the other day?'

'I've come to say goodbye properly. It was all a bit chaotic last time.'

'Yes, it was indeed. You look great, by the way.'

Jimmy's hair had been cut shorter and he had lost more weight. He was wearing trendy jeans and a polo shirt. Contact lenses enhanced his brown eyes and he was clean-shaven. He looked years younger.

'It's all that bloody sex. Cali the insatiable, I call her. She's not coming today; she sends her love though.'

'Lucky you,' Simon chipped in. 'Ruby's right, you look great, pal. And do you know what the best thing is?'

'No more fuck, shit, bollocks? I know. I still do it when stressed. But Cali must have shagged it out of me. I'm so happy.'

'Well good to hear. You are indeed a case study we can use for future Bow Wowers.'

'Anyway, here, before the others arrive and get jealous.' Jimmy handed Ruby a large Clarins bag.

'Jimmy! You shouldn't have.'

'I should. It's from both of us. You're an angel in disguise, Ruby Stevens. What you did for me…it's changed my life.'

'Anyone could have done it.'

'But they didn't – you did.'

Ruby felt tears pricking her eyes. It felt good to have helped somebody.

'And for you, Reverend.' Jimmy handed Simon a carrier bag. The tall vicar pulled out a bottle of vodka, a pot of Vaseline and a framed photo of Fanny the wonder dog.

Jimmy winked at him. 'We weren't sure what to get you, but thought you'd appreciate at least one of these.'

Simon hurriedly put it all back in the bag and smirked. 'Wanker.'

'From a man of the cloth too,' Jimmy laughed.

Ruby went to the back kitchen and filled Simon's vodka mug. She helped herself to one too. She flicked the kettle on, and as she bent down to open the biscuit cupboard, she felt a hand gently cup her bum cheek.

'How you doing, sexy lady?'

She turned around. 'I'm good, thanks.' The Fireman had

replaced his usual T-shirt with a smart, blue shirt. He looked extra hot and she felt a tingle in her nethers.

'How are your knees?' he asked her.

'I look like I've fallen over in the playground.'

'I can just imagine you in a gym skirt and bunches.'

'Nick Redwood!'

'Come on, you lovely lot – let's sit down, shall we?' Simon summoned his disciples. 'Right, firstly, for those of you who don't know Jimmy, stand up please, Jim.' Jimmy stood up and did a little bow. 'This young man here is a volunteer who will be able to answer any of your questions, and run some of the sessions when I can't make them.'

Ruby thought it felt weird with Cali and Ellie not there any more, but it was great they had moved on.

Simon was on a roll. 'Jim is one of our positive stories. He came in here very disturbed due to the loss of his wife. He was a shadow of the man he is today.'

Jimmy remained standing. 'Yes, I was a bloody mess. I suffer from Tourettes, I didn't care about my appearance. I smelled. But a lot of you may relate to that. You lose the will sometimes. It's hard. You think you'll never be able to carry on a normal life without that person. The whole "time is a healer" analogy is so well used, but that's because it's true.'

He coughed and carried on. 'And for those of you here who are dating widows and widowers, we need you. You don't think we do, probably, half the time. But bear with the person you are with. I'm proof that there is light at the end of those long, dark tunnels.

'While I'm standing up, I want everyone to give Ruby, at the back of the room there, a big round of applause. She turned me from a tramp-like useless piece of shit to the man in front of you today.'

Everybody clapped. Ruby reddened. The applause subsided, but Jimmy didn't.

'I feel great, I've got a job I enjoy – and not only that, I met somebody here, and I love her very much. Maybe Simon you should set up a Bow Wow Dating Club?'

'Maybe later,' Simon responded, secretly thinking he couldn't imagine anything more horrendous. 'And thanks, Jimmy, for sharing.'

'While we're being so caring and sharing, can I say something too?' Nick was usually so shy in a group.

'Fire away! Hah! Get it? Fire away.' Nobody laughed at Simon's weak joke attempt.

'I just want to say that Ruby deserves more than a round of applause.'

'Oo-er missus.' Jimmy put his hand to his crotch.

'Jimmy, please don't lower the tone.' Simon shook his head while shielding a smile.

Ruby raised her eyes to the ceiling. It was very flattering but also very embarrassing to have such a fan club.

'She's been here for all of us. I can't tell you how she first helped me, but what she said just did it for me. I'm moving forward with my life now.'

Ruby felt she might cry. Behind his bravado, Nick was such a soft, caring man. She took in how smart he looked.

The Fireman carried on, 'I've decided today is my last Bow Wow too. You are all great and Simon, man, you are an inspiration. I will miss you all, but it's another step forward to feeling better.'

'This door is always open, Nick. Even if you just want to pop in for a chat.' Simon was sincere. 'I'm really chuffed for you, mate. Well done.'

Ruby called after Nick as he headed down the church path. They had been the last to say their goodbyes to Simon. She always carried a torch as it was so dark around the churchyard. Now, when Nick turned round, she held her torch under her chin to make her look zombie-like. He put on a fake terrified face.

'What's up, Rubes?' he asked. 'I thought we'd just said goodbye.'

'You know you said you would miss us all?'

'Yep.'

'I just wanted to say, I really will miss you too.'

'Ruby, I work down the road from your house. I live less than a mile from you. We are going to stay mates. Aren't we?'

'I…er…'

'Let me capture this moment on film,' Nick laughed. 'A tongue-tied Ruby Stevens. How very rare.'

She pushed him with affection in the ribs. 'Look, I'm going to my holiday home in the Lake District tomorrow morning. Just need a bit of time out from the real world. I know you mentioned you've got a week off and I just wondered if you wanted to, maybe, come up?' She paused. 'As friends, of course.'

'Of course.' Nick pushed his tongue into the side of his cheek.

'Nick! You don't have to, it's fine. My mate Fi, who you met at the pub a while back, and her boyfriend James are already there, so I would understand if you didn't want to come.'

He took her hand, lifted it to his face, and kissed it. 'Sorry, Ruby, I'm just joking with you. I'd bloody love to come. I could do with a change of scenery too, so it's perfect timing.'

'Really?'

'Really. I was just going to do some DIY in the flat, but that can wait. So what's the plan?'

'I was going to get the train up tomorrow morning.'

'Sod the train, Rubes, I'll drive. I've got an old camper van, another hobby in itself. It'll be fun.'

'If you're sure, that would be amazing. It's so just so beautiful up there. We can be proper tourists. I'll show you all the good bits.'

'Well, then it's a date. I'll pick you up at midday from yours.'

Ruby kissed him on the cheek. 'Perfect. How exciting. I do love an adventure and you will just adore Daffodils, I know it.'

Nick walked back to his flat with a big smile on his face. He looked to the sky and spoke under his breath. 'Milly. My darling Milly. I hope you're not cross, but she has got such a good heart, I know it will help heal mine.'

Ruby awoke with a feeling she hadn't had for a while – excitement.

She was up to date with her dressmaking and could spend a few guilt-free days with the lovely Nick at Daffodils; one of her very favourite places. The garden needed a good sort-out and a burly fireman would be able to help her.

At noon on the dot, Nick drew up outside the flat, smiling and waving as he got out of his old, beige camper van and slid open the side door quickly to avoid the heavy rain that had just started falling.

Ruby laughed to herself. She loved camper vans and knew it would be great fun. She also noted how handsome her travelling companion was. She took a deep breath as she thought of the last time she had packed for a trip.

Dittisham had been so special and Michael had made such an effort. The Devonshire village had become a close second-favourite place to her beloved Lakes, and she suddenly felt sad that she hadn't been able to work it out with the lovely author. But he obviously had made his choice with Emily or he would have come back to her by now. She must have been right that he didn't love her, that it had all been too soon for him, and he hadn't got over his ex like he thought he had.

Maybe she was being rash inviting Nick to Daffodils, but there was no need to rush things. The Fireman was a very good friend, and if things developed, so be it. She would just keep a clear head and see what happened. It would be nice to have him around, especially as Fi and James had rekindled their love and were currently constantly fawning over each other.

'Ready, girl?' Nick looked over to Ruby in the passenger seat and grinned.

'Ah, I need to do one thing first.' She reached into her handbag for her phone. 'Turn this bloody thing off. I've changed the answerphone, so clients know when I'm back. Mum and Sam know where I am, and Fi and James are expecting us early evening, so all is good. Peace at last.'

'What a fantastic plan. I will do the same. And Ruby?'

'Aha?' Ruby had half an eye on her phone.

'Thanks for inviting me. I know Daffodils is a special place for you…and was for George.'

'Well, it's good that it's being filled with special people again then, isn't it?'

Nick stuck his bottom lip out and felt warm inside. They pulled away and Ruby caught sight of Margaret waving wildly under a torn red umbrella.

'Pull over a sec, Nick.' Ruby wound down her window.

'I didn't know you had a handsome chauffeur to take you up there, duck,' cackled her neighbour.

'You know me, Margaret, a toy boy in every port.'

'Well, have a good time anyway, love. You…and the chauffeur.' The old girl winked discreetly at her young neighbour.

Ruby shook her head. 'Gotta love her.'

'She seems like a wise old bird.'

'Wise all right. She's taught me a lot, I can tell you.'

Nick tooted, turned up the radio, and sped off. Intent on their chatter, neither of them noticed his beloved camper van splashing a tall, bespectacled man walking up the road with his black Labrador.

CHAPTER SEVENTY ONE

Michael had got in from his run, sweaty, tired but hopeful. He thought back to what Cali had said. 'You have to try and gently fill the holes in their hearts that were blown open by grief.'

He had tried but clearly not hard enough. His last text from Ruby had been that she missed him and wanted to meet, but then she had disappeared off the face of the earth. Maybe her phone was broken? Each time he had tried to call her, it was as if she was cutting him off. He didn't text her as he couldn't bear the thought of her not replying. He would just have to try and catch her at her house again.

However, he was hesitant because of what happened last time. Women! If only he could work them out. Maybe she had been drunk when she had said she missed him. Was she still with the husband lookalike? The whole business was driving him mad. But something was stopping him from giving up, and that something was so obviously love.

Barney barked. 'I know, boy, you're hungry. Let me sort you out.'

Michael lit a cigarette as he reached for a tin of dog food, and then stubbed it out immediately. What was he thinking? He didn't need to smoke. He'd just been for a run, for goodness sake. Screwing up the packet, he put his foot on the bin pedal. Then he got the packet back out of the bin and poured water over it. There was no way he could retrieve them now. As he grabbed a fork from the drawer, he suddenly thought of Ruby and the amazing sex they'd had in the Dittisham cottage. She loved it when he was sweaty. Oh, how he fancied the arse off that girl. He started to feel the usual heat in his groin – not a good look in running shorts. Good job he was in the privacy of his own home. As soon as the bowl was on the floor, Barney began to wolf it down noisily.

Michael clicked open his laptop. Emily, the bitch, was going to get it in more ways than one. It had really thrown him seeing her. He couldn't deny she looked great, but beauty with her was definitely skin-deep. She was an ugly person and he was quite glad that his mate had instigated his getting away from her. He wasn't sure if he could even write about having sex with her any more, but he would try.

***Let Love Win* by Michael Bell**
Chapter 27: *Emily sauntered into the bedroom in just a sexy pink underwear set and a pair of black four-inch stilettos. Michael didn't even look up, he was so intent on finishing the chapter he was writing.*

She bent over the bed and pulled her panties to the side with her fingers. 'Fuck me from behind – and now.'

'But your tummy – it might hurt you or the baby.'

'Oh, Michael, just do it, will you. I want your cock in me good and hard.'

Despite the raunchiness of it all, Michael still had to think of Ruby to get an erection. Emily had turned into some sort of sexual deviant since being pregnant, and although he couldn't complain, it just made him want Ruby all the more. He had a connection with the fun red-head. The only connection he had with Emily was the baby growing within her.

Fantasising about Ruby coming into the room, pulling him off Emily, then sitting astride him as Emily masturbated on the bed next to them made him come really quickly.

'Oh, darling was that it?'

'Emily, I'm writing.'

'This bloody book better be a bestseller, is all I can say.' She harrumphed and stormed to the bathroom to shower.

'Bloody hell, every time,' Michael said aloud as his hard-on throbbed through his running shorts. He vowed he would write a thriller next time. It would save him wasting so much writing time!

Once he'd cleaned himself up, he sat back at his writing desk. What should he do with Emily? Should they go through with having the baby? It was too late for her to lose it. Maybe it could turn out it wasn't his. Brilliant! She could have been seeing someone else all along too… Hmm. It was too early in the book though, he was only on chapter twenty-seven. No, he would keep on having inane sex with her and carry on seeing Ruby – that would be more exciting for the reader. But then again, what about poor Ruby? It wasn't fair on her that he was with another woman. He would never do that to her in real life. He cared for her way too much. And the readers might begin to hate his character.

He groaned and pushed his glasses up onto his head. What was he going to do with the real Ruby? It was so difficult. She obviously wasn't interested any more as she would have followed up on that text and not completely bloody ignored it. Sod it, he would call her. Damn – her phone was off! He hoped that she was all right. He showered quickly and grabbed Barney's lead.

'Come on, boy, we're off out for walkies again. I need to know what the hell is going on.'

'You twat!' Michael cursed as a camper van sped past him as he was rounding the corner to Amerland Road, soaking both him and Barney.

He took a deep breath as he knocked on Ruby's door. He felt excited and scared at the same time. Margaret appeared out of nowhere, sporting a red umbrella.

'Oh, hello. Michael, isn't it?'

Michael smiled. You couldn't beat a nosy neighbour; thanks to them, at least you always knew what was going on.

'Yes, hello, Margaret. How are you today?'

'Bloody sick of this rain, I know that.'

'In June too, you'd think it would be sunny.' Why did old people always talk about the weather? Michael thought back to his May deadline. That was how long he had been going to wait for Ruby. Well, the deadline was way past and he was still hanging in there. The time had just flown!

'She's not here, duck. Look at you, you're soaked through. Why don't you come in and get yourself warm and dry?'

Barney shook himself, making Michael even wetter.

'If it's not too much trouble.'

'Of course not. Bert is snoring as usual. I'll be glad of the company.'

Margaret lit her old gas fire and gave Michael a towel to get the worst of the water off of him. She went to the kitchen and returned with a tray laden with a metal tea pot, three china cups and saucers, a plate of custard creams, and two schooners of sherry.

'Ruby's favourites.'

'What, the sherry?' Michael laughed.

'She'd kill me telling you, but she does love a sherry, actually. You don't have to have one if you don't want to, but I thought it would warm you through.'

Michael drained his glass in one go and screwed up his face. 'Blimey, that's sweet.'

He took off his glasses and rubbed his eyes. They felt sore from too much writing. He put them into their case and placed it on the tray.

'I thought you might be partial to sweet things, what with courting our Ruby.' Margaret also downed her sherry, then poured herself another. 'Well, it is Saturday.' She bent over to put the bottle on the floor and farted without even noticing. Michael decided to ignore it, despite even Barney wincing at the smell. The black Labrador let out a little whimper then flopped in front of the fire.

'Courting is not quite the word.'

'Oh, well, she speaks highly of you, young Michael.'

'Does she? Really?'

'Yes. She was shaken to the core when George was taken, but you put a smile back on that pretty face of hers.'

'Not a big enough one, obviously.'

Margaret, ever the matchmaker when she knew it was right, was aware that she couldn't divulge too much information.

'You just need to talk to her.'

'I've been trying. But her phone is either off or it cuts off.'

Margaret didn't dare say that she knew she had been hanging up on him since she had caught him with Emily. But, as he had the dog with him, she guessed that Ruby might be right.

'So...single at the moment are you, Michael?'

'Yes, yes, I am.'

'I didn't know you had a dog? Ruby never said.'

'She wouldn't have. I only just got him. Ooh, listen to that rain.' Michael didn't want to get into an Emily conversation with someone like Margaret, as he was sure, especially now she was on the sherry, she would get the wrong end of the stick and not relay it properly to Ruby.

However, he had to ask the question that had been on the tip of his tongue since he had arrived.

'So…um…do you know where she is? Ruby, I mean.'

'Gone to her place in the Lakes. The poor girl has been working so hard, and with her volunteering too, needed a break. She hasn't had a holiday all year. Well, apart from a couple of days in Devon with you, that is.' Michael was quite taken aback at how much Ruby did tell Margaret.

'That's great. She loves it up there. You're right – some time away will do her good.'

Margaret didn't think he'd be saying that if he knew she'd gone with The Fireman.

'So…er…do you know who she's gone with?'

'Oh, some old friends of hers, that's all,' Margaret blustered. 'Another sherry, duck?'

'No thanks, the tea's just fine.' Michael reached for a biscuit. He didn't dare ask what friends, it made him sound like a stalker. He was annoyed that she hadn't spilled names, but Ruby was right, she was a wise old bird.

Michael finished his tea as Margaret poured yet another sherry. Bert and Barney snored in unison. The old girl then dropped off too, but shook herself awake after a few minutes.

'Sometimes,' she said drowsily, 'a letter works the best out of anything. There's some paper and a pen in the bureau.' She pointed to the antique in the corner. 'Now, there's no time like the present. If you write to her, I will make sure she gets it, I promise. She's turned her phone off, you see. I know that much.

Said she wanted some peace.'

With that, the old girl promptly fell back to sleep. Michael had to laugh. Here he was in a nigh-on stranger's house, surrounded by three snorers, while the woman he loved was away with goodness knows who. At least he had an explanation concerning her phone this time.

A resounding clap of thunder caused Barney to stir slightly. Michael stroked his ears gently. 'It's all right, Barn.'

Well, sod it. There was no point trekking home in this foul weather and he didn't have spare cash for a cab. He looked at the blank page. For a second, he had a vision of Emily on his shoulder sneering, 'Hah, call yourself a writer.' But he *was* a writer and write he would.

He scribbled the black biro on the inside of his hand to get it to work and then lifted his head to the ceiling in thought.

Dear Ruby…

CHAPTER SEVENTY TWO

'You took your time,' Fi shouted from the chaise longue in Daffodils' luxurious sitting room.

'Have you seen the weather?' Ruby replied. 'And Nick's van only goes sixty miles an hour at downhill.'

'A van, you say?'

'It's a camper van, you snobby cow,' Ruby shouted from the kitchen.

'Here.' James handed Ruby a glass of wine and kissed her on the cheek. 'Have this and stop abusing my lover.' He shook Nick's hand. 'Nice to meet you, mate. Beer?'

'Great, thanks.'

Ruby went to see Fi.

'Can't believe it's bloody June,' she grumbled. 'This weather is awful.' Then she looked at Fi's stomach. 'Blimey! You're huge.'

'Tell me about it.' She went to a whisper. 'Not even four months and I'm already like a baby elephant. Mind you, I am eating my way through a tub of pecan ice cream a day. I quite like the fact I can eat what I want when I want.'

'Well, don't go too mad. You know how much you hate exercise and it will all have to come off.'

'Oh, Rubes, don't go all sensible on me now. James and I are having sex again, at it like rabbits, thank goodness. So I will burn it off later.'

'I'll make sure I take the twin bedroom the other end of the landing then?'

Fi kept to a whisper. 'Twin, yeah, right!' She smirked. 'Don't tell me there's no hose action on the cards then?'

'There's not.'

'Why not? He's well cute.'

'I just want to do something properly for once – you know, get to know him.' Ruby also couldn't bear to sleep in the double bed where she had made passionate love with George on countless occasions either.

'You wait, another couple of wines and you'll be rubbing The Fireman's shiny helmet.'

'You're so wrong and so coarse.'

'No, I'm oh so right, my little ginger minger.' Fi stretched out on the chaise. 'I bloody love it here.'

'So do I. It's just so calming, isn't it? I can feel Lucas around us as well. Camping it up, wafting house spray around, and pouring the largest brandies you've ever seen. I wish I'd known him for longer.' Ruby suddenly went quiet. 'Why do people have to die too soon, Fi?'

'My mam says it's because they are too good for this world, and I believe that. George didn't have a bad bone in his body. How you feeling now, anyway?'

'I'm so much better, actually. I was thinking the other day that without fail, every single day, I would wake up and the first thing I would think of was him not being here any more. But now I don't. I think about my day ahead. And it's just certain things that trigger my memories of him.'

'I guess that will happen forever.' Fi started munching gherkins from the bowl on the side table.

At that moment, James appeared and stoked up the fire. Nick plonked himself down on the sofa next to Ruby.

'You should be doing this, mate,' James laughed.

'Ha ha. No, thanks. Can't believe you had to light it. On the upside, it's supposed to cheer up tomorrow, so maybe we could go to Derwentwater like you suggested, Rubes? I quite fancy a walk.'

'Yeah, sounds good. You up for it, you two?' Ruby looked to Fi.

'I'll see how I feel,' she said. 'Just walking around the village may be enough for me, to be honest. Millbeck is so pretty and I'm not up for a big hike with bump on board.'

James walked over to her, knelt down, and rubbed her tummy. 'It's so exciting. I can't wait for us to be parents.'

'I just can't imagine Fi changing nappies and doing night feeds. You wait, she'll have two bottles made up, one full of red wine for her and the other with milk for the baby.'

'Not funny, Rubes. I will be the perfect earth mother, you wait and see.'

'I'm sending her back to work and being a house husband.'

'Hmm. I hadn't thought of that. Nah. I need a break.'

Nick piped up. 'A break? That's the funniest thing I've ever heard. Coping with a baby will be the hardest thing you've ever done in your life.'

'Look at the guru over there.' Ruby grimaced at her friend's words. She hadn't told Fi Nick's tragic story. She jumped up quickly, put her hand out to him, and directed him back to the kitchen.

'Come on, Fireman Redwood, let's unpack.'

When they were out of earshot, she squeezed his arm. 'Sorry about that – they don't know what happened.'

'Rubes, it's fine. You are so sweet. But seeing Fi pregnant does bring back memories.'

'I bet it does. Just being here holds a lot for me too.'

'Maybe I shouldn't have come.'

'Don't be silly. I really wanted you to.' Ruby went to him, put her hands on his cheeks, and brushed his lips with hers. 'It will be good to get to know each other outside of the bloody Bow Wow.'

'That place is such a laugh, in a way. I mean, Simon, love him to death, but what is he all about?'

Ruby chuckled. 'Oh, he's just one of life's eccentrics. And the world would be a worse place without them. A bit like Lucas, who left me this house.'

'Indeed, but let's look forward now, eh? Onwards and upwards for us both, Miss Designer Pants.'

'Miss Designer Pants?'

'No worse than you calling me The Fireman!'

'Oops.'

'Yes, oops,' Nick teased her. 'Right – come on, now it's stopped raining. Let's get those bags in.'

CHAPTER SEVENTY THREE

Dear Ruby

I am bizarrely sitting in Margaret's front room writing this. She is snoring, Bert is snoring and my reacquired dog Barney is snoring too.

I, however, am thinking. Thinking about you. I don't want to make this a massive essay, because in short my feelings haven't changed from the day I met you.

You were so sad and distraught at losing your precious wedding ring, but I knew from that moment, looking at your beautiful pale face and into your moist green eyes that I wanted to sweep you off of your feet and protect you forever.

I love you, Ruby Stevens. I cannot get you out of my head. I've tried. I think sometimes I wish I had never met you, as never before has someone affected me like you have. Every waking moment it is you on my mind. Silly things I think about daily. Like the way you bite your thumbnails when you're anxious or throw your head back and laugh in that infectious way. The little squeaking noise you make as you are about to come. There is nothing about you that I don't like. Well, apart from the stupid piece of you that doesn't realise how much I do care about you.

And that guy, the one I saw you kissing at your door. Of course I know now it wasn't your precious George. How could I have thought that of you? I was just hurt and angry and lashed out. How dare I? And for that I will be forever sorry.

I don't blame you for seeing other people. After all, it was me who told you to go away and think about what you wanted, and now I regret that. We met too soon, perhaps. But then again, maybe if I had kept on your case, then I would have smothered you with enough love to win you over. I don't know.

I felt sick for days after we rowed at The Bow Wow Club. Another thing that I am immensely proud of you for doing. I could see how much respect everyone has for you there. But again, it was such a bloody shock seeing you, when you hadn't told me you were volunteering.

It had taken a lot for me to go along and say my piece and I was just so embarrassed to see you. I didn't want you to see me as a weak man, Ruby. I am strong and will always be strong for you.

The day I saw you at the door I came to apologise for the row at the Bow Wow, got you flowers and everything: I would have said all these things then.

I am even writing a novel and you are the heroine. It's good too – well, it could be nothing less with you as the star, now, could it?

I've thankfully got rid of my demons about Emily jilting me too, by writing about it. Weirdly, she rang me. Not to apologise or anything civilised like that. No, she was moving into a flat that didn't take pets so poor old Barney didn't fit with her life any more and had to go. I have to say I was delighted to get my boy back. It had crippled me to lose him more than my fiancée and best mate, to be honest. He has also kept me sane in my loneliness without you.

I know you are away, I'm guessing with Fi. She will make you laugh and help you to enjoy the precious time off that you so need and deserve. Hopefully a change of scene will help you to think about us too.

I know that you care about me, Ruby, even if you never said it. You don't make love to someone like we did without feelings being involved. I could sense the love between us. Felt like I was drawing it from your pores. It was immense, in fact.

Oh, I'm harping on now, sorry. It would be so much easier for me to be saying all these things to you face-to-face, but your phone has been off and is still off. That's why I'm here actually. Was coming to see you again, with more roses (I think I should buy shares in that flower stall at East Putney tube!). I got your text saying that you missed me and wanted to see me, then you disappeared off the face of the earth.

And the main reason I was coming to see you was to tell you again that I purely and simply love you.

I hope when you get this you have had the best time away and have a big smile on that beautiful face of yours.

Call me a romantic old fool but if it's meant to be between us then love will win, I just know it.

In fact, Ruby, just bloody call me, will you!

Michael X

CHAPTER SEVENTY FOUR

'Ruby? Ruby? Are you awake?' Nick whispered as he pushed open the door to the twin room she was sleeping in.

'I am now.' She turned on her bedside light and sat up in the single bed, pulling the duvet up to cover her modesty. She put her hand to her head. 'Shit, I feel groggy. Must have got a premature hangover.'

'Well, we did put some back, didn't we? But it was our last night in this beautiful place, so we were allowed. Anyway, budge up, you.'

'Nick! It's three o'clock in the morning and there's barely room for me in here, let alone a muscly fireman.'

'I heard a noise.'

Ruby giggled. 'Don't be such a wuss. This old place creaks and groans all the time. It's not haunted, if that's what you think. I've stayed here on my own countless times and have never felt anything spooky.'

Ruby shuffled over and tapped the mattress next to her. 'I can't promise I'll keep my hands to myself.'

'What's a broken promise between friends, eh?' Nick took off his T-shirt, revealing a tight pair of Calvin Kleins, and slipped in beside her.

Ruby suddenly became conscious of her sleep breath and sticky-up hair. 'Erm, quite a lot actually.'

'Yeah, that was a silly thing to say. Look, let's snuggle up. I can always get in the other bed when you've warmed me up.'

Compared to Michael, it felt funny being in the crook of Nick's arm as he didn't have an ounce of fat on his honed physique. She put her hand under the covers to straighten down her T-shirt and swept his pants by mistake. The Fireman was rock hard.

'Ooh sorry, a firm hose, how mouthwateringly delicious.'

'Ruby.' Nick propped himself up on one elbow. 'Stop joking.'

'What do you mean?' He pulled her towards him and kissed her really gently.

'Nick, I...' She pushed her warm mouth onto his and felt her way around his toned back. As much as it felt gorgeous and safe being here right now with him, she was still not sure.

'I want you to be the first,' Nick whispered in her ear.

She looked straight into his tearful eyes and nodded, completely getting it.

She thought back to how tender Michael was with her when they had first slept together. How important he knew it was for her to feel safe and loved.

Nick had pre-empted this moment so much he had even brought condoms with him.

So – The Fireman and Miss Designer Pants made pure, simple love in a single bed in a beautiful cottage in the magical Lake District. No fireworks, no fuss. Just a mutual respect and understanding.

CHAPTER SEVENTY FIVE

Bert woke himself up with a snore and half-opened one eye. He reached for his glasses and looked at his watch. 'Good. I haven't missed it.' He spoke aloud and turned to the racing page of the paper that was still folded neatly on his lap. He smiled at the sleeping Margaret and the nearly empty bottle of sherry beside her. Two glasses on the tray? He'd completely slept through a guest. Wouldn't be the first time he'd done that, that was for sure. It couldn't have been our Ruby, he thought. Because whoever it was had left some sort of designer spectacle case behind.

He shuffled to the kitchen, burping as he went in search of a piece of paper. Still half-asleep, and noticing one of Margaret's familiar Basildon Bond blue envelopes propped up against the metal tea pot, he began to write down his runners for the evening meeting at Windsor on the back of it.

CHAPTER SEVENTY SIX

James appeared in the beautiful front room of Daffodils rubbing his eyes. He spotted Fi in her dressing gown lying on the velvet chaise. The French doors were open on to the magnificent garden that Nick and Ruby had worked so hard at tidying up the day before. The soothing noise of the stream nearby and the birds singing made for a perfect morning greeting. The pregnant Fi already had her hand in a bowl of gherkins.

'You're up early, darling.'

'I know. Sorry if I woke you. The sun came streaming through the curtains at six a.m. and I couldn't get back to sleep. Then I heard the door slam at eight. The two of them must have gone walking like they said they were going to. Bloody early though.'

'I went out like a light after all that wine, but I'm sure I stirred around three and heard them shagging.'

'Nah, I don't think Ruby feels that way about him or she'd have done it on the first night. You know what she's like with the younger ones.'

'Look at you, Miss Prissy Pants. You had me for the first time right on that chaise longue, to be exact, in broad bloody daylight. Anyone could have walked in.'

'I fancied the arse off ya, that's why.'

'And do you still?' James said matter-of-factly.

'Don't be an eejit, of course I do. Now go and get me a cup of that Bovril.'

'Yuk.'

'I know. Why can't I crave something decent? The ice-cream's all right but bloody gherkins and a beef drink!'

Fi lay her head back and rubbed her tummy. James was back quickly with a steaming mug of Bovril which he placed on a side table next to her. He kissed her on the forehead.

'You look even more beautiful now you're pregnant, you know.'

'Blimey, it's me who kissed the Blarney Stone, not you.'

'I mean it, you silly mare. I love you, Fiona O'Donahue.'

'Well, I guess that's a good bloody job as you're going to be hopefully spending the rest of your life with me and baby Kane here.'

'We could have another. Why stop at one? Now that we know we can do it so easily. Maybe even pick sperm from the same father so they are blood siblings.'

Fi felt slightly sick and knew it was nothing to do with the pregnancy. She closed her eyes so as not to lie with them.

James pulled a pouffe over and sat facing her. He took both her hands in his.

'I know you slept with someone, Fi.'

Fi gulped. 'No…I…'

He put his hand up to stop her carrying on. Then he lifted her left hand and kissed the top of it. 'I know you so well – but it's OK. It is. I pushed you to it. I pushed you away on purpose, not thinking for one minute you'd hang in there and let yourself be treated so badly. You are usually such a strong woman.'

Tears flowed down Fi's cheeks. 'But our love was stronger.'

James gulped back his own tears as she continued. 'And as for fancying you? I adore you. I've loved you since the minute we practically broke the springs on this thing. You are my world, James. And I'm so bloody sorry.'

'Does the father know it's his?'

She knew she had to tell one last lie. It would be too complicated otherwise. James was clever, but she just hoped that even he, with his first-class degree in Law, hadn't managed to work this one out. The law of averages would say that a very tall, black, orange-haired, camp vicar of the parish would be the last suspect on his list.

'God, no! It was a one-night stand. You know what I'm like with sex. I just needed it and it was on a plate. I should have been born a man!'

'For that, I'm glad you weren't.'

'And I was cross with you, because you did hurt me and I didn't understand why you were being so cruel when I had done nothing wrong. I just wish you had talked to me. I could have shared your pain.'

'I know, I behaved appallingly. At the time I was convinced that I was no good for you, that I should set you free. That's how much I love you, Fi. Set you free so you didn't have to stay with someone who couldn't do what he was put on this earth to do.'

'That's bollocks. It doesn't make you less of a person if you can't have children. In fact, I think it makes you a stronger one. If you can deal with that being thrown at you, you can deal with anything. I love you no less for it. Come here.'

She pulled him forward and cradled his head in her heavy bosom.

'Yes, I did wrong but we were going to have a baby that wasn't ours anyway. And I didn't have to go through the worry of whether the IVF would work or not. The father will never know, but he was a good man, I could tell, and our baby will be amazing.'

'What if he sees you with the baby and puts two and two together?'

'That won't happen.'

'How can you be so sure?'

'One, he's not from London and we did use a condom. He just didn't know that it split. And before you ask, I went to Tony's clinic and got checked out for anything nasty.'

When James stood up and walked away from her, Fi began to panic. Shit. He knew it was Simon's baby. He knew she had lied again. This would be the last straw for him, however much he loved her.

'James, I know I've been a complete whore but let's move on from this. I know we can make it work.'

Fi bit her lip. Mentioning the clinic had obviously wobbled him, despite everything he had just said. Why couldn't she just keep her mouth shut sometimes? He was a bloke, he wouldn't probably have even thought to be worried about that.

Knowing he was a thinker, she saw little point in running after him. Instead, she had just started to doze off when his familiar voice stirred her.

'Of course we can make it work, you stupid cow.' She opened her eyes, smiled, and then burst out laughing.

For there, standing in the doorway, was the usually quiet and reserved Mr James Kane with a beautiful diamond engagement ring hanging by a pink ribbon from a very erect penis. He put on a thick Irish accent.

'Now get this *on* your fecking finger and get those filthy knickers *off*.'

CHAPTER SEVENTY SEVEN

'Bugger!' Michael couldn't find his glasses anywhere. He was always mislaying them. He hated contacts but they would have to do as he couldn't possibly write without them. He was feeling tetchy for not smoking and because he couldn't wait to talk to Ruby.

Seeing Margaret had made it worse in a way, made him feel closer to Ruby by association.

He clicked open his laptop. Barney sighed heavily on the floor by his feet.

***Let Love Win* by Michael Bell**

Chapter 29: *Michael didn't know why he hadn't thought of a letter before. So much easier than dealing with the sexy, feisty red-headed Ruby face-to-face. She could sit and read it quietly. In fact, he remembered her showing him the letters that Lucas had written when he had left her Daffodils in his will. She had been touched by them. Let's hope she would feel the same about his. Maybe now this would be it? She would come to her senses and love would win.*

Michael cringed as he heard the back door slam. 'I'm home, Pooky – and guess what the mumsy wumsy-to-be has got to show you?'

Emily swanned into the study. 'Just look, more of that delicious lacy underwear – your favourite. Shall I?'

Michael was just thinking that he quite fancied a shag.

'You shall – and make sure you wear it with those red four-inch stilettos of yours.'

'Come on, big boy, come on – let me ride you harder.' Emily pounded down on Michael. Despite her now pendulous pregnant breasts bouncing in front of his eyes, he shut them.

'Oh Justin!' Emily cried out as she came. Michael sat bolt upright and pushed her off him a little too roughly. 'Justin? Who the fuck is Justin?'

'Er...I was just listening to Justin Timberlake's new single in the car, must have been on my mind. I mean, how hot is he?'

'Hah! Yes, of course. Justin Timberlake.' Michael got up off the bed and pulled on his dressing-gown. 'How silly of me not to think of that.' He had fire in his eyes. 'Not Justin – my best mate Justin – then? Nah, of course it wouldn't be, couldn't be. My darling sweet little Emily fucking MY BEST MATE!' he shouted as loud as his voice would allow.

Michael had to stop typing and go to the loo. With the sudden memory of his best mate doing the dirty with Emily in real life, his tingle from writing the sex scene had completely gone.

He just had to get over it. And he hoped by changing his mind and putting it earlier in the novel, this might help him. It wasn't the fact that he wanted Emily back, it was just the betrayal by his best mate and the actual moment when he caught them at it. It was so hard to bear. He couldn't even relive the actual scenario in his novel, it would have hurt too much.

He snapped his laptop shut. His head wouldn't allow him

to write any more today. He could tell Emily what a slag she was in chapter thirty. She would end up as a single parent with no money as her parents would disown her and Justin would have already moved on to the next best not-pregnant thing. Her selfish heart would be broken and he would live happily ever after with Ruby. *The End.*

He took a deep breath and thought of Ruby. Pretty, vibrant, funny, kind, sexy Ruby. How he loved that girl.

He didn't know exactly when she would be back but guessed it must be soon. Surely Margaret had given her the letter? What if she didn't want to call him? What if she had gotten over him? After all, he had been a complete dick when he turned up at the Bow Wow. Maybe she was still seeing matey boy dead husband lookalike? Maybe she had even gone away with him? He began to feel angry and sad at the same time. If love was going to win, it was taking its bloody time to get to the finishing line.

He got up to fill the kettle when there was a knock at the door. Barney sat up and began to bark loudly. Strange. Only a handful of people knew where he lived. Opening it tentatively, a frown crossed his face as he saw who it was.

'Micky boy.'

Michael couldn't manage any sort of noise. It was actually a comfort to see his best mate, but he also wanted to punch him right in the face.

His friend stood in the doorway as tall as his five foot eleven frame would allow. 'Fancy a pint, mate?'

The big man nodded slowly.

CHAPTER SEVENTY EIGHT

Ruby and Nick were puffing hard as they walked up Skiddaw. The colours, sights, and sounds of the bright summer morning touched every sense. The scenery around them really was quite breathtaking.

'I thought I was fit,' Nick panted.

'You are that.' Ruby poked him in the ribs.

'I can't believe you got me up so early,' he grumbled. 'With a hangover too.'

'But look around you. It was worth it, wasn't it?'

'Yeah. It's stunning, Ruby.'

'Here.' She took his hand. 'Just look.'

The views over Derwentwater were simply breathtaking. The sun warmed their faces. Birdsong filled the air. It was a perfect moment.

'Shall we sit for a moment, get some food in us?' Nick suggested. 'I'm bloody starving.'

'Deffo.' Ruby unpacked the coffee flask and some currant buns she'd buttered earlier. 'Quite the Famous Five, aren't we?' she joked.

'All we are missing is a Julian, George, and Timmy.'

'Definitely missing a George, that's for sure.'

'Oh, Rubes. I'm sorry.'

'Don't be silly. This place is full of him and I like that. It's good to have memories. In fact, up here is where I declared my undying love for him.'

'That's sweet. What a wonderful place to do it.'

'Not quite. I had slated his fiancée, he went mad, and then I realised how I felt about him. He said it was too late, stormed off, and a mountain rescue team had to find me.'

'No!' Nick bit his lip but had to laugh. 'That is so terrible but funny at the same time.'

'I know. But imagine being up here in the winter and not being able to see a way down? I was shitting myself. I kept thinking of Lucas to keep me going. This is where I threw his ashes. I feel him around me too. I loved Lucas. He was so special to me. Such a wise and charismatic man.'

They ate the buns then lay back on the grass looking up at the bright blue sky. After ten minutes of lying in silence, Nick lifted himself onto his elbow and looked down at Ruby.

'Thanks for last night. It was really special.' He kissed her gently on the nose.

'Yes, it was lovely. Sex with someone you care about is the best sort.'

'This is special too, Ruby. This moment with you.'

Nick lay back down and they held hands, looking at the sky and continuing their silence.

Ruby thought back to throwing the remains of Lucas Geronimo Steadburton at the sky. James and Fi had been with them too, and had laughed that she had carried him up in a plastic container, knowing that the gay, debonair, BAFTA-winning actor would have much preferred being carried in a silver goblet of some sort.

Now what was it he had said in one of his letters to her? She spoke aloud. '"Dance like nobody's watching; love like you've never been hurt. Sing like nobody's listening; live like it's heaven on earth."'

'What did you say?'

Ruby repeated it. 'It's Mark Twain. Isn't it amazing?'

'Especially the love like you've never been hurt bit.' Nick sat up. 'We need to do that now, Rubes.'

Ruby sat up and leaned on his shoulder. 'Nick, I…er…I do really like you…'

'Carry on. I'm waiting for the "but".' Then Nick laughed. 'I'm teasing you. Go to him. If what I've done for you is made you realise you should be with a man you love, then what a reason for us to have met.' Ruby jumped up. 'I bloody love him, Nick. It's this place. It makes me see sense! Lucas makes me see sense.' She had tears running down her face. 'I've been such a cow. Michael has been nothing but good to me and for me – and I have treated him like shit.'

'He will understand. You're ready for happiness, Ruby, and he seems a top bloke. I mean, the fact he came to the Bow Wow Club to try and understand you better – that alone makes him decent.'

'Yes, it does. Suddenly everything seems clear. I'm so sorry though. About us, I mean.'

'Ruby, I cannot think of anyone else I would have rather made love to since losing Milly. It's another thing to tick off the list in the *Bereaved Road to Recovery Guide*, and only you would understand that. Don't get me wrong. I think you are amazing. I love your company. But if we are being honest with each other, we're a stepping stone. Our common understanding of grief does bind us but we are not The One for either of us. We met each other for a reason. And it makes me feel warm to think that they are looking out for us, up there.'

Ruby hugged Nick tightly, pulled away, then kissed him hard on the lips.

'I love you, Fireman Redwood, and I hope you will always be in my life.'

'The feeling's mutual, Miss Designer Pants, and if things don't work out with the big lad then we can always be friends with benefits.'

'It's a win, win then. I'm glad you feel the same way! I mean, how often does that happen in affairs of the heart?'

'Let's hope more than we think. I mean, look at us with Milly and George. True love.'

'And that's what makes it all the sadder. Losing your baby girl too. Oh, Nick.'

'It hasn't killed me, so all it can do is make me stronger. I will never forget them, Ruby. Like you will never forget your George. But we either lie on the floor face down and bash our arms around like toddlers and scream, or we get up, brush ourselves down, and get on with it.'

Ruby threw her arms in the air dramatically. 'Yes, let's live like it's heaven on earth.' She started to run back down the hill.

Nick caught up with her and swung her round. 'You dramatic old cow.'

'I am just dancing like nobody's watching. Milly, George, and baby Annabel with be with us forever. We can draw from their love. There can never be too much love in our hearts. I feel so good. I feel so free.'

'Good. I've never seen you look so happy and it suits you. Now come on, you've got a man to catch.'

CHAPTER SEVENTY NINE

'Thanks for not punching me, mate.'

Justin and Michael supped on their pints in a busy Clapham bar.

'Well, it wouldn't be a fair fight, would it? I'd have knocked you into next Tuesday.' Michael's six feet four stature made even the five feet eleven Justin seem small.

'I'm truly sorry, Micky. I acted like a complete wanker.'

'Yeah, you did. You hurt me badly. And if so much time hadn't passed I might not be quite so calm with you. But you did me a favour, taking on that silly bitch.'

'Likes her things, doesn't she? Even my City bonuses had trouble keeping up with her handbag fetish. Good tits though.'

'Fair point,' Michael nodded. 'But that's about it when you dig a little deeper.'

'I can't believe I put a woman in front of a friendship. Shit. What a bloody twat.'

'Yeah, you are. But, it's taken balls for you to confront me and I respect that. How did you find out where I lived?'

'She told me she was dropping the dog off with you, so I asked her.'

'Oh, right. How are you doing anyway?'

'I've realised that being single is where it's at – for the moment anyway. Loving the ladies, like in the old days. Speaking of which...'

Two blondes walked in, clocked them, and made for the bar.

'The one with long hair is well fit.'

Michael shook his head. 'I should have known it wouldn't have lasted long with you and Emily. There is a word, "commitment", in the dictionary, which I don't think you've found yet.'

'Hah! And how're you doing, now you've got over your best mate being a complete dick?'

'I'm good, actually. Work has picked up and I started writing that novel I always harped on about.'

'Blimey. What's it about?'

'It's a love story.'

'What? Look at you. Micky Bell, romantic author.'

'Don't take the piss. It's good. I'm enjoying it.'

'So, who are you basing your heroine on then? Please don't say Madam Want It All.'

'Don't be stupid. The only person she ever loved was herself. No. I've met someone. But I'm not telling you about her in case you steal her too.'

'Don't be like that. I was just starting to feel better.'

'She's called Ruby. A bloody decent girl. Good laugh. Sexy too.'

'I'm really pleased for you, mate. How long have you been seeing her then?'

'Well, that's the point. I'm not. Her husband died a couple of years ago and it's been hard graft. There were times when we were close but I knew she was still thinking about him, and it was tough. I said we should have a break and now she hasn't come back. I stupidly thought absence would make the heart grow fonder.'

'Bloody women!'

'Tell me about it.'

'So what are you going to do?'

'I've written her a letter.'

'You're so soft.'

'No, I'm a writer, and if I can't convey how I feel on paper then there's no hope. I love her, mate.'

'Well, I hope it works out.'

'If it doesn't, I'm tempted to go away for a bit. I can do my writing anywhere and I'm sick of that shithole of a flat. It's not good for Barney anyway.'

'Well, let me know where you go if you do. I've missed you, mate.'

'Justin Thompson, you're going all soft on me, now there's a thing.'

'Fuck off. Now, come on, they're showing a game at the Blandford this afternoon if you fancy it? Oi, oi. Or maybe not. Budge up mate, looks like we've got company.'

The two blondes from the bar were walking towards them. They looked and sounded a little rough around the edges.

'Do you mind if we share your table? It's packed in here.' The short-haired one squeezed up close to Michael. 'You're a big boy, aren't you? Tall, I mean.' She rubbed her hand right up his thigh.

Justin laughed. 'Small feet he's got, though.'

The girls seemed quite drunk and giggled. They noticed the boys' empty glasses. 'Going to the bar, are you?' the long-haired blonde enquired. 'If I give you the money, can you get us a couple of Chardonnays?'

Justin stood up. 'Don't be silly – I'll get them.'

'I thought we were going to watch the football?' Michael wasn't in the mood. Justin made a face that Michael understood very well.

'OK. One more it is. Let me come to the bar and help you.'

With a drink in each hand the boys headed back towards their table. It had been occupied by a group of lads and the girls were nowhere to be seen.

'Cheeky bitches, they've gone.' Justin was not amused.

Michael put his hand to his now empty left pocket. 'Thieving bitches, more like. She has my phone.' He put his hand to his head. 'Can I use yours to call the police?'

'You'll never get it back, mate.'

Michael sighed at Justin's negativity. Yes, momentarily it had been good to see him. But a sad realisation had dawned on him: the person in front of him was effectively a stranger now. He had brought nothing but trouble to his door before, and here he was, doing it again.

The experience of being betrayed had no doubt helped Michael to grow as a person. And he knew now, for sure, that he didn't want someone he couldn't trust or rely on in his life any more.

He headed for the door and glanced back.

'You're right. I don't think I'll ever get it back.'

CHAPTER EIGHTY

Ruby sang along to the radio as she hung her washing on the clothes line. She had so enjoyed her time at Daffodils, and now that she understood it was Michael she wanted, a certain calmness overtook her.

If he was back with Emily then he still had to know how she felt. He said he loved her. Surely he hadn't gotten over her that quickly? He would have gone back to his horrible ex on a whim, and Ruby was sure that she could win him over. His wife had been unfaithful and he didn't deserve that. No, Mr Strong Hands was not getting away from her that easily. She was ready for him and was excited at the prospect of sleeping with him again.

She had no regrets about what had happened between her and Nick. In fact, it had been a good thing: it helped her understand just how much she did want Michael.

Her night with Nick had felt right, though. It had made her see that a fling with the likes of Harry was just a short-term gratification, and that it had made her feel awful afterwards.

She had thought it best to text Michael in case Emily was around when she rang. She had drafted it and redrafted it at least fifteen times. She had one chance to get it right and she didn't want to blow it. She finished up simply stating, *I want to see you. I've missed you a lot! I await your call. Love R Xx*

That had been two days ago. She went through different scenarios in her head. It had definitely been delivered. Maybe he was waiting to be alone if Emily was on the scene? Or maybe he had given up on her? I mean, if he was all loved up with *her* now, then what could he say in reply? She would give it another day and would then send another one. It was annoying he didn't have a set office as she didn't dare just turn up at his flat in case *she* answered the door.

She switched the kettle on and opened the fridge.

'Damn!' She had run out of milk. She slipped on her flip-flops and headed to the corner shop. Margaret was scrubbing her step as she walked past.

'Hello, duck,' called the old lady. 'Long time no see. Did you have a good time in the Lakes? Phew, that's that done. I'm just about to make a cuppa; will you come in and have one with your old neighbour?'

'I was just going off to get milk to make one, so I will do. Thank you.'

Ruby followed Margaret into the kitchen. Bert was out in the back garden weeding.

Ruby noticed the familiar-looking glasses case perched on top of the microwave. 'You've got the same glasses case as Michael.'

Margaret raised her eyebrows. 'They are Michael's. Bugger! I forgot all about him coming round.'

'He came here?'

'Well, he came to see you. Literally the day you went off to the Lakes with The Fireman.'

'You didn't tell him I was with someone, did you?'

'Ruby! Of course I bloody didn't.' The old lady looked

contrite. 'I had too much sherry, as usual, and I conked out. He must have got up and left while I was sparko. Oh no, it's all coming back to me now!'

'What? That sounds serious.'

'No, it's not. I just suggested that he wrote you a letter.'

'A letter, you say?' Bert echoed as he came through the back door to wash his filthy hands.

'Yes, you know – when Michael came round the other day? You were asleep, and then I fell asleep. He said he was going to write a letter.'

'I don't even remember him coming round.' Bert poured some washing-up liquid onto his hands, then looked up. 'Shit, I do recall something. I needed a bit of paper so I wrote my horses on the back of an envelope I found by the kettle. I took it to the bookies.'

'Oh Bert, you silly old sod. Please don't say you threw it away?'

'Hmm, what did I do with it?' He scratched his head.

'You are useless!' Margaret said crossly.

'Don't you go on at me, Maggie. You were the one in a Bristol Cream coma.'

Ruby tried to remain calm. 'OK, Bert, think back if you can.'

'Ha. I remember now. I saw your name on it, Rubes, so I took the letter out.' A wry smile crossed his face. 'The bloke was pouring his heart out.'

'So where did you put it?' Margaret was frosty.

'Have you got a usual place you put paperwork?' Ruby's voice was getting slightly higher.

'This drawer.' Bert rifled through it. 'It was on that smart blue paper she uses.'

'Out of the way, let me.' Margaret began to flick through each piece of paper carefully, but nothing came to light.

'Maybe you did take it to the betting shop?' Ruby had slight panic in her voice now.

'No, love. It'll be here somewhere, I'm sure,' Margaret soothed.

Ruby gulped. Bert put his hand to his white scruffy hair and shut his eyes. He began mumbling and pacing around the kitchen.

'Woke up. Couldn't find paper. Walked to kitchen. Found envelope.' He moved into the front room and began pacing around again. Then, suddenly he punched the air.

'Bloody eureka.' He pointed to the shelf on the fireplace and to the wedding photo in which Ruby and George smiled sweetly back at him. 'It's behind there, sweetheart. Makes total sense now. That husband of yours is taking care of it.'

Tears pricked Ruby's eyes. She hurriedly pulled out the now-crumpled sheets of paper.

'I have to go home and read it, right now.'

'Yes, go on, duck,' Margaret said excitedly. 'And then tell me exactly what he says.'

'A funny little squeaking noise, eh?' Bert chipped in.

Ruby threw herself down on her bed and began to read hungrily.

I love you, Ruby Stevens. I cannot get you out of my head. I've tried, oh how I've tried. I think sometimes I wish I had never met you, as never before has someone affected me like you have. Every waking moment it is you on my mind. Silly things I think about daily. Like the way you bite your thumbnails when you're anxious, or throw your head back and laugh in that infectious way. The little squeaking noise you make as you are about to come. There is nothing about you that I don't like. Well, apart from the stupid piece of you that doesn't realise how much I do care about you.

'I can't believe it.' Ruby shouted, completely overwhelmed that Michael felt the same way. She had got completely the wrong end of the stick. He loved *her*. Wanted to be with *her*. Tears flowed down her cheeks. She had to go to him. She quickly dialled his number, and it went straight to answerphone.

She rang for a taxi, pulled on her favourite summer dress, and smudged her lips with gloss.

On reaching the ugly Clapham block of flats her brain froze. What number was it again? Thirteen, that's right. Unlucky for some but her favourite number. She pressed the button for the lift. It was taking an age. She headed for the stairs and began to run up, two at a time.

Puffing heavily, she rattled the knocker as hard as she could. A girl with lank black hair and smoking a roll-up was putting her key in the door next to Michael's.

'He's not here, sister. Saw him go off with a holdall and that dog of his a few days ago.'

'Oh. He didn't happen to say where he was going, did he?'

'Said that if I heard anyone knocking and asked where he was, just to say FBI to them and they would understand. Goodness knows what he meant. Maybe he's joined them or summink. I bloody hope not.'

Ruby kissed the dirty-looking girl on the cheek.

'Thank you! Thank you so much.'

CHAPTER EIGHTY ONE

'Nick, I owe you big time,' Ruby shouted from the window of his camper van as she sped away from the fire station, Devon-bound.

Once she had reached the M5 she started to feel slightly panicky. She wondered why exactly Michael had gone to the Ferry Boat Inn, especially if he had been so intent on seeing her. It seemed strange. She remembered a conversation they'd had months ago when he had said that if ever he was in trouble then that was where he would go. She recalled saying they should have the same pact.

She really hoped that Michael wasn't in trouble and suddenly began to doubt if she was doing the right thing. I mean, she was travelling for hours to see him. What if he had a secret lover down there? Or if he was in some sort of scrape that he didn't want her to know about?

No, she was being ridiculous now. He had written the letter to her just days ago and had spelled out his love for her. Maybe she should call him? She pulled over onto a hard shoulder and did just that. The call went straight through to voicemail. Well, there was a chance he was in the FBI, as you weren't allowed to use phones in there. Saying that, he hadn't answered his phone for days. She imagined all sorts of terrible scenarios and began to feel slightly sick.

It had been such a journey to get this far with him and she just hoped that everything would be all right, that they could work it out once and for all. Their relationship over just the space of a few months had been a catalogue of disasters. Getting her bag stolen, then falling over in the street on New Year's Eve, and then Michael getting the wrong end of the stick – well, sort of – about her and Harry.

But in all of this, Michael hadn't really put a foot wrong – apart from screaming at her in the churchyard. But he had every reason to do so. She had been seen kissing someone who was the spitting image of her husband in broad daylight, after all. Poor, sweet Michael, she couldn't wait to make it up to him.

She began to think how quickly life can change. Six months ago, she hadn't made a dress for over a year, and since then she had fulfilled the dreams of at least ten brides. She hadn't even heard of the Bow Wow Club and the wonderful characters she had met through it. Simon would be a friend for life, and as for Nick, he was such a beautiful man and they had been in the right place at the right time for each other. Something which doesn't happen often enough.

Finding love, she acknowledged, was all about timing. Her mother had said that to her once and she had been so right. It made Ruby wonder how anyone actually got together with regards to age, compatibility, wanting children or not, where to live, and so many other things that came into the equation of life.

But Michael was so right for her. She fancied the pants off him, but most importantly she loved him and he loved her. They were good for each other. Wanted the best for each other. She was proud that he was writing his novel and he was so supportive of her in every single way.

Thankfully, it was still light as she turned right at the Sportsman's Bar and headed down the long winding road to Dittisham. She would just park up, head to the Ferry Boat Inn, and pray he was there. If he wasn't, she would just wait for him to arrive. It was so close-knit down here that someone would have seen a six-foot -our man and his black Labrador and know where they were staying, she was sure.

She locked Nick's camper van and began the walk down the very steep hill to the pub. It was a beautiful evening and the sound of gulls and the boats filled her heart with hope. She smiled as she heard children squeal as they caught crabs down on the pontoon and the bell ring for the ferry, and she thought back to the special time they had spent in Dartmouth before she had ruined it all by having a strop.

She crept past the pub door and tried to peek in, but couldn't. She really needed a drink anyway, and was sure they would make her feel welcome.

Tentatively walking in, she noticed Slugger, the bespectacled barman, in his usual position. He recognised Ruby from Valentine's Day and smiled broadly. She put her finger to her lips to shh his greeting.

Her heart did a massive leap when she saw her handsome man sitting in the window seat that housed her favourite water view in the world. Barney was asleep under the table.

She very quietly took a seat opposite her lover, then cleared her throat lightly to get his attention. Barney opened one eye, then went back to sleep. Michael looked up.

'Hello there.' Ruby's voice slightly faltered.

Michael swallowed hard. He bit the inside of his mouth then exhaled deeply as she continued.

'My name's Ruby.' His eyes filled with tears as his pretty table companion went on, 'You're very tall.'

'And you're very ginger.'

'I've had a terrible year.'

'What's made it so awful? Tell me, Ruby.'

'There was this man, see. I met him outside a Tube station. I'd been mugged. He was really kind. Had really strong hands. But he did something terribly wrong.'

'Ah, right. What exactly did he do wrong then?' Michael reached over and took both her hands.

'He told me he loved me. Told me far too soon.'

'How unthinkable is that?'

'I know, I mean – how dare he do something so rash? But this man, this man...' Ruby started to get choked, '...he is the most beautiful person in the world. He pulled me out of a serious darkness and made it light again. He made me feel loved and safe and wanted. And I feel terrible that I treated him so badly when he didn't deserve it at all.'

'So, if you saw this man again, what would you say to him?'

'I would tell him that I love him. I love him with all my heart. And I would quite happily spend the rest of my life with him.'

'OK – well, I think if you said *that* to him, then he really would quite like it.'

'Really?' Tears slowly ran down Ruby's cheeks.

People on tables either side of them, and even Slugger, were now listening intently.

'In fact, I know he would.'

Michael jumped up from his chair and got down on one knee next to Ruby.

'I have never doubted my love for you. From the minute I set eyes on you I knew you were the girl for me, and if you'd marry me I'd be the happiest man in the world. So...Ruby Ann Stevens, will you please bloody marry me?'

Ruby took a deep breath as the tears kept flowing.

'So?' a dozen voices echoed around the cosy pub.

'Yes! Yes, of course I will marry you. Well, as long as you promise to write a happy ending, that is?' At that precise moment, the soft-toy otter whizzed up to the top of the bar on its weighted string – triggering the bar bell to ring and the whole bar to erupt in rapturous applause.

EPILOGUE

So The Author and Miss Designer Pants found true love.

Brought together by George's twin brother – although no one would ever know that, of course.

The treasured *Rubes & George forever X* wedding ring would remain close to the never-forgotten landscape gardener.

And dear old Margaret had been right all along. That not only had there been space for someone else in Ruby's once fragile heart, but that there was proof that ol' devil called love *doesn't* have a calendar.

THE END

ABOUT THE AUTHOR

Nicola May is a rom-com superstar. She is the author of fourteen romantic comedies, all of which have appeared in the Kindle bestseller charts. Two of them won awards at the Festival of Romance and another was named ebook of the week in *The Sun*. She lives near Ascot Racecourse with her black-and-white rescue cat, Stan.

Find out more at www.nicolamay.com
Twitter: @nicolamay1
Instagram: author_nicola
Nicola has her own Facebook page

ALSO BY NICOLA MAY

The Ferry Lane Market Series:

*

Welcome to Ferry Lane Market
Stars Align in Ferry Lane Market

The Cockleberry Bay Series:

*

The Corner Shop in Cockleberry Bay
Meet Me in Cockleberry Bay
The Gift of Cockleberry Bay
Christmas in Cockleberry Bay

*

Working It Out
The School Gates
Star Fish
The Women of Wimbledon Common (formerly the *SW19 Club)*
It Started With a Click (formerly *Love Me Tinder)*
Christmas Evie
Better Together